# QUANDARY
## DETECTIVE CARLA MCBRIDE CHRONICLES
### BOOK 4

## NICK LEWIS

ROUGH
EDGES
PRESS

**Quandary**
Paperback Edition
Copyright © 2023 (As Revised) Nick Lewis

Rough Edges Press
An Imprint of Wolfpack Publishing
9850 S. Maryland Parkway, Suite A-5 #323
Las Vegas, Nevada 89183

roughedgespress.com

Paperback ISBN 978-1-68549-243-4
eBook ISBN 978-1-68549-242-7

*For Shelley, Jim, and Rick*

# QUANDARY

# CHAPTER 1

I t wasn't Red Brewster's first rodeo. For the past twenty years, he'd called the Kentucky High School baseball championship game. In his stellar sportscasting career, his play-by-play voice was iconic. Before he continued his broadcast, he glanced at the on-deck circle as Philip Devaney warmed up. Red's pulse and respiration ramped up; he knew what Devaney was feeling. He had experienced that same nerve-racking tension thirty years ago as a Stallion. Like the professional that he was, he took a deep breath and continued his final play-by-play soliloquy.

"Alright, fans, here we go. The Stallions are down to their last out. The state championship trophy hangs in the balance. With the bases loaded and behind by three runs, it's a do-or-die moment for the Stallions in the bottom of the seventh inning. It all comes down to Devaney, the Stallions' all-star first baseman. Can he keep this rally going? Well, folks, we're about to find out."

Relief pitcher Roy Gullett, for the Altmont Tomcats, had a ninety-five mile-per-hour fastball. He threw nothing but heat, and everyone knew that. However, his wildness put him in this precarious position. After a visit from his coach, he'd settled down and struck out the next two batters. It had all come down to Gullett's flame-throwing fastball against Devaney's quick and keen, eye-hand coordination. A lot was at stake as Red's iconic voice continued the broadcast.

"Devaney steps into the batter's box as deep as he could, waiting for the pitch. Gullett takes his wind-up and flings the ball toward home plate. Devaney takes the pitch, strike-one the umpire signaled. Folks, I can't believe he took that waist-high pitch right over the plate. I wonder if Devaney is playing a game of cat and mouse? We'll soon find out."

Devaney stepped out of the batter's box to calm his nerves. He knew a state championship was riding on the last at-bat of his high school career. The Stallions had never won a state championship in any sport. This is the closest any athletic team had ever come. Everything was riding on his shoulders. After Devaney took a deep breath, he once again settled in the batter's box as far back as he could. He knew what was coming; Gullett threw nothing but heat. At ninety-five miles per hour, he didn't need an off-speed pitch to keep batters off-balance. His wildness took care of that.

Gullett nodded at the catcher, then took his wind-up and smoked Devaney again. Strike two, the umpire screamed. Devaney signaled timeout and stood outside the batter's box to calm himself. After a deep breath, he took his stance deep in the batter's box once more. He was now ready for another fastball and a chance at a hero status. With Gullett in his stance, he nodded at the catcher once more. While waiting on the pitch,

Devaney focused on Gullett's right hand as he went into his wind-up. There was nothing different in his motion or delivery, and Devaney guessed fastball all the way.

As Devaney expected, Gullett delivered more smoke toward home plate. Devaney timed the waist-high fastball perfectly, and a thunderous crack filled the stadium. The ball sailed high and deep toward left field. As Devaney approached the first base bag, he watched the ball soaring toward the fence. After rounding first base, the left fielder leaped high as the ball sailed over his outstretched glove. As Devaney crossed home plate, pandemonium erupted on the field and in the stands. He had done it, a grand slam to bring home the first state championship to Oakmont High School.

Although Red was supposed to be impartial, he couldn't control the emotions flooding his soul. Once a Stallion, always a Stallion, he believed. With his voice cracking with emotion, he continued his broadcast.

"There you have it, folks. The Stallions have captured the Kentucky High School Baseball Championship in grand, heroic fashion. What a game, and one for the record books. Go Stallions. Congratulations, state champs. Stay tuned for post-game interviews after these brief messages."

As the celebration continued in the stadium, Red made his way down to the field to interview Stallions' head coach Gabe Cook and the game's most valuable player, Devaney. Finally, catching up with them in front of the Stallions' dugout, he began his interview.

"Coach, congratulations. What is going through your mind right now?"

"Well, Red, it's unexplainable what I'm feeling.

These kids worked hard all year, and they deserve all the credit, especially Devaney. I couldn't be prouder of him."

"Philip, congratulations on being named the tournament's most valuable player."

"Thank you, Mr. Brewster, but I owe it to Coach Cook and all the guys. It was a team effort."

"Of course, tell me about your last at-bat. Were you trying to out psyche Gullett?"

"Everyone knew what was coming—nothing but fastballs. He felt he had my number as he struck me out in my first two at-bats. I knew he was cocky and felt he could just blow it past me again. So, yeah, by taking the first two pitches, I wanted him to think he had my number again. So, yeah, I played a game of cat and mouse waiting for that right pitch, and he threw it."

"Well, I guess it all worked out. What's next for you guys?"

"What else? It's time to celebrate with the Diamond Brotherhood at my father's cabin. Umm, here he comes now. Thanks, go Stallions!"

As Philip hugged his dad, Red continued interviewing Coach Cook. As chants of "We are the Champions" filled the stadium, members of the Diamond Brotherhood gathered around Philip's father as he explained the ground rules for the celebration.

"Listen up, everyone, those are the rules. I'll be checking in on you from time to time, so behave, and no girls, and I mean that. Once you are there, no one leaves. Does everyone understand that?"

The Diamond Brotherhood nodded in unison.

"Philip, one last thing. Everyone's car keys go into the safe in my bedroom, okay?" Philip nodded. "Great, I'm proud of every one of you. You each have your whole life in front of you. Be safe and make smart decisions, okay?"

After everyone nodded, each player dispersed, heading toward the lake house. It wasn't long after arriving that the celebration began. Chants of "We are the Champions" rocked the cabin as the beer started flowing. A couple of hours later, a knock on the door startled Philip. He parted the window curtains, and a lustful grin grabbed his soul.

# CHAPTER 2

## THIRTY-FIVE YEARS LATER

With the lowest crime rate in the state, Oakmont was growing by leaps and bounds. Its proximity to Lexington, Louisville, Cincinnati, and Knoxville, made it the perfect place to work and raise a family. With excellent schools and a renowned university, industries and retail businesses flocked to the community. Furthermore, because of its revered and sought-after quality of life, Oakmont had morphed into a viable retirement destination. The sky was the limit for the city, and the current city commission touted their leadership as the driving force behind its success.

Mayor Lester James and City Commissioners Bryan A. Walters, Rich Masterson, Barry Stewart, and Philip Devaney were on cloud nine about Oakmont's past accomplishments and rosy future. However, that all changed when the senseless murders of five citizens two years ago shook the city to its core. Although the mayor and city commissioners continued to relish in Oakmont's success, the recent violent crime wave began to overshadow their leadership. Mayor James had taken most of the heat for the city's fall from grace as one of Kentucky's safest communities. His opponent used the rise in crime to his advantage, making the mayor's re-election bid closer than any before.

Furthermore, the city commissioners' race was also the tightest in recent years because of this influx in violent crimes. In the primary election, Masterson, Stewart, and Devaney finished in the top three. Wilson Bortel, CEO of Freedom National Bank, who finished fourth, and Walters, CEO of Oakmont Trust and Savings, who finished fifth, would battle it out for the fourth seat on the city commission.

Bortel's platform focused on the violent crime wave, while Walters focused on Bortel's unimpressive civic record. They often clashed publicly throughout the campaign because their banks were fierce competitors. In the final forum before the general election, Walters accused him of allegedly buying votes. However, Bortel vehemently denied such allegations. Although Walters finished his campaign with as much mud-slinging rhetoric as possible, winning another term was in jeopardy.

With the campaign finally over, Commissioner Walters looked forward to election day. However, this one was painfully different. In the past, he awoke beside his gorgeous wife, Cynthia, excited and confident of being victorious. Having breakfast with her was always an essential part of that winning tradition. Unfortunately, on this election day, she was not by his side when the sun's warmth flowed through the bedroom windows. She had fought a courageous battle against breast cancer and lost. Although he wanted to win another term, without her by his side would make it a bittersweet victory. On the other hand, losing would devastate him as she could not comfort the heartbreak and emptiness in his soul.

With his mundane and lonely breakfast over, Walters arrived at the bank at his usual time. Over the past four-teen years, his election day routine consisted of no appointments or meetings, a long lunch with Cynthia, and voting together. However, today, after a few morning appointments, his lunch was short, and the ride to his voting precinct was lonely and full of bittersweet memories.

After voting, he turned left onto Tate's Creek Park-way, taking the long way back to downtown. He was in no hurry to experience the loneliness inside his office. While passing the next intersection, a white sedan turned right, keeping a safe distance behind him. After traveling a half-mile, a traffic light was just ahead. With it green, he sped up, hoping to get through it. However, as it turned yellow, he hit the brakes. As he waited, the white sedan pulled up behind him.

As he did routinely, he checked his rearview mirror. For some strange reason, seeing the white sedan and the two men inside sent his pulse racing. He never looked good in a beard, he thought, but the driver of the white sedan wore one well. Returning his gaze to the traffic signal, it had turned green. The driver of the white sedan, being an impatient jerk, laid on the horn. Disgusted and fuming, Walters shot him the bird and turned left.

While glancing in the rearview mirror, the car was gaining on him. At the next traffic signal, the white sedan pulled up beside him. After the passenger door window lowered, profanities irked him. As the light turned green, the white car sped away. Walters slowly pulled away, wondering why so many people were impatient assholes these days.

After returning to the bank, he passed the afternoon away until it was time to visit McGruder's for what he hoped would be another victorious celebration. Unfortunately, if it were a victorious one, it would be lonely and bittersweet. Although his son would join him, hopefully, for a celebratory beer this evening, it wasn't the same without Cynthia at his side.

Rising from his desk, he walked over to the doorway, watching customers move about without a care in the world. Suddenly, two men entered the front entrance and approached one of the tellers. Recognizing them as the two men in the white sedan, he quickly closed the door and returned to his desk. He promptly brought up the security cameras on his monitor and watched the two men conduct their business. Given his uncomfortable encounter with them earlier, paranoia crept into his fragile psyche.

The two men seemed harmless and left the bank after conducting their business. Wanting to make sure they were gone, he opened his door and walked to a window with a view of the parking lot. With the white sedan gone, he breathed a sigh of relief. He then walked over to the teller and asked to see the check. He didn't know a man named Parker Jarrell and hoped he would never have an encounter with such an impatient jerk ever again.

As his banking team left for the day, he walked to the front door and secured it. After returning to his office, loneliness grabbed his soul. Opening one of the doors on the credenza, he pulled out a bottle of his favorite bourbon, Blanton's. He grabbed his favorite Waterford crystal rock glass, and within seconds, two fingers' worth of the amber liquid called his name. Sniffing its alluring aroma, he savored its smoothness as it went down. Closing the door, he sat at his desk, wondering how he would handle tonight's outcome, win or lose, without Cynthia by his side.

# CHAPTER 3

After finishing his Blanton's, Commissioner Walters stopped at the county clerk's office. The early returns were not promising. He was not one to hang around the courthouse waiting for the final results. His celebration venue had always been McGruder's, and tonight would be no different. However, this evening, he would go it alone for the first time in his life. Even though Cynthia wouldn't be there in a physical sense, he firmly believed her spirit would join him at the bar.

With the television centered directly above the bar, he kept track of each race, especially his. The latest scroll at the bottom of the screen had Bortel leading him by seventy-three votes. It had been a hard-fought and nasty race, and Walters believed he had done his best. With only two precincts left to report, he still held out hope that the citizens would allow him to represent them for another two years.

As he swirled his glass around, melting ice clinked against the sides. Downing the diluted remains of Blanton's, he held up the glass towards Sam. She knew what that meant. Within minutes, another Blanton's on the rocks called his name. After a long sip, he stared at the empty stool to his right. As bittersweet memories of Cynthia flooded his mind, a lump in his throat grabbed his soul. While wiping a few tears from his eyes, his focus returned to his drink.

Blanton's had been his faithful companion most every day, making his loneliness temporarily manageable. After Cynthia died, his job and the city commission consumed his daily regimen. In the evening, Blanton's provided him the comfort to make it through to the next day until he'd do it all over again.

Although Cynthia had repeatedly told him to find true love after she was gone, he couldn't bring himself to pursue any serious relationship. However, he still had manly needs, and one-nighters quenched his sexual appetite with no strings attached. That was the perfect antidote for his sexual cravings until that special woman came along, capturing his heart as Cynthia did many years ago.

While glancing at the screen, the fat lady had sung on his reign in city government. Losing by seventeen votes, he knew a re-count would automatically occur. However, he didn't hold much hope for it to swing the results in his favor.

Taking another long swallow of Blanton's, he placed it on the bar and turned to his right once more. The emptiness was devastating. The glass of Chardonnay he bought earlier had grown warm and stale. Glancing at the television screen, Sam knew it was his last hurrah. With his glass empty again, Blanton's called his name once more. Within seconds, its numbing power did its best to soothe his heartbreak. Sam wasn't concerned about over-serving him because she could always call his son to rescue him. Lately, she had done that a lot, and it concerned her. While handing him the drink, her smile did its best to ease his sorrow and disappointment.

"Sorry, you lost. This one is on the house. I'll call your son when you are ready to go home, okay?"

After nodding, he turned to face Cynthia's spirit next to him. "Honey, we had a great ride, didn't we?" Dead silence smacked him in the face. "You want a fresh glass of Chardonnay to celebrate my defeat?" The eeriness tugged on his heartstrings like never before. "That's what I thought."

While silence and heartbreak exploded in his soul, he pointed at the glass of Chardonnay. Sam knew what that meant. It wasn't the first time she'd seen him like this. Within a minute, she placed another glass of Chardonnay on the bar. Sam smiled and squeezed his cold and clammy hand, comforting him as best she could.

While acknowledging her, he returned his gaze to Cynthia's invisible spirit. After reaching for her hand on the bar, cold emptiness and loneliness grabbed his soul once more. Taking his drink in his hand, he savored all of Blanton's subtle nuances. Gently clinking the glass of Chardonnay with his drink, he murmured, "cheers." As the final election results flashed on the screen, he realized he was the only incumbent city commissioner not re-elected.

After hanging his head low, he placed the palm of his hand on his forehead and closed his eyes, hoping to end his sadness and sorrow of losing the election. While silent sulking had run its course in his soul, the lights flickered several times. Muted shadows boomeranged throughout the pub. A swooshing sound emanating from the front entrance seized his attention. After turning toward the front door, awe-and-shock grabbed his flushed face while Sam's rosy cheeks turned ghostly pale. As a beautiful lady entered, time stood still. Suddenly, an empty beer glass shattered on the floor. While catching Sam's bug-eyed expression, he mouthed, "no way."

As the color drained from his face, Blanton's burned as it went down, leaving him breathless. Coughing, he held up his glass toward Sam once more. After this unexpected entrance, he hoped another bourbon would clear his mind and return him to reality. Turning toward the mysterious, haunting lady, she sat at the far end of the bar. Her stare was hypnotizing.

While stunned beyond belief, Blanton's calming power did little to ease his anxiety. This beautiful lady, the spitting image of Cynthia, sent his pulse racing. As he rubbed his eyes continuously, her haunting beauty pounded his soul with uncertainty and fear. He wondered whether his wife had a twin sister she never knew existed. As the lady's devouring eyes met his, her seductive expression held his intense gaze. At that moment, he knew this beautiful lady was real and not an aberration of too much of one of Kentucky's finest bourbons.

Sam delivered him his fourth drink of the evening. With his drink in hand, he walked gingerly toward the lady, hoping not to stumble and embarrass himself. As he sat on the stool beside her, her sultry silence captivated him. Nodding at Sam, he motioned her to bring the glass of Chardonnay to him. Sam placed it on the bar in front of the stool to his right, where Cynthia always sat. Picking it up, Bryan offered it to the mysterious lady. She gently took it in her right hand, and her sensual lips met the rim of the glass. As she savored Cynthia's favorite Chardonnay, Bryan held up his glass toward her, and she gently tapped it.

As she whispered "cheers" in his ear, her warm breath aroused his senses. Her sultry voice played games with his psyche. Her warm whisper ignited his subconscious being, and his mind began to wonder what was happening. Somewhere in his past, he had heard that voice before. With the silence and tension fading away, he stared deep into her soul, waiting for his subconscious voice to answer him.

"I haven't seen you in here before. I'm Bryan Walters."

As her stare bored deep into his glassy eyes, her sexy and irresistible voice replied, "Nice to meet you, Bryan. I'm Angela, Angela Clark. I went by the name Angie when we were growing up, but I prefer Angela now, okay?"

After a puzzled nod, Bryan took another sip of Blanton's. It controlled his raw emotions. While admiring her flawless face, her hair rested squarely on her shoulders. Her scent mesmerized him, a smell he knew all too well. Umari Seduction by Shadé was Cynthia's perfume. A deep breath of its alluring seductiveness ramped up his anxiety to a new level. He couldn't believe his eyes; he thought for a moment that he might be hallucinating, or Blanton's addictive power finally took over his soul. However, when Sam introduced herself to Angela, the angelic and sexy voice was real and alluring to anyone. She was real, maybe too real, they both realized.

# CHAPTER 4

The lights flickered once more, casting shadows across Angela's mysterious face. As her haunting brown eyes captivated him, a weird connection to her jolted his soul. In his mind, a vision flashed from his youth. Furiously shaking his head, Blanton's met his lips once more. After swallowing the eight-year-old bourbon, he sighed heavily. Somehow, somewhere, he knew that voice from his past, but where, he couldn't recall.

"Angela, have we met before, or do we know each other somehow?"

"Hmm, you don't remember me, do…you…Bryan?" As his face grew warm, his eyes searched his subconscious world. "I believe they used to call you Bailey. As I remember, you always bailed out on every curveball bearing down on you, right, Bryan?"

More confused than ever, his forehead glistened under the fluorescent lights. After another sip of Blanton's, he wiped his brow, taking a deep breath of her sensual aura. As he strained to remember all of the Angies in his past, one finally jolted his soul.

"Seriously, Angie Clark, am I right?" Her alluring nod grabbed his soul. "No way. You don't look anything like you did back then. What's it been, thirty-five years?"

"Umm, something like that."

"You moved right after your senior year, right?"

"Uh-huh, that's right. We ended up in California. Do you remember my mom?"

"Umm, yeah. Barclay, right?" She nodded. "A beautiful woman, as I recall."

"Yeah, she was. Remember, she worked for your dad, Alex, during his campaign for the state senate. Umm, that's until she got pregnant with Lenny, which she always told me was an unfortunate mistake because the timing wasn't right."

"What do you mean?"

"Ask your dad?"

"My dad, he's dead. What does that have to do with Lenny?"

"You know, never mind, you wouldn't understand. You were young and naïve, just like me."

"Umm, okay. What happened to Lenny? He was what, six years younger than us?"

"Yeah, something like that. Anyway, when he finally came out of the closet after graduating from high school, my parents disowned him. He couldn't take the hurt. He was rebellious and got in some minor trouble. Eventually, he moved where he would fit in better. I haven't heard from him since that day. Both my parents are dead now."

"I didn't know. I'm sorry to hear that." Nodding, Angela tasted the developing nuances of the Chardonnay.

"Are you okay?" Nodding again, she smiled. "You must know, I did like Lenny, hmm, you know?"

"Yeah, all you guys did, the infamous Oakmont Diamond Brotherhood, as I recall, right?" He nodded and enjoyed Blanton's spicy character. "You guys always made fun of him, even called him queer bait a lot. He didn't seem to mind because he thought you guys were his friends. I knew differently, and that bothered me. It still does today."

"Angela, we were just young jocks joking around. We meant no harm." She offered no response and took a big sip of the wine. "Tell me more about your life."

"Umm, of course. After graduating from high school, I joined ROTC at the local university where we lived. I did my time, and it changed me mentally and physically. I became a strong woman, a black belt in karate. I can take care of myself. I even took some acting classes, was in a few plays, and for a while, I even thought I wanted to be an actress. But that didn't pan out. I discovered I loved delving into people's minds much more. You know, finding out what makes them tick."

After nodding, Bryan's intense stare admired her haunting eyes and lustful smile as she continued opening up to him. "Eventually, I got married, had a son, don't know where he is now either. I'm divorced now. I have a great career as a behavioral psychologist. Even authored a book, you should read it sometime. I think you would find it very interesting. Anyway, two years ago, I moved back here. Not sure why, but something strange brought me back home, even brought me here tonight. Anyway, umm, you remember me now, right?"

"Yeah, I do. Uh, we had some classes together our

sophomore year, maybe our junior year as well. Hard to remember everything that happened back then."

"Uh-huh. I wasn't pretty or sexy back then. Had braces, and wore black-rimmed glasses, remember?" Remaining silent, another sip of Blanton's warmed his face once more. "You know, I never told this to anyone before. Umm, I don't even know why I'm telling it to you now. Anyway, I had a mad crush on you back then." Awkward silence grabbed him as another sip of bourbon burned as it went down. "Well, I did. I can't believe you took advantage of my gullibility and naiveness back then. Anyway, that's water under the bridge now."

While his mind drew a blank about what she was referring to, the burn of Blanton's left him gasping as his pulse exploded in his soul. Silently, he stared at the television, hoping things would change in his favor. After reviewing the results scrolling on the bottom of the screen, he wanted to forget what happened thirty-five years ago. Deflecting her mysterious, probing eyes, he moved the conversation in a different direction.

"Umm, what about your cousin, Bambi? I remember you two were very close."

"Yeah, we were like sisters. Why do you bring her up?"

"Umm, no reason, she just popped up in my mind. She was something else as I remember."

"Yeah, she was. All the boys liked her, even you. Uh, enough about her, tell me all about your life? What makes you tick, Bryan?"

"Umm, been in Oakmont all my life, went to college here, majored in banking and finance, worked my way up to CEO, was in city government until tonight. I lost my wife, Cynthia, to breast cancer about two years ago. In many ways, you remind me of her."

"How so?"

"Umm, hard to explain."

"Well, I'm sorry for your loss. Did she go to school with us?"

"Nah, I met her in college. She's from Cincinnati, Ohio."

While Angela finished her last sip of wine, Bryan sniffed his glass; Blanton's aroma was all that remained. Signaling Sam for two more drinks, she approached him, shaking her head.

"Sorry, Bryan, got to cut you off. Let me call your son."

"Nah, I'm okay."

"No, you're not. I'm calling your son." After pulling out her iPhone from her back pocket, she found his number from her recent calls.

"Sam, hold on for a moment." She nodded as Angela's haunting eyes zeroed in on Bryan's glistening forehead. "Bryan, I'll take you home. We're old friends, right?"

Angela's mesmerizing voice captivated him. As he listened to her, his eyes gravitated to her delectable and perfect curves. Everything about her reminded him of Cynthia's sensual body. As his lustful mind and hormones began awakening, he wondered where this evening might go.

"Okay, yeah, yeah, sounds good, Angela. Sam, she can take me home. I'll be fine. We're old friends."

Satisfied that Bryan would not be driving home, Sam put her phone away. While moving their glasses and

wiping off the bar, she watched Bryan's charming drunk-
enness in action.

"Hmm, Angela, maybe, umm, when we get to my
home, umm, maybe we can have a nightcap, umm and...
er, we can, you know what I'm talking about, right?"

Angela rolled her eyes and sent a flirtatious smile at
his lustful eyes. As she bit her lower lip, a tantalizing,
sultry wink along with her irresistible scent ignited his
lust for her all the more. Smiling back at her, he placed a
Ben Franklin on the bar. He told Sam to keep the change;
she'd earned it. Angela grabbed his arm as he slid off the
stool. With him close to her aroused curves, an eerie
feeling bolted throughout his body, sending his pulse
racing.

As they left, Sam felt sorry for Bryan. She knew he
was a lonely man, and Blanton's was his only friend
these days. Although Angela's motives were questionable, maybe a one-night stand with her would help move
his life in a different direction. Bryan was on a self-
destructed path fueled by too much alcohol and loneliness. He needed something to change his life before it
was too late. Maybe Angela had the right prescription to
save him.

# CHAPTER 5

With Angela's BMW X3 parked a block away, they would walk past Wilson Bortel's bank, where his victory celebration was still in full swing. While walking toward her car, Bryan's alcohol-induced lustful mind craved Angela's curves in motion. Oblivious to his surroundings, he paid no attention to anything or anyone else. On the other hand, Angela was in complete control of her emotions and hormones. She was always aware of her surroundings; she'd learned that the hard way.

Across the street, a pearl white Porsche 911 glistened in the yellowish glow of the old-world streetlights that gave downtown Oakmont its old-world charm. A car of that significance was uncommon in the city. Its unique dark tinted windows created an invisible shield for anyone inside or its contents. Glancing at the Porsche several times, she wondered why such a car of power graced the streets of Oakmont.

Continuing toward her car, she held his hand firmly, squeezing it ever so often. Her touch continued to ignite his dormant hormones as he fantasized about a night of steamy passion with her. After sneaking another glance at her perfect curves in motion, the heat was building in his groin. While imagining her next to him in his bed, his heart raced faster and faster.

Because his mind was on her tantalizing body, he hadn't realized the noise coming from Bortel's bank. He abruptly stopped, glaring at the celebration taking place in the lobby. The disappointment of losing the election to such a smug-ass jerk smashed the lustful fantasy playing out in his mind. As he murmured four-letter vulgarities under his breath, Angela watched anger devour his flushed face, his thumping heart. Tugging on his arm, he forcefully shook off her grasp.

Across the street, Preston Geronimo sat in his pearl-colored power machine, watching Bryan's rage erupt as he stood glaring at the victorious celebration going on inside the bank. The door on the Porsche opened slightly, letting the coolness of the evening enter. With one foot out, he watched Bryan's rage escalate. Abruptly, something told him to let it play out. Moving his leg back inside, he closed the door. Within seconds, an open window allowed him to experience the ensuing fireworks.

"Bryan, let's go so I can get you home, where you can sleep it off."

"Look at that asshole, Angela. He thinks he is a real hotshot now. I'm going inside to show him a few things."

"That's not a good idea, especially the shape you are in."

"I'm fine, Angela."

"No, you're not. Let's go, Bryan."

He shook her grasp from his arm, walked to the door

of the bank, and glared inside. Angela wondered where Bryan's anger might take him next. She grabbed his arm once more, but he shook it off. Quickly jerking the door open, he entered, motioning her to follow him. Once inside the lobby, Bortel's supporters were oblivious to them standing there. However, it didn't take long for Bortel to spot Bryan's anger across his face. Approaching his with arrogant cockiness, Bortel pushed his drunken outrage.

"Well, well, Mr. Walters. Have you come to concede? I've been waiting for your call. All the votes are in, and I won. I'm sure you will ask for a recount, but it won't make any difference. Just man-up and concede."

"Screw you. We'll see about that, you asshole. I heard rumors that you bought votes, and that's how you won. You're a cheater, plain and simple."

"That's crazy. You're drunk, but most of all, you're a sore loser." Angela's sexiness caught Bortel's wandering eyes. He smiled, moistening his lips. "Miss, you might want to get him out of here before something ugly happens."

"Listen, you asshole. Leave Angela out it, or I'll…"

"Or what?"

Wilson's campaign manager, Grant Persinger, watched this verbal altercation escalate, as did Preston Geronimo from across the street. Seeing the glare and glassiness in Walter's eyes, Grant quickly approached them as Walters drew back his fist, ready to strike. As he launched his knockout punch, a firm grip immediately prevented Bortel's jaw from shattering. Bryan turned, scowling at Angela, who held a firm grip on his wrist.

"What the hell did you do that for?"

"You're wasted. I didn't want you to get hurt, but

more importantly, make a fool out of yourself, which you may have already done."

"I can handle myself. You're the one who made me look like a fool."

Bortel backed away from Walters, laughing and taunting him. "I can't believe you let your bimbo stand up for you. What a coward you are." Continuing laughing and ridiculing him, Angela quickly met Bortel face to face. While her haunting eyes grabbed his soul, her inviting cleavage captured his lustful eyes. After noticing them, her powerful knee sent him grabbing his crotch and gasping for air. Anguishing in pain, he glanced up at her. Flaunting her cleavage in his face, she smiled, taunting him all the more. Visibly anguishing in pain, he watched Angela and Bryan leave the bank. Glancing back at Bortel, who was still gasping for air, Bryan flipped him an emphatic up-your-ass-bird.

Reaching her car, she unlocked the doors, and he slid into the passenger's seat. After Angela was securely behind the wheel, she glanced at his drunken posture. She scolded him for not using a seatbelt. After buckling up, her ample cleavage and her well-toned thighs re-ignited his lustfulness. With his hormones reaching the ignition stage, his hand found her right knee. As he moved it upward, she quickly smacked his hand. Embarrassed like an exploring teenage boy, his hand rested quietly in his lap as he gathered his composure. While glancing at her scowl, his face grew warm and distant. Probably embarrassed, Angela thought. However, she needed to clear the air. After reaching for his hand, her touch eased his disappointment and anxiety.

"What's going on in that mind of yours, Angela?"

"Uh, when I asked you about Bambi, you seemed cold, that it bothered you."

"I'd rather not talk about it."

"Something happened to her, right?"

"It was a tragic ending. You know, she ended up pregnant. Her parents couldn't handle it. They moved away before she began showing. Long story short, she gave birth to a boy, complications from delivering her son eventually took her life. Are you satisfied now?"

"I'm sorry, I didn't mean to upset you." Silence smothered the car until the powerful purr of the Beamer growled. "Listen, Angela, when we get to my home, will you come in for a nightcap?

"Maybe. What do you have in mind?"

"Just a nightcap, unless you want something more, you know what I mean, right?"

While rolling her eyes, a sultry smile flashed across her face. As a lustful grin met her gaze, his primal urges erupted as the car pulled away from the curb. His house was just a ten-minute drive away. Pulling into his drive-way, she cut the engine as silence captivated them. With her hand on the gear shift, he reached for it just as she pulled it away.

"I guess we're here."

"Yeah, we are. Will you come in for a nightcap? I promise I'll behave, of course, that's if you will."

"Well, umm, we'll see. What do you, umm, really want, Bryan?"

# CHAPTER 6

Angela's sultry-seductive voice grabbed his lustful mind. Quickly rolling her eyes, a flirtatious smile fueled his jets all the more. He promptly exited and walked around the car, opening the door. While moving her killer-like legs toward him, his eyes gravitated to the short, tight leopard-skin skirt. Breathing deep to calm his raging lust, he extended his hand to her. Grabbing onto it, she maneuvered her tall frame out of the car. As she stood in front of him, her mesmerizing stare tempted him. However, he promised to behave and cooled his raging hormones. As she scanned his house, he led her up on the expansive porch. Opening the door, they entered his lonely, lifeless, but beautiful home.

"Wow, you've done well for yourself."

"Thank you, make yourself at home while I fix us a nightcap."

Angela nodded, and he entered the kitchen. As he poured two glasses of Chardonnay, his phone rang. It was a quick and harsh conversation. While waiting for Bryan to return, she scanned the great room. The portrait above the fireplace took her breath away. As she stared at it, Cynthia Walters' eyes bored holes in her soul. Anxiety erupted in her veins as she stood breathless, seeing her likeness in the portrait. Remaining fixated on Cynthia's stunning beauty, her seductive sexiness, Angela was oblivious to Bryan standing behind her.

"Beautiful and sexy, wouldn't you say?"

"Shit don't sneak up on me like that. But yeah, she is beautiful, sexy, and her eyes could seduce anyone. Maybe even me. She even looks a lot like me."

Turning to face him, two glasses of Chardonnay called their name. She studied his stare at the mesmerizing eyes of the portrait. Handing her the glass of wine, it kissed her sensual lips. Its many nuances lingered on her palate. Nibbling on her lower lip, she moistened it, tormenting his lustful eyes.

"Nice, I always found the taste of pears and lemons together are quite sexy and seductive. What is this?"

"Caymus Mer Soleil Reserve?"

"Haven't had it before. Expensive, I presume?" Bryan nodded. "Umm, Cynthia's favorite, right?"

"Of course. Why don't we relax on the sofa?"

"Yeah, why not. Noise must travel far in this house, probably the hardwood floors. I don't mean to pry, but I couldn't help hearing your conversation. Uh, you seemed disturbed. Is everything okay?"

"Yeah, just my nosey neighbor across the street. She wanted to bring over a package of mine delivered to her house by mistake. I told her I had a visitor, and this was not a good time. It's nothing to worry about."

Sitting side by side on the sofa, the alluring nuances of the wine began its seduction. Taking another lingering sip, Angela placed her glass on the sofa table. Her engaging eyes met his as he took a long drink. Gently, she took the glass out of his hand and placed it on the table. While leaning in, her kiss soothed his troubled and lonely lips. Tasting her sweetness, her sexiness, he searched for more of what she was willing to offer. Her deep, exploring kisses swallowed his powerful lust. As her engorged breasts touched his soul, his hormones exploded. She responded to his arousing tenderness. While her sultriness, her sexiness, left him gasping, he wanted all of her, and now. As their hormones reached the ignition stage, she backed off and stood up. Gasping, he met her flirtatious smile. Rising and breathing heavily, he wanted all of her and couldn't wait any longer.

While watching her eyes move in the direction of the master bedroom, he took her hand, led her to his bedroom, and closed the door. While exploring each other's wants and needs, heat, lust, and passion erupted in a hot fury behind closed doors. As their hormones ravaged their souls, their bodies collided with raw passion and excitement. Expressions of fulfillment and gratification echoed off the walls. Finally, becoming one, silent pleasure captured them. With her head resting on his shoulder, he caressed her back. Her breasts kissed the hairs on his chest, leaving him gasping for more of her. Playfully, her fingers gently tickled his hairy chest, kindling his fire and lust all over again. Kissing her forehead, she let out a big cleansing sigh.

"Umm, what are you thinking?"

"Uh, back then, you know, when we were growing up, I had this huge crush on you, as I mentioned earlier. My secret fantasy was to melt into your arms and make passionate love to you all night long."

He smiled, continuing to hold her sexiness next to

him. His primal urges began to search for more of her vulnerability, her burning uncontrollable passion. Exhausted from the effects of pure ecstasy, she drifted off to sleep in his arms. As she breathed peacefully, he closed his eyes, saying goodbye to Cynthia forever. As he absorbed Angela's soft and silky sexiness next to him, he believed he could find true love again, and maybe with her.

As a new day filtered through the curtains, freshly brewed coffee aroused his senses. Rubbing his eyes, he turned over, expecting Angela's sensuous curves under the sheets. However, empty disappointment squashed his lustfulness. After a quick bathroom stop, he followed the aroma of freshly brewed coffee emanating from the kitchen. His lustful thoughts expected to see her seductive presence waiting for him. Instead, empty silence grabbed his soul. Next to the coffee maker, a note under an empty coffee cup grabbed his attention. Picking up the cup, he immediately tossed it in the trash. He no longer needed it. He said goodbye to Cynthia last night.

Fetching his coffee cup out of the cabinet, he poured himself a cup to calm his anxiety. Smelling its robust aroma, he savored the nuances of Starbucks Dark Roast as Angela's seductive scent lingered on his body, in his soul. Putting his cup down, he picked up the note smelling its alluring scent. At first, a subtle smile spread across his face only to morph into a questionable scowl of anxiety.

Tossing the note into the trash, he quickly entered the great room, hoping Angela was relaxing on the sofa. With a disappointing frown, he returned to the kitchen, picking up his coffee and taking a sip. While sitting at the kitchen island, he wondered what the note meant.

Turning on the television, Commissioner-elect Wilson Bortel, in all his smug righteousness, boasted about his victory. Not what he wanted to see after reading the note and his altercation with him last night. He flipped the bird in his face and quickly turned off the television. After carrying his coffee to the great room, he placed it on the mantel. Reaching for his wife's portrait, he finally took it down. Putting his index and middle finger to his lips, he pressed them on her lips for a brief moment.

"Honey, you told me if I found love again, to embrace it. I will always love you, you know that, but it's time to let you go."

Although the portrait was just a mass of canvas, paint, and brush strokes, her spirit answered him and set him free to love again. Smiling, he carried it to the basement. Placing it on a shelf, he covered it with the blanket Cynthia knitted for him while fighting her courageous battle with cancer. Returning to the great room and his coffee, he sat on the sofa staring at the emptiness above the fireplace. While breathing deeply, Angela's scent still lingered on the couch. Disregarding the note's warning, he realized it was time to embrace true love again. He wondered whether Angela was the person to help him find peace and happiness once more.

# CHAPTER 7

Preston Geronimo entered McGruder's before the lunch rush. While being his first visit to the pub, he was unaware of all the beers on tap. After scanning the pub from front to back, side to side, he chose a stool just underneath a television at the front of the u-shaped bar. He counted twenty on one side and saw more beer taps through a window-like opening. After counting those, he guessed they had a total of about forty, quite impressive for a bar in Oakmont, he thought.

Before long, Sam fronted him and introduced herself. To her, the man appeared to be in his late forties or early fifties, wavy black hair, probably professionally colored, she thought. Clean-shaven and handsome, his pink button-down oxford dress shirt under a black V-neck sweater conformed to his well-toned body.

"What may I get you, Mr....?"

"Preston Geronimo, but most people just call me Geronimo. What do you recommend, Sam?"

"West Six Amber Ale, a craft beer from Lexington. May I offer you a taste?" He nodded and glanced at the television above him while she drew a sample of the beer.

"Here you go."

"Thank you, ma'am."

After smelling the beer's aroma, the amber ale tasted just as well, smooth and not too hoppy.

"Hey, Sam, this is fine. Draw me one."

Sam left, and a minute later, she returned with the West Sixth, placing it in front of him. "You want to start a tab?" He nodded and tossed his credit card on the bar. "Great, is there anything else I may get you?" He shook his head while glancing up at the television. "Just holler at me when you are ready for another beer or want to order something to eat, okay?" A man of few words, he nodded, and she went about her duties.

On the television, a breaking news flash caught his attention. He waved at Sam. She approached him, noticing he couldn't take his eyes off the screen. "Would you turn up the volume, please?" After grabbing the remote and adjusting the volume, Kiersten St. Clair's sexy voice filled the pub.

"Just in, incumbent City Commissioner Walters has lodged a formal inquiry into allegations that Commissioner-elect Bortel engaged in illegal vote-buying. As you know, he won by a mere seventeen votes. Commissioner Walters has filed a formal request for a recount and recanvas as well. Hold on, everyone, Mr. Bortel just left the courthouse." After approaching him, Kiersten's mic was in his face. "Mr. Bortel, is there any truth to Commissioner Walters' allegations of illegal vote-buying?"

Agitated by her question, he vehemently responded, "Absolutely not, I won fair and square. And last night, he stopped by my celebration at the bank. He was drunk and upset that he lost and threw a punch at me. If it weren't for that floozy lady friend of his, I would be filing assault charges. He's a sore loser and will pay for this one day. I've got to run, no more questions."

"Thank you, Mr. Bortel." Turning to face the camera, Kiersten continued her report. "There you have it, folks. Stay tuned for further developments in this situation that isn't going away anytime soon. Now, back to your normal programming."

Geronimo motioned Sam to cut the volume. Downing the last ounces of his beer, he held his glass toward Sam. A minute later, another West Sixth Ale was on the bar. Taking a long draw, he put it down.

"Sam, I assume someone in law enforcement owns this place."

"Well, sort of. Two professors in the Department of Justice and Safety at the university started it a long time ago. Initially, a hole-in-the-wall, they moved, built a new place, that one burned down, and now we are here.

"Hmm, I like it."

"So, Geronimo, I haven't seen you in here before. You live in Oakmont?"

"Nah, never been here before, just visiting. Let's say I lived most of my life on the west coast. I heard of this place from a friend and thought I'd give it a try. What's McGruder's specialty?"

"Rueben on grilled marble rye. Can I put an order in for you? Comes with homemade chips, or you can add fries or onion rings for a dollar more."

"Okay, sounds good. Are the onion rings homemade?"

"Of course. That's the only way to serve and eat them, right?"

Nodding, Sam left to put his order in as he continued to survey the pub. Besides the law enforcement motif plastered on the walls, coat of arms flags hung from the steel trusses giving it that classic Irish feel. It was one of a kind and the in-place in Oakmont.

As he savored the West Sixth, a swooshing sound emanating from the front entrance grabbed his attention. Three gentlemen entered and looked for their favorite booth. Recognizing one of them as Wilson Bortel, the man on the breaking news segment, he followed their path where they took the corner booth. Sam immediately greeted them and left.

Within minutes, two other men entered through the side entrance and took a seat on the other side of the bar. Studying Bortel, Geronimo was startled as Sam placed his Reuben and onion rings in front of him. After smelling the aroma of corned beef and sauerkraut, his mouth began to water. The onion rings were thick and golden brown, just like the homemade ones his mom made years ago. After one bite of the Reuben and one crunch of the golden crispy onion rings, a thumbs-up greeted Sam's cheery smile.

Geronimo was good at watching people and reading lips. He glanced at the two men sitting on the other side of the bar. Their conversation appeared meaningless to him. Sam approached them and took their order. Ironically, they chose West Sixth Amber Ale as well. Sam drew the beers and put them in front of them. Geronimo continued to watch them as they took a long draw of their beers. After putting their beers down, one of the men locked eyes with him.

Breaking the man's stare, Geronimo directed his gaze at Bortel and his two friends. Although he didn't know any of them, he still was interested in their conversation. As he ate the delicious Reuben and onion rings, he kept an ear to the discussion in the corner booth. While good at reading lips, it was apparent the conversation centered on Commissioner Walters' allegations.

As Geronimo took his last bite, he noticed Bortel and his friends badgering Sam. He could see that things were heating up, and she was visibly upset. Being the gentle soul he was, he walked over to inquire if everything was okay. While standing at the booth, Bortel's smirky grin met Geronimo's badass posture.

"Sam, is everything okay?" She wiped a few tears off her flushed cheeks. "Mr. Bortel, I assume. Leave the lady alone, okay?"

"Mr...."

"Geronimo."

"This is not your concern, so bug off."

"Right, I just made it my concern. Sam, just let it be. He is clearly a jerk."

"Sam's friend, Commissioner Walters, is the jerk, sir! He almost attacked me last night."

"Yeah, he is my friend, and he would have kicked your ass, you jerk!"

Sam returned to the bar while Geronimo settled things with Bortel. He could easily take him in a heartbeat, and it wouldn't be pretty. After an exchange of unpleasant pleasantries, he returned to his seat at the bar. Sam noticed his glass was empty and placed another beer in front of him.

"Thanks. Bortel is such a jerk and always tries to hit

on me even though he's old enough to be my dad. This one's on the house. Thank you."

After nodding, Geronimo's reassuring smile eased her anxiousness. "He won't be harassing you anymore, I promise you."

She nodded and headed for the kitchen. Geronimo glanced at the two men on the other side of the bar, then finished his West Sixth Amber like a college student during rush week. After she returned from the kitchen, Geronimo motioned for his bill. After leaving a generous tip, he stood up and glared at Bortel on his way out.

# CHAPTER 8

The past few days, tranquility flowed through the Oakmont Police Department. Detectives Carla McBride and Bernie Kowalski were enjoying the downtime to their advantage. This past year had been incredibly difficult for them. However, the past two cases had brought them closer together. Although they were not partners when this unprecedented crime spree began, they were now a confident and formidable team. They were forced together by Police Chief Brock Evans during The Black Rose case. In that case, Bernie suffered gunshot wounds for the first time in his career, while Carla, unfortunately, notched her first kill. Through all of this, they became faithful partners.

Ever since Beth Pendergast joined the police department, she quickly became a valuable member of their team. A forensic psychologist and profiler, she was instrumental in solving a fifteen-year-old cold case that haunted each of them to this day. Beth's current cold case involved a young woman found in a ditch at the city cemetery some twenty years ago. Since no one came forward to identify her, she was considered a loner and homeless. Furthermore, with little evidence to go on, the case quickly turned stone-cold.

While reviewing all the files with Beth, a well-dressed gentleman entering the police station caught Carla's eye. The big clock on the wall showed ten o'clock. Murmuring under her breath, Bernie caught a glimpse of him as well. Bryan, "The Crusher" Walters, son of Commissioner Walters, had been a person of interest in Alaina James Gonzalez's death in The Black Rose Case. After being cleared, neither of them had had any contact with him since that day.

"Bernie, what's he doing here?"

Shrugging his shoulders, he continued reviewing the transcripts from the Angel Hardesty cold case. Carla observed Bryan's demeanor as he registered with the receptionist. Fear, anxiety, and uncertainty painted his face as he sat, waiting to see someone. Within minutes, Chief Evans met him. After exchanging pleasantries, they walked to the chief's office. While passing by Carla and Bernie, Bryan's worried eyes met their stoic faces. Bernie watched them enter the chief's office, and then the door closed.

"Hey, Carla, I wonder why Bryan is visiting the chief?"

"Who cares? It probably doesn't involve us."

"How do you know, are you clairvoyant now?"

"I just know, dickhead, trust me."

"Right, and you've never been wrong before, have you?"

Carla rolling her eyes, brought a smirky smile to his face momentarily. However, it quickly disappeared as Chief Evans appeared from his office, with Bryan following. They entered the conference room just off the hall-way. Within a minute, Chief Evans appeared from the conference room, heading straight to them. After seeing a concerned scowl across his face, they knew their down-time was about to change. With him stopping at their desk, it confirmed they had a new case. And somehow, it involved Bryan "The Crusher" Walters.

They accompanied him to the conference room. On the way, he explained the reason for Bryan's visit. After entering the room, Carla and Bernie sat opposite Bryan while Chief Evans sat at the head of the table.

"Detectives, I assume you remember Bryan, son of Commissioner Walters." Both nodded. "His father has been missing for a few days, and he wants our help." Acknowledging him, he continued, "Bryan will tell you what he knows. After that, you can ask questions, okay?" They nodded once more, and he motioned Bryan to begin.

"Detectives, I want you to know I asked for your help to find my dad. Chief Evans says you're the best he has. I know several months ago we got off on the wrong foot, but it all worked out, no hard feelings on my part."

"Bryan, we apologize for not handling it differently. We were just doing our job."

"Of course, Detective McBride. As I said, no hard feelings." They both nodded as he continued. "My dad hasn't been at work for the past couple of days. He called me Wednesday morning, saying he needed time off. I thought nothing of it at the time. However, when he didn't show up today or contact me, I got a little worried."

Bryan paused to take a deep breath and then contin-ued. "After checking with his administrative assistant, I called his cell, no answer. I tried it a second time, went straight to voicemail. I ran by the house, looked around. He wasn't there, nor was his silver Jaguar. He's never done this before."

"Okay, Bryan. When was the last time you saw your dad?"

"Detective Kowalski, this past Tuesday, around seven o'clock, I met him at McGruder's for a beer. He always spent election night there with my mom. This time it was different. My mom passed away about two years ago. Breast cancer took her life." A short pause provided Carla and Bernie the opportunity to offer their condolences. "Thank you, anyway we had a drink together talking about my mom. He said he would see me tomorrow. I wished him good luck in the election and left. That's the last time I saw him."

"You said you stopped by his house. What time was that?"

"Detective McBride, right after work last night, around six o'clock. I used my key to get in the house."

"Did anything seem suspicious to you, you know different, or out of place?"

"Yeah, the alarm was off, and my mom's portrait above the fireplace was missing. I thought that was very strange. Burnt coffee was in the coffee carafe, and that was unusual. His bed was unmade, as well. Dad was anal about those things. Something is not right."

"Did he have any enemies that you know of?" Bryan shook his head. "Okay, if you don't mind, we will run by the house and check things out?"

"Sure, here is my key. The code to the security gate is 1745, while the code for the garage is 2482."

"Okay, we will go through the house and garage, see

if anything suspicious catches our eye. We'll let you know what we find out."

"Thank you, Detective McBride."

"Sit tight, you two, I'm going to walk Bryan out, and I'll be right back."

Several minutes passed, and the chief returned with the same worried expression as before. Glaring at them, he continued.

"I don't know what is going on with Commissioner Walters, but something is dead wrong here. Let's give it our best and find him. Unless there are any questions, get the hell out of here and find him, now."

# CHAPTER 9

Located in Camelot Estates, an exclusive upscale gated community outside the city, Commissioner Walters' house was a twenty-minute drive from the station. After keying in the code at the security gate, Commissioner Walters' house was on Mahogany Way. The two-story brick home was impressive. An inviting porch spanned the front of the house, giving it that classic southern charm.

A well-manicured lawn and shrubbery validated Commissioner Walters' son's comment about his dad's meticulous and anal habits. Pulling into the driveway, Bernie put the car in park, then cut the engine. After they exited, a driveway led to a three-car garage at the rear of the house. A covered breezeway connected it to the home. Behind the garage, a wooded area spanned the entire side of the street. Scanning Mahogany Way, the peacefulness of the neighborhood offered no cause for concern.

"Carla, I'm going to check out the garage. Why don't you check the mailbox and meet me back there?"

Carla nodded and proceeded to the beginning of the driveway. A large mailbox and a newspaper tube were built into a brick column showcasing the house number. Retrieving the mail and newspapers, she walked toward the garage to find Bernie. With the garage door up, a silver Land Rover stood ready to tow a boat. While in the other bay, a 2010 pristine red Corvette convertible waited for its driver to rev it up. Both car hoods were ice-cold; nothing seemed disturbed.

Satisfied with their inspection of the garage and grounds, they walked back to the front of the house. While walking up on the porch, its massive white columns gave it a persona of power and prestige. Knocking on the door, they announced themselves in case Commissioner Walters was home. Silence flowed back at them.

Although it wasn't an apparent crime scene, they drew their service weapons and turned on their flashlights just the same. Inserting the key in the lock, Bernie turned the doorknob. Opening the door slowly, it creaked. Carla announced herself once more; again, silence rang out. Opening the door further, Carla stepped inside, shining her flashlight around. Bernie followed with his flashlight beaming.

As they scanned the great room, blackout shades and drapes created an eerie morbid atmosphere. Shining her flashlight up the staircase to the landing overlooking the great room, Carla paused for a moment, seeing something that looked out of place. Her beam of light focused on the railing's attachment to the wall, then to the floor directly below. After catching her breath, she tapped Bernie on the arm, he flinched.

"What?"

"We have a problem. Point your flashlight at mine."

As his beam of light joined Carla's, his scowl met her eyes. "Shit, that's a big problem, alright. Umm, who is it?

"It looks like Wilson Bortel."

"Who the hell is he?"

"Come on, man. He's been in the local news a lot lately. He edged out Commissioner Walters in Tuesday's election. Walters filed a complaint with the election board for possible illegal vote-buying."

"Umm, I'm still drawing a blank."

"Forget it, dickhead. He's likely dead, but I'll check for a pulse anyway. Then we'll check the rest of the house before calling it in."

Bernie nodded. After checking for a pulse, she shook her head several times. Dividing up, they quickly searched the rest of the first floor, all clear. They moved on to the second floor, all clear as well. Returning to the great room, Bernie found a light switch that illuminated it. Bortel's naked body straddled the table. Blood-stained glass lay on the floor below the table. The word "cheater" written across his chest sent their mind wondering. After turning off the lights, they returned to the porch.

"Carla, I don't know about you, but that is a little freaky and weird."

"Yeah, while I call Chief Evans and give him the bad news, you call for a forensics team and the coroner, okay?"

Bernie nodded and walked down the steps to make his calls while Carla sat in a swing at the far end of the porch to call Chief Evans. After a few rings, he answered, and she put him on speaker.

"Chief, you remember the famous line from Apollo 13, you know, Houston, we have a problem?"

"Of course, what's that got to do with Commissioner Walters?"

"Nothing, because he's not here. However, his opponent, Wilson Bortel, is. He's dead as a doornail with the word 'cheater' written across his chest."

"Umm, that's not good."

"No shit, chief. Forensics and DJ are on the way. We'll keep you informed. You better bring Commissioner Walters' son in right away. We need more answers. Also, put a BOLO out on his dad and the silver Jaguar."

The call ended, and Carla joined Bernie sitting on the porch steps. Looking up and down the street, he shook his head numerous times.

"Carla, how does this happen in this neighborhood? It's so peaceful and quiet."

"I don't know. We live in a sick, demented world, where anything is possible."

Twenty minutes later, forensics pulled into the driveway, followed by the coroner, DJ Franklin. As forensics gathered all their equipment, Sherry, the department's manager, approached them.

"Carla, what do we have inside?"

"A dead and naked Wilson Bortel is lying on a massive, shattered glass table. Anyway, we carefully went through the house. We didn't touch a thing. However, we discovered an unlocked back door. You might want to dust it for prints."

Sherry rolled her eyes and sent Carla a crooked dirty smile. She gathered up her team, made assignments, and entered the house to comb it from top to bottom. After she left, DJ met them on the porch.

"Wow, you guys seemed to find a way to get along finally. I thought the chief was out of his mind when he made you partners." Double birds met his crooked grin. "Must have known something no one else did. Well, anyway, so we have Wilson Bortel inside. I always knew politics was a dirty game, and now it looks like it's a deadly one, wouldn't you say?"

"Yeah, maybe. We're going to canvas the street while you do your thing. No use for us to be in your way. We'll catch up with you later."

"You got it, Bernie.

As DJ entered the house, they began canvassing. Carla took the street's right side while Bernie took the other side; they would meet at the security gate and guardhouse. After canvassing, neither found anyone at home. The unattended guardhouse had one camera on the front and one on the back. Looking through a window, electronic equipment, probably a video recorder, appeared lifeless. A sign listed the security company's contact information, and Carla took a picture of it with her iPhone.

# CHAPTER 10

Striking out on their quest to find any residents at home, they returned to Commissioner Walters' house. Inside, a flurry of activity met their gaze. Lying on the tables several feet away, Bortel's body, covered by a white sheet, contained more questions than answers. Standing and staring at the balcony railing, DJ looked confused with a questionable expression on this face.

"DJ, update, please?"

"Bernie, time of death, based on everything I know, probably at least eighteen hours ago."

"You did say eighteen hours ago, right?" He nodded. "That puts the time of death at around Eight or Nine PM yesterday."

"That sounds about right, Carla."

"Well, that's not good. Commissioner Walters' son said he stopped here after work, around Six PM. He told us his dad wasn't home and nothing was disturbed."

"Sounds like a problem to me, and to make matters

worse, he may have been dead when he came flying off that balcony, but the autopsy will determine that."

"Damn, DJ, anything else?"

"Yeah."

Handing a note to Carla, she read it and gave it to Bernie. Reading it aloud, "He cheated. He deserved to die." Passing it back to DJ, Bernie sniffed his hands, bringing a curious expression to his eyes. He thought he recognized the scent. However, he wasn't sure where and thought nothing more of it.

"Well, DJ, that explains the word cheater on his chest. Shit, this is not good. It sounds like we have a sicko out there, or Commissioner Walters took matters into his own hands." DJ nodded and glanced at the railing on the balcony, then returned his gaze to Carla. "And now, Commissioner Walters is missing."

"Missing?"

"Yeah, DJ. That's why we're here in the first place. When Commissioner Walters didn't come into work, his son became concerned and asked us to check things out. To make matters worse, he was the only incumbent not re-elected. Could be a possible motive."

"Guys, this all doesn't make any sense. Good luck."

"Thanks DJ, now we have to find Commissioner Walters wherever he is. What a way to end the week, right, Bernie?"

"Yeah, crime never takes a day off, and now, we'll be working the weekend. So much for that family gathering, I was looking forward to."

Carla and Bernie appeared in a daze as Sherry approached them. She and Carla were not bosom buddies per se. However, they managed to get along better since the last case. Carla always wanted answers yesterday.

Sherry, on the other hand, was thorough and deliberate and didn't care what Carla wanted. She liked explaining everything in every little detail, which pissed off Carla to no end. Love-hate described their relationship, mostly hate.

"Sherry, what do you have, and let's make it quick, okay?"

"McBride, what's got your panties in a wad today?" Carla threw her an in-your-face bird. Sherry rolled her eyes and motioned them to follow her. Entering the master bedroom, she took her black light out. Slowly moving it over the unmade bed, dried semen glistened on the sheets.

"Shit, that's a lot of sex going on this bed. Someone was horny, and someone was hot to trot. I guess that makes for a lustful night."

"Yeah, smell that pillow, Carla?"

Carla walked around the bed, leaned down, smelling the scent. "I don't recognize it. Certainly nothing I would wear. Any ideas, Sherry?"

"Umm, Shadé, you ever hear of it?"

"Uh, yeah, but who the hell wears that stuff these days?"

"I do, bitch."

"Yeah, Carla, my wife, Lydia, does, too. You have a problem with that?"

Ignoring Bernie, "What's it called, Sherry?"

"Umari Seduction."

"Umm, not for me. Eros makes me feel like a natural woman, you know, a real woman."

Bernie interjected, "Really, well, uh, all I can say is whoever was in this bed seduced the hell out of someone else, presumably Commissioner Walters. Must have been his lucky night, umm, that's a lot of sex for anyone, even me." In an instant, Bernie rubbed his arm. "Damn, Carla, why did you do that for?"

Carla rolled her eyes and directed her gaze to Sherry. "What else you got?"

Although Sherry had seen this movie before, her face warmed as she continued, "Guys, now follow me to the kitchen."

After entering, Sherry reached into a white garbage bag and pulled out a coffee cup with Cynthia's name painted on it. Then she pulled out a note and handed it to Carla.

"Read it aloud, Carla."

"Okay, Bernie. It says, last night was the best. However, you better watch your back from now on."

"Carla, smell it." Sniffing, she handed it back to Sherry. "Recognize it?"

"Umari Seduction?"

"Right, Carla. You guys, whoever was in that bed, likely wrote this note. Now, follow me upstairs to one of the guest bedrooms."

Following her, they entered the first bedroom at the top of the stairs. Sherry pointed to the bed, where pillows and covers were in disarray.

"Guys, more semen on the sheets, and the scent on the pillows are the same. Those are the big things I wanted to show you. We'll get everything back to the station and see what else we find."

Carla and Bernie returned to the great room and went out on the porch, scanning the street, looking for security cameras. Two had them, and they proceeded across the street. They had already knocked on every door on the entire street; no one was home. Jotting down the house numbers, they would come back later to see what those security cameras could tell them.

Before crossing the street, movement at the guardhouse caught Bernie's eye. It appeared to be a van from the security company. Tapping Carla on the arm, he pointed toward the entrance. Quickly walking to the guardhouse, anxiety ran through their bodies. Finally, reaching it, the door was open. A technician dressed in a company uniform was working on one of the machines.

"Excuse me, sir, I'm Detective McBride, and he's Detective Kowalski. We'd like to ask you a few questions."

"How can I help you?"

"Can you pull up footage from last night?"

"Sorry, that's why I'm here. I received a report that the video recorder wasn't working. Whoever called it in was right. The last recording was from two days ago. Not sure what happened, but it's fixed now. Anything else I can help you with, Detective Kowalski?"

"No, thank you, sir, sorry to bother you."

Walking back to the house in silence, they wondered what would be next in this case. They've had weird ones in the past, however, this one was already shaping up to top them. Maybe their most challenging one since becoming partners. The house now had crime tape everywhere; forensics and the coroner were gone. Walking to Bernie's car, Carla was ready to open the passenger door and call it a day, however, Bernie proceeded toward the garage.

"Where are you going?"

"I got a hunch. Follow me."

Carla caught up with him as he walked past the garage toward the wooded area bordering all the houses on the even side of the street. Scanning the wooded area, Bernie noticed a path into the woods. He turned to Carla, "Let's take a hike and see what we can find."

"Really, in these shoes."

"Suck it up, partner."

"Bite me, dickhead."

Bernie smiled and entered the woods with Carla trailing in her brand-new designer sneakers. The further they went into the woods, the muted shadows swallowed the sunlight creating a spooky atmosphere. Finally reaching the end of the path, a county road ran parallel to it. On the other side of the road, more dense woods. While scanning the berm, fresh tire tracks and footprints were visible. Carla pulled out her iPhone and took several photos.

# CHAPTER 11

After returning to the crime scene, Carla called Sherry to inform her of the tire tracks and footprints. Still fuming about her dirty designer sneakers, Bernie ignored her continuous four-letter barrage on him. Walking down the driveway, movement from the house across the street caught Bernie's attention. Tapping Carla's arm, he pointed at the home across the street. A woman had just exited a white Nissan Murano heading for the mailbox. After retrieving her mail, she stepped up on her porch, unlocked the door, and entered.

When they reached the front of Walters' home, crime scene tape blocked the entrance to the cold and dark porch. Proceeding across the street, they walked up the steps, and Bernie rang the doorbell. Within minutes, the door opened. A stunning, petite brunette greeted them, introducing herself. They promptly flashed their badges, grabbing her attention.

"Mrs. Tierney, I'm Detective McBride." He's my partner, Detective Kowalski. We'd like to ask you a few questions."

"What's going on over there? Is Bryan, okay? What's with the crime scene tape? Did somebody die? I hope it wasn't him. Did somebody, uh…?"

"Slow down with the twenty questions, Mrs. Tierney."

"Detective McBride, please call me Bobbi, you know, short for Barbara." Carla nodded as she continued to barrage them with questions. "You know, I always thought Bryan would be a good catch and all. You know, he stayed faithful to his wife until the very end. Anyway, how may I help you?"

Bernie jumped in, pointing up at the security camera, "Ma'am, does that work?" She nodded. "Is it possible to review footage from yesterday evening, say from five o'clock on?"

"So, what's going on? I saw the coroner's van leave as I entered the gates?"

Carla chimed in, "It's a death investigation, that's all I can say."

"Oh my, it's not Bryan, is it?"

"No."

"If it isn't, then…who?"

"Mrs. Tierney, may we see the video footage? You may even help us catch the killer?"

"Oh, of course. Please come in. The video recorder is in my office at the back of the house. Follow me. May I get either of you anything to drink?"

"No, I think we are good, right, Carla?"

Carla nodded. Walking down a long hallway, Bobbi entered her office, and after a few keystrokes, the video footage was on the monitor. Offering Carla, a chair at her desk, she sat down while Bernie leaned over her right shoulder as the video began to play. Bobbi returned to the great room where her wine called her name.

Needing to view several hours of footage, Carla hit the fast-forward arrow. As the sun was setting, muted shades of darkness gave way to the artificial glow of the night. After an hour or so, Carla stopped the video and glared at Bernie. The only car on the video pulled into the garage of the house next to Commissioner Walters. He shook his head, exhaling a disappointed sigh. Carla repeatedly murmured one of her favorite four-letter expletives under her breath.

Walking into the great room, Bobbi sat comfortably with a glass of red wine as the gas fireplace created a warm and cozy space. Hearing their meaningless chatter, Bobbi rose to greet them.

"Well, detectives, did you find what you were looking for?"

"Did you see anything strange at the Walters' residence over the past few days?"

"Sorry, Detective McBride. Once I'm home, I don't venture outside. I'm not a nosey neighbor, like some other people in this neighborhood. Clarissa, his next-door neighbor, practically threw herself at him. At least, that's what I heard. She is kind of weird, single and attractive, but just plain weird. Maybe a little off upstairs, you know. I keep my distance from her. You know you can't be too careful these days."

"Right, thank you, Mrs. Tierney."

"Of course, Detective Kowalski."

"We'll be on our way. You've been a big help, Bobbi."

Walking them to the door, she bid them goodbye. As she closed the door, a sultry smile met Bernie's curious eyes, and her sensual perfume brought a smile to his face. Walking off the porch, the sound of the deadbolt securing the delightful home caught their attention. While crossing the street to Bernie's car, he broke their disappointed silence.

"Carla, she's strange, don't you think?"

"What do you mean?"

"Oh, for someone who declared she wasn't a nosey neighbor, she seemed very interested in Commissioner Walters' welfare."

"Yeah, maybe she is lonely and available, you know?"

"Umm, maybe. She did give me, you know, a smile and that look."

"Really, and what look is that?"

"You know, like someone that's on the prowl, hot to trot, enjoys a roll in the hay."

"You wish, dickhead, get your mind out of the gutter. Let's see if Bryan Walters' son is with Chief Evans yet. We need answers and fast."

"Oh, one other thing, Carla."

"Now, what, dickhead?"

"She wears Umari Seduction, same as on the pillow of the bed and the note."

"Seriously, you think she is...?"

"Nah, she's a sweetie."

"Well, I don't know about that. Didn't you notice them...you know?"

"Oh, yeah, how could I miss them?"

"Not the girls, dickhead. They're impressive, I'd say. However, she is very muscular, with very little body fat, and her legs, well, they could certainly do some damage around a man's neck. She's definitely in great shape for her age."

"Uh-huh. Person of interest, umm, I don't know. However, these days anything is possible."

"Right, we'll need to do our due diligence and check her out."

"Whatever you say, McBride."

While traveling back to the police station, Carla called Chief Evans and found out Bryan, "The Crusher," Walters would be there when they arrived. Bernie was driving like a slow turtle, but ever since The Black Rose case, Carla had learned how to ride shotgun and smell the roses.

Bernie turned on Sirius XM radio to The Blend. As Jimmy Buffet's "*Come Monday*" faded away, Tim McGraw's "*Live Like You Are Dying*" filled the cabin. Car karaoke took over as they both sang along word for word. Ever since they became partners, it had become their anthem for living. It's about living and cherishing each day because you never know when it's your last. They knew that all too well; the events of The Black Rose case that sent Bernie to the hospital with gunshot wounds. While there, he discovered prostate cancer had grabbed his soul. He began to think about smelling the roses more often.

Pulling into the police station's parking lot, Tim McGraw belted out the final lyric of *Live Like You Were Dying*. As they entered the station, muted chatter filled the common area. A quick stop at their respective mail-boxes, they both walked past them with smiles on their faces. They loved seeing emptiness staring back at them.

Walking down the hallway toward Chief Evans' office, the voice of a worried son echoed off the walls.

Seeing them approaching his office, Chief Evans motioned Bryan to follow him to the interrogation room. Carla and Bernie arrived at the entrance about the same time as they did.

After entering, thick silence exploded as the door closed. With everyone seated, Bryan's demeanor reflected a son that was scared as hell about his father's whereabouts, a father he loved dearly. Even though Bryan was an All-American linebacker during his playing days, he had a sensitive, emotional side. As he wiped a tear from the corner of his eye, he said, "Please tell me what you found at my dad's house?"

Carla wasted no time digging her claws into him. "Bryan, where's your dad?"

"I don't know. I have no idea. Dad didn't answer his cell, so, uh, I'm clueless. What's going on?"

"Bryan, we found Wilson Bortel dead at your father's home."

"Shit, was my dad there, Detective McBride?"

"No, but he's now a person of interest in the death. We have a BOLO out on him and his Jaguar. So, if you know where he might be, we need to know now. Was he seeing someone?"

"Odd question, why?"

Bernie, tired of playing second fiddle to Carla, interjected, "Although we haven't confirmed anything yet, his bedsheets reflected a night of continuous sex, semen everywhere, even in the bedroom upstairs. Do you have any idea who his partner might be?"

"As far as I know, he's seen no one since my mom passed away. He couldn't find it in himself to move on, love someone else. That's why Blanton's became his friend, well, I guess, his liquid lover. Detectives, I don't know anything else. The last time I saw him was at McGruder's. Alone, as usual, he was nursing a Blanton's, while a glass of chardonnay sat on the bar where my mom always sat."

"Bryan, if you can think of anything, please get in touch with us. Carla and I will visit McGruder's to see what we can find out."

"Thank you. I don't think my dad is capable of murder. It's not who he is."

Carla said, "Bryan, sometimes we think we know people, even family, like the back of our hand when we don't. I hope you are right about your dad."

# CHAPTER 12

McGruder's had bittersweet memories for Carla and Bernie. In their past cases, the Irish pub, with all its Irish influence and law enforcement friendliness, became their second home. Although bad memories were ever-present when Sam waited on them, McGruder's was instrumental in helping them solve their past three cases, and Sam had returned as well.

The pub's silent atmosphere was like the calm before the storm. The local clientele was still fighting the rat race, which gave them quiet solitude to finding answers to questions they didn't even know they wanted to ask. Instinctively, their investigation was always open-ended, always expecting the unexpected while ruling nothing out of the realm of possibility.

After entering the pub, their usual corner booth just off the main entrance was vacant. Carla slid into her side with a perfect view of the main doors and large windows facing Main Street. Sitting in the booth, Bernie squirmed side-by-side, trying to get comfortable. Carla, used to his quirky antics, rolled her eyes at him.

"Do you have to do that every time we're in here? People probably think you got a wedgie going on or something even worse."

As an indiscreet bird met her gaze, he continued to find his comfortable position as Sam arrived.

"What brings you here this late in the afternoon? I figured you would've already called it a day. Anyway, what can I get you each?"

Carla glanced at Sam and then at her iPhone—4:27 flashed on the screen. Almost quitting time, she thought, but then again, they had a high-profile case to solve.

"Bernie, what do you say? We are going to be here a while, so, why don't we, uh, you know…?"

"Just spit it out, McBride. What's your problem?"

"Bite me, dickhead, let's have a beer while we ask her some questions about the other night."

"Whoa, wait a minute, guys, about what night?"

"Sam, bring me a Yuengling, and bring Miss Sourpuss a…"

"Sam, bring me a Smithwick's and gather up your laptop. We need to look at the video from Tuesday night, okay?"

"Yeah, one Yuengling, one Smithwick's, and the laptop. Hmm, it sounds like it's going to be an interesting afternoon. Anything else?"

"Yeah, put a double order in for fried hot banana peppers, right, Bernie?"

He nodded, then glanced at the television above the bar. Breaking news flashed across the screen. "Ah shit, all hell is going to break loose now."

Carla's eyes lit up. Bernie pointed to the television

screen. Turning her head, she said, "Yep, it was just a matter of time." Sam returned with their beers, placing them in front of them. "Would you please turn up the volume?"

Sam directed her gaze to the television, grabbed the remote off the bar, and the breaking news segment playing out grabbed their attention.

"This is Kiersten St. Clair reporting from the residence of Commissioner Bryan Walters. Our sources tell us a body found inside his house is allegedly Commissioner-elect Wilson Bortel. Details are sketchy at this point. We hope to update the story as more information becomes available. Now, back to your regular programming."

"So, this is why you're here. I'll get the laptop."

After the clinking of the glasses, this fishing trip was on. After sipping on their beers, Sam placed the fried hot banana peppers with complimentary condiments in the middle of the table.

"Okay, guys, the laptop needs to charge a little more. It will probably be ready by the time you finish the peppers."

"Sounds good. Did you work Tuesday night?"

"Yeah, what do you need to know, Carla?"

"Was Wilson Bortel here that night?"

"No."

Bernie never liked Carla controlling the conversation. After all, he was the senior detective. As Carla was ready to respond, Bernie quickly jumped in, "But Commissioner Walters was, right?" Sam nodded, and he continued, "Tell us all about that night while we are devouring these scrumptious hot banana peppers, okay?"

Sam glanced at Carla, who nodded. She pulled a stool

from the bar and sat at the end of the booth. Over the next ten minutes, she explained the events of that night in detail while they finished off the peppers.

"So, this mystery lady, a spitting image of Commissioner Walters' deceased wife, shows up and rescues him. Coincidence, hmm, what do you think, Bernie?"

"Umm, that's strange, alright. Maybe it will make more sense once we've seen the video."

As semi-dried suds stained their beer glasses, Sam grabbed them and left to replenish them. Returning with two full glasses, she left again. A few minutes later, Sam placed the laptop on the table.

"Here you go, guys. You know what to do. If you need me, just holler."

While staring at each other, Carla threw Bernie "the look," and soon, Bernie got up and slid in beside her. With the video already loaded, she placed the cursor on the play-arrow and tapped on the trackpad, starting the video. Several minutes later, the video ended with Angela Clark and Commissioner Walters leaving the pub. Bernie glanced in Sam's direction, catching her eye. After a minute or so, she was standing at the booth. While cleaning up the remains of the banana peppers, she carried the empty plastic baskets back to the kitchen and returned.

"So, this mystery lady's name is Angela Clark, isn't that what you said?"

"Yeah, Carla, let me show you a picture of Cynthia Walters."

After pulling out her smartphone, she brought up a photo of Bryan's previous election celebration two years ago. Handing the phone to Bernie, they both were in awe of the likeness to Angela Clark. Giving the phone back to

Sam, Carla noticed Bernie's glass was empty, so she downed the rest of her Smithwick's.

"Yuck! Bernie, please, remind me never to let that beer get warm again, okay?" She wiped her mouth and took a drink of water to wash away the strong taste in her mouth. "Okay, that's quite interesting. What else can you tell us?"

"Let me pull up another video from the next day." After a few strokes of her finger, the video filled the screen. "Here you go, I'll be behind the bar, just wave at me, and I will explain what went down."

Carla hit the play-arrow, and Wednesday afternoon's drama between Sam and Bortel played out on the screen. After the three-minute segment finished, Bernie waved at Sam. She quickly returned to the table, sitting on the stool, ready to explain what went down. As before, they listened as she explained in detail what took place.

"Who was the guy coming to your rescue?"

"Yeah, him. Preston Geronimo said he was just visiting, and he lived most of his life on the west coast. I haven't seen him in here since that day."

"Why did he get involved?"

"Not sure, Bernie. Bortel was getting loud and belligerent, trashing Commissioner Walters. Said that Commissioner Walters and Angela stopped by his celebration accusing him of buying votes, even tried to throw a punch at him, but Angela grabbed his wrist, stopping him."

"Who are the other two men that walked out after Preston Geronimo. From what I see, it's apparent there was a stare-down between them and Bortel?"

"Parker Jarrell and Colt Lassiter, strange guys, you know, maybe they were gay. One of them was wearing a woman's perfume. Parker, the guy in the beard, was older than Colt. Anyway, that's about all I know. They drank beer and played pool. The funny thing is, they were here Tuesday night before Angela arrived. They ordered beers, played pool, and left a few minutes after Bryan and Angela. That's it. What's going on, Carla?"

"Bring us our bill, Bernie's buying. We need to get to Bortel's bank before it closes. And by the way, we need copies of those videos."

# CHAPTER 13

Several minutes later, they were heading to Freedom National Bank. On the corner of Main Street and Jackson Avenue, it was the second-largest bank in the city. With Oakmont Trust and Savings being the largest, that caused rifts between Walters and Bortel. Although it had nothing to do with politics or city government, it was one of the driving reasons Bortel ran for city commissioner in the first place.

Only a short walk from McGruder's, they arrived as an individual had just locked the main doors to the bank. Two detective badges clicked on the glass doors startling him. After unlocking the doors, Carla introduced themselves and entered. The identification badge on the man's sport coat read John Vickers, Vice President, Commercial Sales.

"Mr. Vickers, may we have a few moments of your time?"

"Of course, Detective Kowalski." After locking the main doors, they followed him to his office. He motioned them to sit in a pair of red-leather winged-back chairs. "I assume this is about the tragic death of our CEO." Bernie nodded. "How may I help you?"

"We need to see video footage of Tuesday evening. We understand Commissioner Walters and a lady friend of his crashed his celebration. We understand the commissioner threatened Bortel. Were you here that night?"

"Unfortunately, I was, Detective McBride. I witnessed the whole confrontation. The commissioner, obviously drunk, confronted Wilson. Shouting occurred. The next thing I knew, Commissioner Walters drew his fist back. That's when I approached them. If it hadn't been for his lady friend, things would have gotten ugly. Wilson called Walters' lady friend a bimbo, and that didn't go well."

"How so?"

While this discussion was taking place, Vickers had already pulled up the video from Tuesday night. Turning his monitor toward them, he hit the play arrow. As the video played, Carla and Bernie mumbled until that moment arrived. As Wilson doubled over, grabbing his crotch, Bernie cringed.

"Detectives, is there anything else I may help you with?"

"When was the last time you saw him or talked with him?"

"Let's see, he took Wednesday off. He was here Thursday. So, I guess it was late afternoon on Thursday. He said he would be out on Friday. Detective McBride, anything else I may help you with?"

"Yeah, we need a copy of the video. Just put it on this thumb drive, if that's okay?"

Several minutes later, they walked towards McGruder's, where Bernie parked his car. After getting inside, Bernie hit the ignition button. While turning on the heated seats, Carla did a quick search for Angela Clark. The only listing in the area was for a behavioral psychologist. The address was just a few blocks away on Water Street.

As they looked at each other, Bernie put the car in gear, pulled away from the curb heading for her business. Carla dialed the phone number listed, and it went straight to voicemail. After listening to her greeting for a few seconds, she hung up and sighed.

"Why the big sigh?"

"Whoever this Angela is, her voice is downright seductive even to me. Glad you didn't listen to her. You'd have to cool your jets."

Bernie smiled and pulled in front of her business. A sign in the yard listed all the particulars of her services. Exiting the car, they approached the small porch. After looking for the doorbell, Bernie's eyes gravitated to an old-fashioned doorknocker on the dark-stained door. Bernie gave it a try and waited. Silence. This time, with a little more force, several thuds filled the porch. No footsteps, just silence.

"I know it's getting late, Bernie, but we need to get Commissioner Walters' son back in for more questioning. I'll call the chief and see if we can get it done tonight."

Walking back to the car, Carla placed a call to Chief Evans. It was short and sweet. Within minutes, Bernie was headed to the police station. A few blocks away, Carla's phone rang. After a short conversation, she hung up and gave Bernie a thumbs-up gesture. The rendezvous with Bryan, "The Crusher," Walters was on.

After arriving, they checked their mailboxes; their

emptiness made them both crack a smile. Not bothering to stop at their desks, they headed straight for the interrogation room to wait for Bryan. The digital clock was pushing Six PM when they entered the interrogation room. It had already been a long day, but it could be an even longer one based on what other information Bryan gave them.

While waiting for Chief Evans and Bryan, Carla plugged the thumb drive into the conference room's laptop. A monitor on the wall displayed the videos they would show Bryan. At 6:00 PM, Chief Evans, accompanied by Bryan, entered the interrogation room and sat at the table. With everyone ready, Carla clicked on the play-arrow. The first video began to play within seconds.

When the mystery lady appeared in the first video, awe-and-shock painted Bryan's face. Flushed, he said, "Freeze it there. This can't be possible." The lady's flawless face stung his soul. "Who is she, Detective McBride?"

"According to Sam at McGruder's, her name is Angela Clark. She is a friend of your dad from his teenage years. You ever heard of her?"

"No, I haven't. What was she doing there, especially on that night?"

"We don't know, but she might have something to do with your dad's disappearance."

As the video continued playing, the awe-and-shock expression never left Bryan's face. It was easy to see this lady upset him. When it ended, the second video from Freedom National Bank began to play. Although the audio was not available, Bryan witnessed a side of his dad he had never seen before. When his dad drew his fist back, he cringed. Carla stopped the video.

"Now, do you think your dad is capable of murder?"

At this point, Bryan didn't know what to think. All he knew was Bortel was found dead in his dad's house, and now his dad was missing. The last person to see his dad alive was a woman who could pass as his mother.

"What else have you got?

Bernie interjected, "Semen all over his bedsheets. Your dad must have had sex all night with presumably Angela Clark. We tried to question her, but she wasn't home, and she didn't answer her phone. Forensics found a note in the kitchen trash can. It read, "last night was the best, however, from now on, watch your back." If he didn't kill Bortel, then he is in real danger. Do you have any idea where he might be, no matter how far-fetched it is?"

After vigorously massaging his temples, Bryan shook his head several times before sighing.

Carla said, "I know this is difficult to take, but think hard while watching this other video. It might have a bearing on this case."

The video from McGruder's began to play. Bryan closely observed the verbal altercation between Sam and Bortel. Two minutes later, the monitor went dark. Bryan rubbed his temples and then faced everyone with apparent fright controlling his eyes.

Carla continued, "Bryan, do you know either of those men in the video. Preston Geronimo is in the pink shirt. The man in the baseball cap went by Parker Jarrell, while the other was Colt Lassiter. Do you recognize any of them, seen them before?"

Studying the faces of both men, he replied, "The man in the baseball cap looks like someone that's been in the bank lately, not sure, but the physical characteristics sure look familiar. The other two guys, never seen them before."

Bernie interjected, "Okay, now, we're getting somewhere. Do you know where your dad could be? Did your dad have a lake house anywhere or a cabin in the woods?"

"Yeah, mom and dad had a small houseboat on Jackson Lake. Nothing fancy or elaborate, just a place to hang out. He put it up for sale as soon as mom died. I don't know if it ever sold or not. He never mentioned it, nor did I ask. They loved the place; surely, he wouldn't take that lady there. However, since she could pass for my mom, maybe he's delusional, or he's trying to relive the great times they had. I don't know what's going on with him."

"Give us the directions, and we will check it out. It's worth a shot. I hope we're not too late."

"Too late for what, Detective McBride?"

"I don't mean to alarm you, but I think your dad is in danger."

# CHAPTER 14

L ake Jackson, a five-thousand-acre lake, rested north of the city. With one way in and one way out, the road followed the topography of the shoreline. Off that road, gravel driveways led to each houseboat or cabin. The twenty-five-minute drive from the police station gave them time to discuss the bizarre beginning of this case. Finding Bortel dead in Commissioner Walters' house didn't make any sense.

Furthermore, based on the coroner's initial examination, Commissioner Walters' home may not be the original crime scene. Discovering fresh tire tracks on the other side of the woods with footprints suggested maybe the killer or killers carried him through the woods and entered the Walters' residence through an unlocked back door. All seemed possible, they thought.

Reflecting in their headlights, the sign for the entrance to Lake Jackson was a right turn away. They weren't sure what they were going to find at the houseboat. Bernie navigated the potholes disguised by the moon's reflection on puddles of water as the tires crunched the limestone gravel road. According to Commissioner Walters' son, the driveway leading to the houseboat was the seventh turnoff after turning left onto the main road. After making a left turn, a car's headlights came into view in the rearview mirror. Bernie continued to glance at the car, which appeared to be a white sedan. He watched it turn left, heading away from Lake Jackson.

While continuing toward the seventh turnoff, a white wooden makeshift sign came into view. It read Walters' Shangri-La. After turning right, the gravel driveway meandered down to the moonlit lake. Just off to the right was a silver Jaguar XF. Pulling beside it, the Jag glistened under the moon. Cutting the engine, they exited the car taking notice of the surroundings.

Sliding his hand across the stone-cold hood, Bernie wiped the excess dew off his fingers. Carla wiped the condensation covering the driver's side window; her flashlight moved throughout the inside. Pulling on the door handle, she smiled. After opening the door, Umari Seduction's alluring scent took her breath away.

Several feet away, split rails outlined the path to the lake. As their shoes crunched the gravel path, an eerie uncertainty crept into their soul. After traveling about twenty yards, the moon's glow reflected on the windows of the small houseboat. As Commissioner Walters' son alluded to, it was nothing fancy, more like an updated pontoon boat. Walking down the floating wooden dock, the plank leading to the houseboat glistened under the moon's brilliance.

Bernie's flashlight moved across the walls and windows of the living quarters. With each step they took along the port side, small waves slapped the aluminum hull creating a Rod Sterling-like atmosphere. Just ahead, a beam of light found the door to the living quarters.

Bernie twisted the knob, and hushed Carla's passive chatter. As he opened the door, an eerie quietness met them. While shining his flashlight around, nothing caught his attention. After feeling about for a light switch, Bernie found it and flipped it. Cold darkness continued to surround them, while the faint scent of Umari Seduction sent their pulse racing.

As Bernie's flashlight moved around the main living space, it appeared no one had lived in it for some time. It was nothing fancy and didn't fit the lifestyle of a bank CEO or, for that matter, an influential city commissioner. A kerosene heater sat on the floor. After hovering her hand over it for a few seconds, Carla felt the coldness of a steel mesh covering the wick. At the back of the living space, an accordion-like door faced them.

Approaching it, Carla positioned herself to the left while Bernie grabbed hold of the wooden handle. On a silent count of three, Bernie pulled the door toward him. As Carla's flashlight moved across the bed, remains of hot sex glistened under the beam of light.

A storm door on the starboard side met their gaze. Carla's flashlight illuminated it shining through the window in the top portion of it, casting its light on a rope tied to the railing.

"Bernie, look there."

"Why are you whispering?"

"Shush, dickhead."

"Seriously, no one's here." Approaching the door, Bernie twisted the knob, pulling the door open. "You first, ma'am."

After walking out onto the narrow walkway, an

anchor-like rope secured to the top rail caught Carla's attention. After Bernie joined her outside, she pointed to the rope and motioned him to give it a pull. Putting gloves on, he leaned over the side, grasping the rope with his right arm. Pulling on it, he raised it several feet, but its weight was too much. When grasping it with both arms, the rope's weight gave way as he slowly pulled it through the water.

Leaning over, Carla grabbed onto the rope, helping him. A few feet to go, a dull thud of metal on aluminum brought disgust to their faces. Carla's flashlight illuminated the rusty anchor. Bernie glanced at her and nodded. Within seconds, the anchor swiftly found the bottom of the lake.

"Shit, Bernie, it's not what I expected."

"What did you expect, a body or a giant catfish?" Shooting the look at him, she shook her head. "Yeah, I've heard there are catfish in this lake big enough to swallow a small child."

"Bite me, dickhead." A smile crossed his face momentarily until the sight of another rope tied to the rail towards the bow squashed it.

"What?"

Pointing toward the rope, Carla turned to face another rope hanging down toward the lake.

"Bernie, didn't know this boat had two anchors?"

"They don't. Let's find what's at the end of it. Maybe it's Commissioner Walters or that big catfish I was telling you about." Instantly, Bernie rubbed his shoulder. "What did you do that for?"

"Don't screw with me. Let's go find out what buried treasure awaits us."

About twenty feet away, another thick nylon rope

hung toward the lake. Leaning over the railing, they both directed their flashlights toward the water. The beams of yellow light disappeared in its murkiness. Handing his flashlight to Carla, Bernie leaned over and grabbed the rope with both hands. A strained expression filled his face. He glared at her; she put both flashlights away. She leaned over the railing, grabbing onto the rope with both hands. Counting to three, they pulled on the rope. She looked at him, he shook his head, and they both let go.

"Carla, I'll call forensics and a diving team. We got nothing but dead weight down there, and it's not a giant catfish."

"No shit, Bernie. Let's give it one more try before we call the water boys and get them mad as hell at us."

"Alright, but I think whatever it is, we're not going to budge it."

Leaning over the railing once more, four hands gave the rope a mighty pull. "See, I told you, Carla, we ain't going to budge it."

"Aren't, Bernie, not ain't. One more try." Bernie's glare produced an in-your-face-bird. He smiled. "On three, okay?"

He nodded. Four hands pulled hard. Suddenly, they stumbled backward. Looking at each other, they peered over the railing. A mass of arms and legs began appearing in the murky water. Reaching the surface, a purplish naked body, face down, floated aimlessly at the end of the rope. As the beam of light crossed the inscription on the back of the body, their eyes flew wide open.

"Shit. I'll call for the coroner and forensics. This case just got more twisted and bizarre, don't you think, Bernie?"

"You don't say, partner. Let's wait in my car until

everyone arrives. Then we will take a run by Angela
Clark's business. Maybe we get lucky, and if not, we'll
call it a night until the body is positively identified and
processed. My vote is for Commissioner Walters. How
about you?"

She nodded and placed the calls. Twenty minutes
later the coroner, forensics, and the diving team arrived.
After bringing everyone up to speed, they made a quick
run by Angela Clark's business. Pulling in front of it,
they exited the car and walked onto the small dark porch.
Bernie used the doorknocker several times and waited. A
few seconds later, disappointing silence ended their
night.

# CHAPTER 15

As Angela Clark pulled into her driveway Sunday morning, dawn's brilliance filtered through the light fog. An unusual mistiness glistened on the roof of her quaint frame house. Cutting the engine, she exited her Beamer and opened the trunk. Grabbing her overnight bag, she promptly approached the door, unlocking it.

Before entering, she picked up the Sunday edition of The Daily Reporter and retrieved her mail. After closing the door and securing the deadbolt, she proceeded up a flight of stairs to her living quarters, where she tossed the newspaper and mail on an old-fashioned roll-top desk. A table lamp on a timer cast yellowish hues down a hallway leading to the kitchen.

Firing up the Keurig, Starbucks French Roast filled her favorite coffee mug pleasing her grogginess. Once finished, she placed it on the small dining table to cool down while retrieving the newspaper and mail. Returning to the kitchen, she sat at the table, savoring her coffee while she separated her mail by importance. Angela, satisfied with her results, tossed the junk mail in the trash. Placing the important stuff in a neat pile, she grabbed the newspaper. After tearing the plastic bag away, she unraveled the tightly banded newspaper in disgust.

Immediately, a big, bold headline seized her soul. Taking a sip of the robust coffee, she mouthed, "Well, that asshole, Wilson Bortel, got what he deserved in the end." For a moment, her mind drifted to her unpleasant encounter with him. After another sip of coffee, the first paragraph rocked her soul once more. While reading further, she shook her head about whether Bryan was responsible for Bortel's death.

Reading the entire story twice, she sat dumbfounded. Taking another sip of her coffee, it had turned lukewarm. She placed it in the microwave giving it a new steaming life. Returning to the kitchen table, she reread the story. Her usual rosy complexion gave way to a fear-laden shade of pale. As her mind pondered the possibilities, she still couldn't believe Bryan was capable of murder. To think he killed Bortel was ludicrous in her mind, especially leaving the body in his own home.

Nauseated from that thought, she poured out her coffee and headed to the bathroom for a hot relaxing bath. Turning on the water, she adjusted it to her liking. While waiting for the tub to fill, she fixed a mimosa to help her relax and take her mind off Bryan. In the past, a steaming bath and strong mimosas were her recipes for forgetting life's curveballs. A strong mimosa, meaning mostly champagne with a splash of orange juice, would hopefully ease the anxiety rocking her soul.

Removing her clothes, she stared in the mirror at her

well-toned body and its sensual curves. She thought to herself, she had worked hard to become irresistible and wanted. Placing her mimosa on the edge of the jet tub, she stepped in and slowly slid under the soothing, swirling water. As the water massaged her sensuality, the mimosa began to ease her mental anguish, but not her concern for Bryan. Although she pondered whether Bryan believed he was making love these past few nights to his deceased wife, she didn't care one way or the other. Although she had been married and had other sexual conquests, her lust for him lay dormant in her subconscious world until this past week.

With the lukewarm water sliding off her aroused curves, she downed her second mimosa. Stepping out of the jet tub, she grabbed a short fluffy robe and headed for the kitchen. As the champagne released its thousands of tiny bubbles, a splash of orange juice flavored it nicely. Walking into the living room, she grabbed the remote for the gas logs, and soon the dancing flames provided the warmth she craved.

Dry and warm, she sat on the sofa fronting the mesmerizing glow of the fire. As the flames danced among the logs, she grabbed the remote for her stereo. Instantly, soothing music complimented the ambiance of the fireplace. Retrieving the newspaper, she devoured it front to back. Quickly working on the Jumble, she smiled. Then she did her best to conquer today's crossword puzzle. After completing two-thirds of it, her mind needed refreshing. Color comics always gave her mind that boost, that jolt to tackle the remaining clues.

Putting her pencil down, she smiled, knowing her brain performed admirably, and her answers were correct. She never knew if they were because she never graded herself. Returning to the bathroom, she dropped her robe staring at her refreshed body in the mirror. After putting on a silky lounging suit over her vulnerable nakedness, she relaxed on the sofa, enjoying the randomness of the flames.

Trying to push thoughts of Bryan and Wilson out of her mind, she pulled up the calendar on her smartphone. She reviewed her schedule for Monday, her afternoon patients were follow-ups, while her morning appointment was a new patient. Preston Geronimo was an interesting name, she thought and looked forward to meeting him.

After familiarizing herself with the afternoon patients, another mimosa called her name. As the French champagne became a dead soldier, she tossed it into the trash. Retreating to the sofa, she opened the tab for her morning appointment again. She pondered his name once more. The unusual name sparked her curiosity as to how parents chose a name for their son or daughter. Did they just like the name, or did they want it for a specific reason, she asked herself?

Preston Geronimo had already filled out an online questionnaire. Reading it thoroughly, she made mental notes of the critical questions, the ones that mattered. Closing the file, she savored the mimosa as her body finally felt the effects of the champagne. Walking gingerly to the kitchen, she opened her fridge, grabbing two eggs, milk, shredded cheese, and fresh mushrooms. Finding an onion, a small zucchini, a clove of garlic, she had the ingredients for her gourmet omelet, hoping to absorb the mimosa buzz controlling her body.

Ten minutes later, she plated the omelet, complimenting it with whole-wheat toast and strawberry preserves. Brunch consumed and dirty dishes in the dishwasher, she retreated to her living room, enjoying the instrumental sounds throughout her living space. As the sounds of violins accompanied by a single cello released the stress in her soul, thoughts of Monday's first patient crept into her mind once more.

# CHAPTER 16

As Angela prepared for her first client of the day, across town at the Oakmont Police Station, Carla and Bernie reviewed their notes regarding this past weekend's bizarre revelations. Bortel's strange death had more questions than answers. Given the circumstances discovered through their investigation, incumbent Commissioner Walters had been their main person of interest until his body was pulled from Lake Jackson late Friday evening, making this case all the more bizarre.

And with each victim having something written on their body, it became one of their most challenging cases. Bortel had "cheater" written on his chest, while Walters had "four more" written on his back. Dumbfounded and stunned at this evidence, complicating matters was the Umari Seduction perfume found at both crime scenes.

Assuming Angela Clark was the person in Commissioner Walters' bed, in his car, and at the houseboat, she was the only feasible person of interest in his murder that made any sense. However, they pondered whether she could also be a person of interest in Bortel's death investigation. Furthermore, Barbara, "Bobbi," Tierney, as far-fetched as it was, was also a person of interest they couldn't ignore, at least in the Walters' death investigation. Her undeniable interest in his well-being piqued their attention right away. She also wore Umari Seduction, another red flag.

As with all their previous cases, names identified them. Thus, the Umari Seduction Case was born. To this point, the case files only contained their notes because the results from the autopsies and forensics were still unavailable. While waiting for that critical information, Bernie contacted the office of Angela Clark and scheduled a noon appointment. Carla, who was skeptical about Barbara Tierney from the get-go, would do the due diligence to satisfy their curiosity as a person of interest.

However, first things first, and that was questioning Angela Clark. After setting up an appointment with her, they researched her separately. Unfortunately, what they found wasn't much help to them. Clean as a whistle, one would say. After a successful career in California, she returned to Oakmont about two years ago. After starting a new practice, the university hired her as an adjunct professor in the psychology department.

Since their appointment with Angela was not until noon, they started their preliminary research on Barbara, "Bobbi," Tierney. Like Angela, the information on her helped very little. She was squeaky clean as well. Ironically, she had moved back to Oakmont about the same time as Angela. Currently, she is a professor in the Department of Justice and Safety at the university. Before that, Truman State University was her employer. She completed her undergrad at the College of the Ozarks before obtaining her Master's in Criminology at Missouri State University. And like Angela, she held a Black Belt in karate.

Finished with their due diligence, they assembled in one of the interrogation rooms to compare and discuss their notes on both alluring and intriguing ladies. Glancing at the clock on the wall, they had about fifteen minutes before their appointment with Angela. While sitting across from each other, Bernie's wrinkled frown piqued Carla's curious eyes.

"What are you thinking, partner?"

"Umm, I like being called that." Her scowl met Bernie's smile. "You know, uh, nothing, in this case, makes sense. If Walters killed Bortel, why leave the body in his house?"

"Yeah, Bernie, I agree. So, who killed Bortel?" After shrugging his shoulders, his eyes glanced at the clock. "Then Walters turns up dead. Who killed him and why? We have a real quandary on our hands."

"Yeah, Carla, I agree with everything you are saying, but we got diddly-squat, nothing, zippo, nada…umm…"

"How many damn adjectives are you going to use to describe where we are, dickhead?"

"As many as I want." Pointing at the clock, he continued. "It's showtime, partner. Hopefully, after questioning Angela, we'll be on the right track instead of sucking air."

Although divers recovered Walters' body late Friday evening, the circumstances surrounding his death remained a mystery to the media. Given his position in the community, withholding his name was equally important. After leaving the interrogation room, they entered the common area of the police station. On one wall, a large flat-screen television consistently displayed the day's news, locally and nationally. While passing by it, a breaking news flash stopped them in their tracks.

"This is Kiersten St. Clair reporting outside Oakmont City Hall. My sources tell us late Friday night, local police pulled a body out of Jackson Lake. Furthermore, my sources indicate it was the body of Commissioner Bryan Walters who was reported missing by his son." At this point, Commissioner Walters' headshot flashed on the screen. "City officials will neither confirm nor deny this. At this point, Chief Brock Evans is very tight-lipped about this situation given the recent death of Commissioner-elect Bortel. He refused to answer our questions earlier, whether the two deaths were related. He said the investigation of both suspicious deaths is ongoing. Well, that will do it for now. We will bring you updates as they become available. Reporting from Oakmont City Hall, I'm Kiersten St. Clair, now back to your regular programming."

Carla and Bernie wanted to keep everything about this case on the hush-hush, however, they knew Kiersten St. Clair was very good at getting information. They knew it was just a matter of time before all hell broke loose, and now it had. Shaking their heads, they exited the police station and headed for Bernie's car. Angela's business was a ten-minute drive from the police station.

Arriving just a few minutes early, they sat in the car, observing a pearl white Porsche 911 in front of Angela's business. They had not seen this car in town before; it is not something you'd forget. The presence of such a car captivated their curiosity. Whoever owned it had money and power.

At five minutes past twelve, a man appeared from

Angela's business dressed in a well-tailored black suit, accompanied by a red bowtie. The man exuding power looked up and down the street, then approached the Porsche.

"Bernie, isn't that the man Sam identified as Preston Geronimo?"

"Yeah, sure looks like him. Wonder what he was doing here?"

"I don't know, but we're gonna find out, maybe not today, but we'll find out one way or the other."

Dressed in a finely tailored suit, Preston Geronimo settled behind the wheel and checked the rearview mirror seeing them. Within a few seconds, the Porsche's power growled several times, and it quickly pulled away from the curb. They thought about going after him, but Angela's interview was more critical, and they exited the car. Besides, a spanking, brand new pearl white Porsche 911 wouldn't be hard to track down in Oakmont, especially since Carla had taken a photo of the vanity license plate. The word "STUD" would provide them with everything they needed to track him down later.

# CHAPTER 17

Once inside Angela's practice, a young lady behind a non-descript desk greeted them. After flashing their badges, Selena led them to a small lounge area. While waiting, Carla glanced around the house. Off to the left, a craftsman-style staircase led to the second floor. The walls accessorized with eclectic canvas art drew her attention, while a tall sofa table exhibited several unusual figurines. She began to wonder whether the motif reflected Angela's personality.

Several minutes elapsed before the striking presence of Angela met their wandering eyes. The video from McGruder's didn't do her justice. Her beauty and grace demanded their attention. While watching her approach them, it was easy to understand how she carried herself and could seduce any man she wanted for whatever purpose, even murder.

While flashing their badges, they exchanged pleasantries with her. Bernie's wandering eyes created a quick elbow to his ribs. Rubbing his side vigorously, Carla flashed him the look. Bernie said nothing and just smiled.

"Thank you for seeing us. We need to ask you a few questions about Bryan Walters. May we go somewhere offering more privacy?"

"Oh, of course, Detective McBride."

Her sensual, seductive voice even caught Carla off guard. Bernie smiled as she led them down the hallway to her office, leaving a trail of Umari Seduction in her wake. As they entered her office, a casual, inviting motif surrounded them. Although there was nothing fancy about the large sofa and two winged-back chairs separated by a square coffee table, it conveyed a comfortable and relaxing atmosphere for her clients. Several books lay on the coffee table, catching Carla's eye. They sat on the microfiber sofa while she sat in one of the winged-back chairs.

"Miss Clark, I see by the book on the table you're a published author. Umm, that's not an easy task. *Manipulation Through Hypnotherapy*...umm, that's an interesting title."

"Yeah, it is. Maybe you should read it sometime, Detective McBride. You know, you might learn a few things."

"Right, anyway, congratulations on the book."

"Of course. Let's cut to the chase. What's this visit about, Detective Kowalski?"

"It'd be a good idea to close the door." After closing it, she returned to her chair, and he continued. "We're investigating the death of Wilson Bortel. I'm sure you know about that." She nodded. "We know from a video we secured from McGruder's and Bortel's bank. You were with Bryan Walters last Tuesday night."

"Yeah, I was with him. What's that got to do with Bortel. What's it got to do with me?"

"We'll get to that in a moment. What's that perfume you're wearing?"

"Really, Detective McBride. What's that got to do with anything?"

"Just answer the question, okay?"

"It's Umari Seduction, one of Shadé's most popular perfumes."

"Yeah, so, I've found out. Anyway, forensics found traces of it on the bed pillows in Bryan's master bedroom."

"So, what. We spent the night together. It was magical." Her seductive smile met Bernie's wandering eyes. "Umm, we made love all night long. We were both exhausted, so I don't deny being there. Consensual sex is not a crime the last time I checked."

"Would you submit to a voluntary DNA sample?"

"I have nothing to hide or deny, Detective McBride."

"Umm, I take that as a yes. Now, what about at Bryan's houseboat? That same scent permeated the houseboat and his car."

"Whoa, what were you doing there?"

"When was the last time you were with Bryan or talked to him?"

"Did something happen to him?"

Bernie fired back, "Just answer the question."

"Umm, Wednesday night, I met him there. We sat in the car for a few minutes before going onto the houseboat. We had another night of passion there, but you know that, don't you?"

Bernie nodded as Carla met her glistening eyes. "When did you last talk with him?"

"Detective McBride, I was with him again on Thursday evening at the houseboat, and I called him on

Friday afternoon, but it went straight to his voicemail. What's going on? Is he, okay?" Watching their eyes and disposition, she knew the shoe was about to drop. "Something's happened to him, right?"

"I'm sorry to tell you this, but he is dead."

Quickly finding her face, her hands camouflaged her emerging tears. Sniffles broke the silence smothering the room.

"I know this is difficult, but we have more questions that need answering." Nodding, Angela plucked a tissue from the coffee table, absorbing the red sadness in her eyes. "What time did you leave the houseboat?"

"Umm, about Eight AM on Friday morning, I had a Ten AM appointment. Bryan dropped me off around ninesh. You may check with Selena, my receptionist. I have nothing to hide."

Bernie, who had been observing Angela's body language, chimed in, attempting to catch her off guard, "Wasn't that Preston Geronimo that just left? Is he a patient of yours?"

"That's none of your business, and you know it. Let's move on, or this interview is over, okay?"

Perturbed at Bernie's surprising question, Carla's fury met his gaze. "Where were you on Friday evening?"

"Detective McBride, I left town and returned Sunday morning, and you may check with Selena if you like. She made my travel arrangements." Carla nodded. "What else would you two like to know?"

"What was the nature of your travel?"

"That's none of your business, as well. My next appointment is in an hour, so we are done here. One other thing, detectives, should I seek legal counsel?"

Although Bernie was itching to chime in, Carla

continued, "Do you think you need to?" As a cold expression painted Angela's rosy cheeks, Carla's eyes bored into her soul for a moment before continuing, "You know, maybe you should. And by the way, don't leave town."

Angela walked them to the reception area, bidding them farewell. While Carla asked Selena for a copy of Angela's travel itinerary, Bernie left and returned with a DNA kit. A few minutes later, they left her office with Angela's travel itinerary and a DNA sample. Sitting in Bernie's car for a moment or two, they observed the windows of Angela's house for any movement behind the blinds. The blinds remained still as a growl of hunger filled the car. As Bernie rubbed his belly, Carla nodded.

Smiling, Bernie replied, "Where to, partner?"

"McGruder's, I need my Reuben fix for the week, and I have a few more questions for Sam as well."

"Such as?"

"We need to know if Angela, Preston Geronimo, or those two other guys have been back at McGruder's. Somehow they're all connected to this case."

"Okay, what about Angela?"

"I don't know about that, but she knows something, I'm sure of that. On the surface, there's no logical motive. However, she was the last person to see him alive, and her perfume is present at both crime scenes. We can't dismiss that, can we?"

Bernie nodded and pulled away from the curb heading for McGruder's. After a quick lunch and Sam's disappointing answers, they arrived at the police station, mentally exhausted and clueless about who committed either murder.

# CHAPTER 18

The atmosphere in the common area was tranquil
this afternoon. Passing by the in-house mail-
boxes, the empty spaces brought a smile across
their faces. Neither wanted to see any mail in them, especially envelopes with demented address labels or ones
without any return addresses as in The Gold Fedora or
The Black Rose cases. Reaching their desks, Bernie sat
down and squirmed in his chair until he was comfortable.

Carla was on a mission heading straight to forensics
to register the DNA sample. Head of forensics, Sherry
Caudill, still at lunch, meant she would have to deal with
one of her assistants, which never made her happy. It
wasn't that she hated Max because she didn't. Carla
always wanted answers from the top; patience was not a
strong suit of hers when killers were on the loose. Regis-
tering the DNA sample, she returned to her workstation,
dejected. While glued to his computer monitor, a scowl
met Bernie's earnest eyes. Shrugging his shoulders, he
returned his gaze to his monitor and grumbled something
indiscernible under his breath.

"Spit it out, Bernie." Ignoring her, he continued to focus on the monitor. "Hey, dickhead, why are you ignoring me?"

Glancing at her gleaming eyes with a smile, he replied, "Sherry gets to you, doesn't she?"

"Screw you, Bernie. Something's got your attention. You know it's against policy to look at porn at work?"

A silent bird met her eyes. "I don't need porn, been researching Preston Geronimo. Umm, you know, that Porsche is something else. And I'd have to say, that tailored suit he wore today was very professional, probably not made or bought around here. He's a slick dresser. Remember, Sam said he spent most of his life on the west coast."

"And?"

"Hmm, get this. He's a private dick with a law degree, and obviously, a very successful one. His specialty is, get this, missing persons."

"So, what's he doing in Oakmont, and what does he have to do with Angela? Is she hunting for someone? If she did write the note found in the trash can, then she knows more."

"Yeah, that's what I was thinking. I called his cell, went straight to voicemail, left a message, now we wait on him to return my call."

"A message, you want to scare him off, dickhead?"

"Nah, I just said I wanted to talk to him about the issue at McGruder's on Wednesday, and nothing more. I thought that was vague enough. Now, hopefully, he'll take the bait and contact me. What did you find out from Sherry?"

"Nothing, she's still at lunch. I don't understand why she takes those long lunches."

"Nooner, maybe?"

Glancing at the big clock on the wall that everyone hated, fifteen minutes past one glared back at her. After rolling her eyes at him, she sarcastically responded.

"Right, who would have her, you know, she's a plain Jane? Shrugging his shoulders, and returning his gaze to the monitor, Carla continued. "Anyway, I put a message on her phone to come and see us as soon as she returns. Max logged in the DNA sample, said he would get right on it, but you know how that goes." Bernie nodded. "I hate waiting. You'd think these days we could get results much quicker."

"Yeah, but, hey, Angela didn't deny being in his bed at his home or the houseboat. We must assume she is telling the truth. Her results will confirm that and nothing more."

"Guess so, but that doesn't give us much to go on, does it?"

"Nope."

He continued his research on Preston Geronimo, while she did the same. Consumed with his search history, Carla didn't feel Sherry's presence looking over her shoulder. Bernie saw that she hadn't noticed her yet and cleared his throat, getting Carla's attention. Glancing at Bernie, his head movement broke her concentration. Carla finally felt Sherry's presence and turned toward her.

"What did you want, McBride?"

"That's a stupid question. Anyway, what can you tell us about all the evidence you collected at either crime scene?"

"Oh yeah, that stuff, umm, join me in the conference room."

After they entered, they sat across from each other while Sherry took the chair at the end of the table nearest them. She loved this part of her job; she was the queen of information and relished that throne. Carla hated it, while Bernie didn't give a shit one way or the other. All he cared about was the information and didn't want any part of their battles.

Staring at her folder, Sherry took a deep breath before her opening comments regarding the evidence from both crime scenes. An annoying hum from the fluorescent lights invaded the silence in the room. Glaring at Sherry, Carla grew warm as her disdain for her was reaching a tipping point. Just as Carla started to lash out at her, she began. Rolling her eyes, Carla grumbled under her breath, distracting her.

"What was that snide remark all about, McBride?"

"Nothing, let's get started."

"Right! Anyway, let's start with the bedrooms. Master bedroom, lots of semen, pubic hairs, and other secretions. One male DNA, one female DNA. Based on what you have told me, we can assume the male DNA belongs to Bryan Walters, and the female DNA belongs to Angela Clark. Now…"

"Sherry, I know you find this interesting, but tell us something we don't know?"

"Of course, McBride. The bedroom on the second floor, now that's where it gets fascinating."

"Shit, Sherry, just tell us."

"Hmm, no patience today, huh, McBride. Anyway, the male DNA is the same as the master bedroom. However, the female DNA, drum roll, please." Two in-your-face-birds met Sherry's playful eyes. "Whoa, you both are on edge about something today. They're not the same. How about them apples, detectives."

Silence captured the room as awe-in-shock eyes wandered around the room, returning to Sherry's shit-eating grin. She loved surprising them and making them wait on the good stuff.

"Sherry, you sure about that?"

"Uh, Bernie, are you doubting me? Well, I double-checked them, and they're not the same. Guess that shakes things up, doesn't it?"

"I guess you can't tell us who they belong to, can you?" Sherry shook her head as silence took over the room once more. "Then what else have you discovered?"

"Patience, Bernie."

Loving every minute of this "whodunit" scenario, she let them mull over it for a moment before responding. As Sherry let them stew a little longer, Carla's face grew warmer and warmer in the smoldering silence. Carla reaching her tipping point, began to open her mouth.

"Keep your panties on, sister, okay?"

As Carla's eyes bored into Sherry's soul, she continued. "Ah, fingerprints, well, the ones found in the master bedroom on the wineglass, the coffee mug in the trash, and the master bathroom. I assume those belong to Angela. However, we did find another set of fingerprints in the upstairs bedroom and bathroom. They don't match the ones found in the master bedroom, bathroom, or on the coffee mug."

Pausing to let them absorb this information, Sherry sent a sarcastic smile at them and then continued. "There were also two sets of fingerprints at the houseboat. One belonged to Bryan, the other to Angela, I assume. Nothing new there based on what you told me. And, of course, the semen belonged to Bryan, and other things, you know secretions, and hair presumably belong to Angela because it matched the evidence found in the master bedroom and bathroom."

Sherry continued to go over the forensic reports' mundane stuff, which didn't shed any light on who might have committed either crime. "Any questions before I go over the cause of death for each?" A quick wave of the hand told Sherry to continue. "Great. Let's start with Bortel. It's simple. Once his body hit the massive glass table at such a weird angle, his neck snapped, instant death. Tox screens indicated a high level of alcohol and a sedative in his system. He also ejaculated sometime before dying. I don't think he just fell to his death. In my opinion, his death was premeditated. Now, Bryan's cause of death, well, he…"

Suddenly, three individuals passed by the conference room window capturing Bernie's attention. With the palm of his hand, he cut Sherry off. Getting up, he opened the door and stepped into the hallway, watching the three individuals enter Chief Evans' office.

# CHAPTER 19

Returning to the conference room, Bernie sat back down. He knew Chief Evans all too well. However, the other two, he wanted to learn more about them. They caught him by surprise, sending his heart racing faster and faster. While taking a deep breath, his expression said it all. With his elbows on the table, he massaged his temples as he sighed heavily. All the time, Carla fumed, wondering who the hell caused this commotion interrupting their meeting. Finally, he met Carla's fuming eyes as he ran his hands through his short dark hair.

"Bernie, what the hell is going on? What, who, please tell me who the hell you saw that interrupted this meeting."

"Umm, partner, you're not going to believe who is here."

"Dammit, you are getting just like Sherry."

Dismissing Sherry's glaring expression, he continued, "Umm, Angela Clark and Preston Geronimo."

"Who is this Preston Geronimo dude, he's hot, and that lady, well she is…"

Even though Sherry was going to explain Walters' cause of death, it could wait. Having Angela Clark and Preston Geronimo in the house by their own accord was more important than any new revelation regarding Walters' cause of death. Simultaneously they glared at Sherry, then got up to leave. As Bernie opened the door, Chief Evans fronted them. He motioned them to sit on the far side of the table and asked Sherry to leave.

Angela and Geronimo entered and sat across from them. Chief Evans closed the door and sat at the head of the table. Silence bounced around the large conference table. Like daggers ready to kill, eyes bored through each other, trying to read each other's minds as the atmosphere in the room grew intensely warm and oppressing. Meeting everyone's curious gaze, Chief Evans cleared his throat, demanding their attention.

"Carla, Bernie, I understand you and Angela Clark have already met." Nodding, they were waiting for him to bring the hammer down on them. "Umm, that's what I thought. Now, please meet Preston Geronimo. She hired him to find her brother." Bewilderment painted Carla and Bernie's faces. Their eyes met each other with uncertainty. "Also, he is a lawyer and will represent her going forward regarding Commissioner Walters' death investigation. Are we clear on that?"

Nodding in unison, they wondered why Chief Evans got involved in the first place. As silence captivated the room once more, he cleared his throat demanding their attention.

"Angela Clark has voluntarily come in to tell us what she knows. Please listen and don't interrupt her. You'll have plenty of time to ask her questions after she's finished, got it, McBride?"

"Chief…"

"Not now, got it?"

Disgust painted her face as she nodded nonchalantly. Bernie wasn't one to interrupt and quickly nodded as well. Given their mishandling of Commissioner Walters' son in The Black Rose case, they wanted to remain in his good graces.

Carla's inquisitive eyes focused on Angela and Preston's facial expressions and body language as Angela began. Over the next twenty minutes, she divulged information regarding her relationship with her brother, Lenny. Gay and a little rebellious, Lenny was, for the most part, a good kid growing up. They learned that after he graduated from high school, he came out of the closet. Disowned by his parents, he left home and was never heard from again.

During her story, emotions ran the gamut. Mostly tears of guilt and frustration flowed, however, a few laughs here and there made it easier for her. All the time she told her story, Carla made mental notes of their expressions, especially Preston. Finally composed, Angela nodded at Chief Evans that she was ready to answer questions.

"Okay, you two, keep your questions to her brother at this point. Even though you interviewed her yesterday, you'll have time to ask any additional questions you have regarding your investigation. Are we clear on that?"

"Yeah, we get it, chief. Angela, we want to know why, after all these years, you have decided to find your missing brother, and why involve us when you have hired him?"

"Detective McBride, I have this weird feeling, or maybe it's a premonition or hunch that he is involved in something terrible. By finding him, I can help him before it's too late or something far worse happens."

"So, you have this feeling. Do you have any evidence to support that? From what I understand, you're not sure he is even alive, right?"

"True, but these weird thoughts tell me something different. So, I must try to find my brother, whether he is dead or alive, to dispel my feelings."

"Okay, why talk to us?"

"I know this is far out, but I believe Lenny, or whatever his name is now, may know something about Bryan's death. I don't know why, but I do. It's just like why I decided to come back here to live. Something brought me back home, and I can't explain that, either."

A few tears resurfaced on her cheeks as Carla and Bernie now had more questions than answers regarding Commissioner Walters' death. This new revelation also threw a big monkey wrench into their theory that the same individual or individuals might have committed both murders.

"So, what makes you think he is connected."

"Detective Kowalski, umm, this may be a little far out since it's been over thirty years since he told me this. You see, Lenny was a little slow and shy. He wanted to be friends with the Oakmont Diamond Brotherhood. Bryan and his baseball buddies made fun of him growing up, but Lenny didn't mind then because he believed they liked him. They used to call him queer bait a lot and made him do things he didn't want to do. That disturbed me. Anyway, he told me he would get even with all of them one day."

"You used the word them."

"Umm, them. Yeah, besides Bryan, let's see, umm, Lester James."

"The mayor?"

"Uh-huh. A guy named Barry Stewart, yeah, and his cousin. Umm, let's see, Philip Devaney and Rich Masterson. They all belonged to the Diamond Brotherhood. Maybe a couple more, but I don't recall all their names. Oh yeah, I believe one went by Petey, not sure if that was his first name or not."

"Okay, that's interesting, right, Bernie? As Bernie nodded, Carla continued, "Some of them are current members of the city commission."

"Umm, I...I didn't know that."

"Well, they are. So, after over thirty years or so, your brother decides to get revenge on these guys for something they said or did when they were kids. I don't buy that. Gotta be something else."

"Hmm, I...I know this is a little far out, Detective McBride."

"Yeah, it is. What aren't you telling us?" Preston met Angela's gaze; she nodded. "Listen, somebody's going to answer that question, okay?" Preston touched Angela's hand and met Carla's wandering eyes.

"Detectives, Angela received an anonymous piece of mail a few weeks ago from someone. Postmarked from a town in Tennessee, but no return address. No fingerprints on it. All it said was it was time for revenge. That's why she decided to find Bryan and warn him. She didn't plan to spend the night with him—it just happened. That's why she left him the note under the coffee cup."

"Where's the piece of mail?"

After reaching in her purse, Angela pulled out an

envelope and handed it to Carla. She pulled the hand-written note out and showed it to Bernie. As they studied it, flashes of the note found at Bryan's home left more questions in their mind. After handing the note back to her, silence captured the room. Carla and Bernie now realized their theories just got blown to hell.

Chief Evans remained silent throughout all this, listening for the right moment to throw in his two cents' worth. Coughing to get their attention, he met their gaze and interjected, "Why don't we take a break, get some-thing to drink, and return in about ten minutes? Everyone okay with that? We have many questions to get to the bottom of this situation."

# CHAPTER 20

fter what turned into a fifteen-minute break, everyone returned to the conference room. At least, Carla knew there was more to this situation than Angela was divulging. If it had anything to do with either of their investigations, she would get to the bottom of it before Angela and Preston left. With everyone seated, silence flowed among them. Fixated on Angela's mysterious eyes, Carla watched them move back and forth between Preston and Chief Evans. It was a period of mind-reading or at least studying body language. Angela's eyes and facial expressions were hiding something important. Carla was sure of it.

Chief Evans glanced at Carla, then at Angela, and said, "Are you ready to continue, Angela?"

"Of course. Detective McBride, what else is on your mind?"

"I want to talk about last Tuesday night. How did you know Bryan would be at McGruder's?"

"Let's say, umm, I stopped at his bank. He wasn't there. His VP, John Vickers, told me where I could probably find him. Later that night, I took a chance he would be at McGruder's."

Bernie was a good listener and intuitive, allowing Carla to handle most of the questioning while he took notes.

"What did you talk about?"

"Uh, you know, past history, catching up on old times."

"What else? What aren't you telling us?"

"He asked me about my brother, which strangely touched me. Anyway, I told him what I just shared with you and nothing more."

"Anything else, no matter how, you know, contrite or odd it may be?"

Angela sighed and glanced at Bernie, who was jotting something down. As her eyes returned to Carla, she continued, "Yeah, umm, there was something kind of off the wall." As Bernie jotted more notes down, her gaze met his quirky smile. When Carla cleared her throat, Angela returned her focus toward her. "Although weird, he asked about Bambi."

"Who's she?"

"She was a cousin of mine. We were like sisters back then."

"Okay, I assume Bambi is a nickname. What's her real name?"

"Joni, uh, Joni Ballard."

"Okay, what was weird about that?"

"Don't know, it just came out of the blue. As far as I knew, they weren't friends. She wasn't someone that would hang around with those uppity-preppy boys. She was different, you know, got around."

"Uh-huh. What happened to her?"

"Well, she ended up pregnant. Umm, their parents couldn't stand the shame and moved away. She gave birth to a baby boy. Unfortunately, there were complications with the birth. Umm...she." A few tears trickled down her cheek, and she wiped them away. "Umm...she died a few days later."

"I'm so sorry."

"Thank you. We lived in California when she died. My mom came back for the funeral. As far as I know, Bambi's parents, George and Karen, raised her son. Even though she was a wild one, she was still a daddy's girl. Her death devastated him, as I recall. I felt I'd lost a sister. Anyway, I understand the boy was a difficult kid growing up. You know he got in minor trouble as a teenager. That's all I know. We lost track of them as they moved around. Not sure where they are now."

"Do you know why Bryan asked about her?" Shaking her head, she dried her eyes. "Do you know the boy's name?"

"Umm, I believe it was either Chase, Chas, Chad, umm, yeah, Chase, that's it. I often wonder what happened to him."

Bernie looked up from his notetaking, meeting Carla's questioning eyes. That name struck a chord with them, and Carla zeroed in on Angela's wandering eyes.

"Angela, have you ever heard the name Parker Jarrell before?" After shaking her head, she continued, "Security video from McGruder's show him, and another man that went by the name of Colt Lassiter was there Tuesday night and the next day. Do you recall seeing them on Tuesday night?"

"Umm, no, and never heard of them either."

Pulling out her smartphone, Carla pulled up the

video. "Here, look at this." Taking the phone, Angela watched the video intently as Preston glanced at Carla and back at the video. "Do you recognize either of these men? They left right after you and Bryan." Shaking her head, she handed the phone back to Carla.

"Are you sure?"

Nodding, Angela glanced at Preston and then back at her. Carla continued to study her eyes and body language. In her mind, she was sure Angela was not telling her everything.

"Do you have a picture of your brother?"

Nodding, she opened her purse, pulling out her wallet. Fumbling through several pictures, she handed a wallet-sized photo to her. Carla and Bernie studied the photo for a moment, trying to visualize if this innocent young teenager could be Parker Jarrell. Turning it over, it read Leonard Allen Clark, sophomore, Clermont Junior High School. Turning it back over, they studied the eyes and then looked at the video, pausing it to look at Parker Jarrell one more time. Although there was a resemblance, they couldn't be sure that the man behind the beard could be Angela's brother.

"Angela, do you have another one of these?"

"It's the only one I have, Detective McBride. You can make a copy of it, if you want."

Grabbing the photo, Bernie went to the copier and made several copies, while Carla focused on Angela's demeanor and body language. Returning to his seat, he handed the photo back to Angela. Placing it back in her wallet, she met Carla's intense eyes.

"Detectives, what else may I help you with?"

Done taking notes, Bernie shoved the notepad

towards Carla because it was his turn to shake her up
a bit.

"Angela, did you kill Commissioner Walters?"

"Seriously, you got this all wrong, Detective
Kowalski."

"Angela don't answer another question. We came in
good faith, and now they are accusing you of murder.
Let's go."

"Preston, I'll answer it. No, I did not kill Bryan. Why
would I? The three nights we spent together were
wonderful. I thought we might have something, and after
my failed marriage, I've been looking for a good man.
Although it was only a few nights, I thought I was beginning to fall in love with him."

"Did he feel the same for you, or was he just
screwing you, thinking it was his deceased wife?"

"Detective Kowalski, this line of questioning is out of
line. Let's go, Preston."

Angela and Preston promptly left in disgust. As questioning glares bounced around the table, silence captured
the room. Although they had made some progress, they
were no further along in either death investigation. As
Chief Evans cleared his throat, it broke the tense silence
smothering the room.

"What's next, guys?"

"We need to talk to Mayor James as soon as possible.
Maybe he knows something she's not telling us."

"I'll arrange it, Carla. Hopefully, we can get him in
here today."

# CHAPTER 21

Commissioner Walters' death had delivered the city government a devastating blow. And making matters worse, Commissioner-elect Bortel's death left the incoming city commission in disarray. Being one commissioner short made it difficult to pass any important public business. However, the city commission had very little vital business to conduct at this time of the year, making it easy to leave the remainder of Commissioner Walters' term vacant. But Bortel's death was a different story. Based on the state constitution, if the position was left open for more than thirty days, the governor could appoint a qualified person.

Although a special election was an option, that would take time to put it together. Besides, there were already three qualified candidates from the recent election that could fill the vacancy. Before the regular meeting, the mayor would hold a special meeting to discuss what was best for the commission. At the regular meeting that evening, the mayor would announce the commission's decision.

Maggie Oliver, the owner of a women's specialty boutique in the historic downtown district, finished just behind incumbent Commissioner Walters. Many in the community were excited when she decided to run because men, mainly the good old boy network, had ruled the city commission for too many years. Citizens felt it was time for a change. The final two candidates, Larry Zimmerman and Paul Girardi weren't well known, finishing seventh and eighth, respectively.

With a special meeting scheduled for five-thirty that afternoon, Mayor James agreed to meet with Chief Evans, Carla, and Bernie at four o'clock. That gave Carla and Bernie a few hours to review Angela's answers and an opportunity for lunch. McGruder's was their go-to lunch venue and allowed them to ask Sam a few more questions. They also hoped they would get lucky and see Parker Jarrell and Colt Lassiter there.

The lunch crowd had dissipated when they arrived. Taking their favorite booth in the corner, Carla took her designated side to watch people inside the pub and on the street. Within minutes, Sam arrived at their table with iced tea. She took their lunch orders and left. After placing them, she returned for some chit-chat with her favorite detectives. She had become like a daughter to them. Studying their faces, she knew they'd had a stressful morning, that their current case was taking its toll on them. After glancing toward the kitchen window, their order was ready. Leaving them to their sulking, she left and returned with their lunch.

"Rough morning, huh?"

"Yeah, you could say that. This case is bizarre. I don't

know that we've had one like this in a long time. Right, Bernie?"

"Yeah, it's strange, and nothing is making any sense, either."

"Guys, is there anything else I may get you or help you with? Just let me know, okay?"

"Sam, we appreciate that. Have you seen those two guys you showed us on the video, you know, Parker Jarrell and Colt Lassiter back in here?"

"Carla, at least not when I've been here. I can ask Mandy to be on the lookout if you like. I trust her not to get involved, you know, as I did."

"That won't be necessary, right, Bernie?" With a big bite of fish in his mouth, he nodded. "I assume Preston Geronimo has not been here as well."

"Nah. You know Carla, it's odd those two guys were here when Bryan was here, and then Wilson, now they're both dead."

"Yeah, we wondered about that as well. You mentioned that one of them seemed older than the other." Sam nodded. "How much older do you think?"

"Hmm, I'd say, umm, probably at least fifteen years or more, especially with the beard. Parker was the older one. Why do you ask, Carla?"

"Just curious."

"Listen, if they have something to do with these deaths, you will let me know, right?" Carla nodded. "Good, are they?"

"Let's say they are persons of interest just like Geronimo and Angela and leave at that. Wouldn't you agree, Carla?"

Nodding, she glanced at her watch, realizing they needed to get back to the station to prepare for their meeting with the mayor. Looking at Bernie, she pointed at her watch.

"Sam, will you get us our check, one check, and Carla's paying today."

Arriving back at the station, they cautiously checked their mailbox, continuing straight to their workstations. Quickly checking their work phones, the message lights were dark. Empty mailboxes they liked, a darkened voicemail light they hated. They were always waiting for that anonymous tip that could help them.

While waiting for their meeting, Bernie Googled Parker Jarrell while Carla searched for info on Colt Lassiter. Bernie struck out on Parker as though he didn't exist. He then searched for Leonard Clark, Angela's long-lost brother. That was a dead end as well. Carla struck out on Colt. However, she found at least one reference to a Chase Ballard. An obituary for George Allen Ballard of Jellico, Tennessee, identified Chase Ballard as his grandson. Chase's mother, Joni Ballard, was listed as preceding her father in death. However, there was nothing in the obit connecting any of them to Oakmont.

The big clock on the wall indicated they had about thirty minutes until the meeting with the mayor. Glancing at Bernie leaning back in his chair, rubbing his temples, Carla gave him a quirky smile that caught his eye.

"What?"

"Did you find anything?"

"Nothing, nada, zilch, how about you?"

"Hmm, Colt Lassiter doesn't exist like Parker. However, I found a reference to Chase in an obit. His grandfather died several months ago, but that's it."

"Well, at least that's something assuming Lenny and Chase are using aliases and are involved."

"Yeah, I'll bookmark it all the same. Hey, I'm going to see if Sherry is in yet. I'm going to ask her if she can do her magic stuff with face recognition. You know, take the photo Angela gave us to see what Lenny would look like today with a beard. It's worth a shot. I'll meet you in the conference room in time for the meeting."

"Good luck with her, and kill her with kindness, right?"

"Of course, I will. Don't look now, but the mayor is in the house, heading right in our direction." Bernie looked up as he passed by them. "I told you not to do that. That scowl on his face means he's pissed about something. I'll see you in a few minutes in the conference room."

# CHAPTER 22

arla and Bernie sat in their regular spots, waiting for Chief Evans and Mayor James to join them. Five minutes late, they entered. While the mayor sat across from Carla and Bernie, Chief Evans closed the door and took his usual place at the head of the table. Mayor James immediately met their gaze. Unfortunately, they had seen a lot of each other lately because of The Gold Fedora case involving one of his golfing buddies, Wylie Adkins, aka Rocky. Wylie's involvement blindsided him, and he couldn't afford to let that happen again.

Although he ran away with his previous election bid, the recent crime spree dented his armor, causing the tightly contested mayoral race just completed. Furthermore, these latest deaths hit too close to home. He needed those murders solved quickly to restore public confidence in his leadership. Tension in the conference room was thick. Chief Evans cleared his throat breaking the cold atmosphere in the room.

"Mayor James, we thank you for coming in on such short notice. We know you are a very busy man, so let's get right to it. Guys, he is up to speed on our meeting with Angela Clark and Preston Geronimo. He is aware of her relationship with Commissioner Walters. Carla, you may begin."

"Okay, based on what Angela told us, you went to high school with her, correct?"

"I do remember her, black-rimmed glasses, and plain-Jane-like. What's this got to do with me?"

Carla pulled up a photo of Angela on her smartphone and handed it to him. The gleam in his eyes said it all as he gave the phone back to her.

"Who is she?"

"That is Angela Clark. Yeah, I know, it's hard to believe, right?"

"Yeah…yeah, it is. Umm, what does it have to do with me?"

Bernie observed the mayor's facial and body language as she continued, "We're not sure. She says you made fun of her little brother, Lenny. You remember him?" Rubbing his forehead, he searched his weary mind for answers. "She told us you and your Diamond Brotherhood boys called him queer bait when you were growing up. Do you remember that? She also said that maybe you guys forced him to do things he didn't want to do."

"What's going on? These questions don't mean anything to me or make any sense. Just cut to the chase, okay?"

"Of course. Commissioner Walters' death may involve Lenny. However, we're not sure there's a connection to Bortel's death. Angela and Preston Geronimo, her lawyer, and a private dick came to us about an anonymous note she received in the mail."

"Where are you going with this?"

"Since the chief has filled you in on everything, you know Lenny is gay, came out of the closet after graduating from high school. After his parents disowned him, he disappeared from the face of the earth. Before he left, he told Angela he'd get revenge one day. Two weeks ago, she got a note saying the time had come for revenge. We assume that note was from him."

While laughing intensely, his face quickly grew flushed. His eyes searched for a sense of normalcy at such an absurd assumption. It left him speechless and sent his pulse racing throughout his body.

"Mayor, are you okay? You seem, well, distracted and flustered?"

"Yeah, I'm fine. I'm just a little surprised that joking around as a teenager would be a motive for murder almost thirty-five years later. Doesn't make sense."

"Yeah, murder never does. However, we think something else is at play. Who were your baseball buddies?"

"Bryan Walters, Philip Devaney, Barry Stewart, Rich Masterson, Chad Hayworth, and Pete Moseley. Unfortunately, Chad and Pete are no longer with us. We all hung around together back in the day, a very close-knit group."

"So, Bortel was not one of your baseball buddies?"

"Nah, as I recall, he was a tennis player and not a very good one. He only lived here for a couple of years. His parents moved because of a new job, why do you ask?"

"At first, we thought the murders were connected, but now, we're not so sure, right, Bernie?"

"Yeah, something just doesn't make sense. Mayor, did you know Joni Ballard, you know, Bambi?"

"Shit, I haven't heard, uh, that name in a while. What does she have to do with this?"

"Maybe nothing, but maybe her son does."

"Son! Shit, I didn't know she had a son" Letting out a big sigh, he continued. "I remember she moved away after her senior year, never heard of her ever again after that."

"Got part of it right, mayor. She moved away because she ended up pregnant. She had a son named Chase. She died a few days later, complications from giving birth, her parents raised him." He deflected Carla's intense stare for a moment. "Mayor, look at me." He met her earnest gaze once more. "Anyway, two men that go by Parker Jarrell and Colt Lassiter were at McGruder's last Tuesday and Wednesday, two days before Walters and Bortel ended up dead. We don't know if they are Lenny and Chase and using those names as aliases. They told the bar manager they were from out of town and left it at that."

Awe-and-shock grabbed his face, while his reddish complexion faded into a pale whiteness. As he searched for calmness, his eyes repeatedly bounced from around the table as he gasped for air.

"Mayor, are you sure you're, okay?"

"Yeah, chief. Umm, I'm speechless at all this. Umm, may we finish another day? I've got a special meeting about the vacant city commissioner position in about an hour, and I need to compose myself, get ready for it."

"Sure, you two don't mind, right?"

Noticing all this information caught the mayor off guard and upset him, they nodded.

"Yeah, we can continue tomorrow if that's okay with you, mayor?"

"Yeah, yeah, umm, that should be fine, chief. Oh, one more question, am I in any danger, McBride?"

"Not sure, just be aware of your surroundings, okay? And don't mention this to anyone until we have more conclusive evidence, alright?"

He nodded and got up to leave. As he met Carla's strained expression, he knew that he and his baseball buddies' safety was in jeopardy. Leaving the conference room, the mayor quickly walked through the common area ignoring everyone, and out to his car. Unlocking the door, he scanned his surroundings. After inside, he locked the doors.

Sitting quietly in the car for a few minutes, he finally started it. Pulling out of the parking lot, he traveled east on Main Street. While glancing in the rearview mirror, two men in a white sedan were following him. While staring at them, his heart raced. He paid particular attention to the man with a heavy black beard. He continued toward city hall with the car remaining a safe distance behind him.

As he drove down Main Street, he glanced in the rearview mirror, hoping the car was no longer following him. However, his heart raced faster seeing it. After passing Avondale Country Club, he glanced in the rearview mirror again, seeing it turn right onto Westover Court. Taking several deep breaths, he quickly drove to city hall.

Back in the conference room at the police station, Carla, Bernie, and Chief Evans sat, wondering what just happened. It was apparent to them that Mayor James was disturbed by everything he found out today, especially that his life may be in danger. They were sure that he knew more, and hopefully, he would cooperate before it was too late.

# CHAPTER 23

After reaching city hall, Mayor James pulled into his usual parking place. In the rearview mirror, cars continued to pass by the parking lot entrance. While breathing a sigh of relief, he cut the engine. Exiting his car, he quickly entered city hall through the back entrance. He entered the conference room where Barry Stewart, Philip Devaney, and Rich Masterson were seated at the table, waiting for him. Also seated were the candidates who were being considered to replace Commissioner-elect Bortel. Members of the media sat against the wall.

Maggie Oliver, Larry Zimmerman, and Paul Girardi would each have five minutes to make their case to fulfill Bortel's term. Although Mayor James felt composed, his face showed otherwise. He felt everyone's glaring stare as he took his seat. While glancing around the table, each person waited for him to begin. After several deep breaths, he sighed.

"Thank you for being here in this difficult time. We have lost two citizens and valued colleagues for no apparent reason. I met with Chief Evans earlier this after-noon, and he brought me up to speed on the investiga-tions. Unfortunately, there aren't any credible leads or suspects at this time. As difficult as it may be, we must move on and do what's best for the city's common good and its citizens. Any questions at this point?"

While glancing around the room, no one had any questions. Everyone was ready to get on with the meeting.

"Okay, we will hear from each candidate, and if anyone does not have any questions, we will move to an executive session to discuss who would be the best choice. We will hold a vote, and if a tie exists, I'll decide who will fulfill the vacant commissioner position. Paul will go first, followed by Larry, with Maggie being last. Are there any questions?

Immediately, Kiersten St. Clair, from the local televi-sion station, was the only person raising her hand. She was the one person he hoped to avoid today. Always a thorn in his side, today was going to be no different. While waiting to be recognized, her stare sent his pulse racing.

"Kiersten, what question do you have for us today?"

"Mayor James, my sources tell me the Walters and Bortel's deaths may not be connected at first thought, is there any truth to that?"

"I will not be answering any questions regarding those ongoing investigations. If you have any questions about this special called meeting or the public's business, you may ask them now. Otherwise, we need to move on."

"Oh, I'm sorry. Umm, is it possible we will see our first female city commissioner?"

"Either Maggie, Larry, or Paul will be the next city

commissioner. Hope that answers your question. Anyone else?" Silence filled the room. "Okay, Paul, you're up."

Twenty minutes later, Mayor James addressed everyone thanking them for their cooperation and attention during each candidates' comments on why each should be selected. He told the media he would announce his decision at tonight's regular city commission meeting.

"Okay, this special meeting is adjourned. We will take a ten-minute break before the commissioners join me in an executive session in this same conference room."

The candidates and media quickly left, followed by the mayor and the city commissioners. Ten minutes later, the mayor and city commissioners reconvened in the conference room. Each commissioner took turns stating their reasons for their choice to replace Bortel. About twenty minutes later, a vote was held, resulting in a tie between Maggie Oliver and Larry Zimmerman.

"As I stated earlier, in case of a tie, I will make the decision and announce it tonight. Now, I want to discuss something very personal and confidential that involves us, our past. It must stay in this room."

Suddenly, silence captured the room. Expressions of bewilderment covered the stoic faces of each commissioner. They glanced around at each other, returning their gaze to the mayor. Barry, a successful lawyer in Oakmont, broke the worrisome atmosphere in the room.

"Lester, what's going on, and how does it involve our past?"

Grumbling from Philip and Rich followed. Philip was a pharmacist, while Rich was an auto dealership tycoon.

"Hold on, guys, calm down, okay? Remember when

we were growing up, we had this young kid named Lenny Clark, remember our bat boy and gopher." Eyes wandered back and forth at each other. "Think, guys. His sister was Angela Clark. You know, the gal that was a little chubby, braces, black-rimmed glasses." Wandering eyes turned into nodding.

"Yeah, I think we all remember." Philip and Rich chimed in. Noticing Lester's flushed face, he continued. "Are you okay? You've been kind of jittery ever since we began the meeting."

"Yeah, sort of. This might come as a surprise, but Lenny may have something to do with Bryan's death." As pale expressions captured, everyone's face, silence exploded in the room. "That's the meeting I had with Chief Evans today, and even a bigger surprise, Angela Clark, she is something else. She's turned into quite the looker. You all remember Bryan's wife. Well, Angela could easily pass for her twin sister if she had one. Anyway, Angela and Bryan hooked up. Furthermore, she is the last person to see him alive."

"Lester, what the hell is going on?"

"Barry, guys, Angela moved back to town a couple of years ago, opening up her practice. She is a behavioral psychologist. Anyway, she received a piece of mail telling her it was time for revenge. That's why she sought Bryan out, supposedly to warn him, and now he is dead."

While showing signs of anxiety, Barry, Philip, and Rich glistened under the fluorescent lights. As wetness began to emanate from their armpits, their eyes continued to search for clarity and calmness.

"You remember, Lenny was strange. We all thought he might be gay. Well, he is. After they moved away from here, he came out of the closet. His parents disowned him. Angela tried to smooth things over, but he eventually left home and virtually disappeared. Before he left, he told Angela, one day, he would get revenge. Angela assumes that means us."

Wandering eyes turned into deeply concerned ones focused on Lester as they looked for answers, clarity, and assurance. While wanting to ask questions, their mouths resembled a nightmarish-like silent scream.

"Listen up, that's not all. Do you all remember Bambi? Well, they moved because she was pregnant. She gave birth to a baby boy, and because of complications with giving birth, she died. Her son, Chase Ballard, was raised by her parents."

Eyes wandered back and forth at each other. Sweat continued to roll off their foreheads; perspiration soaked their shirts from the anxiety and the pure fright in their souls.

"I only tell you this because after I left the police station, two men in a white sedan seemed to follow me for a short distance. One man had a dark beard like one of the men on a video from McGruder's they showed me. Those two men were in the pub election night, the same time as Walters and the next day when Bortel had lunch there. All of this might be nothing, but you need to be aware of your surroundings."

Again, the silence was smothering the conference room. Each commissioner was struggling to find calmness.

"Guys, why don't we get some fresh air and compose ourselves? We've still got about an hour before the city commission meeting. We'll reconvene in about ten minutes, not a mention of this to anyone, got it?"

Nodding moved around the table. They all got up and put their suit coat on to hide the anxiety in their souls. Leaving as calm as possible, they exited the city hall through the back entrance.

# CHAPTER 24

F orty-five minutes remained until the regular city commission meeting began. Mayor James and the three remaining commissioners reconvened in the conference room to discuss the mayor's riveting information. Dusk morphed into cold darkness outside while yellowish amber light filled the conference room. A funeral-like silence pounded the walls as everyone contemplated everything they had heard earlier. Ever since they were kids, they were still a close-knit group. Each wondered which event from their past was coming back to haunt them with a vengeance.

"Lester, I think you scared the hell out of us. I'm not sure why, but we need to hear more."

"Barry, guys, you all know we did some stupid things a long time ago and never thought any of it would come back to haunt us."

Strained expressions moved around the table; each knew what he meant. Anxious silence continued to chill the room as all eyes came back to him.

"Were any of you aware of Bambi's pregnancy?"

Wandering eyes flowed between them for a brief moment.

"Lester, where does Bortel come into play here? He was never part of the Diamond Brotherhood?"

"Right, Barry. At first, everyone believed both deaths were connected, however, after Angela came forward on her own accord, the police are not sure anymore. Although it is possible Bryan did kill Wilson, why leave his body in his house? It doesn't make any sense. Until these murders are solved, we all need to be vigilant about our surroundings. I'm to meet with them again tomorrow. Perhaps, I'll learn more. If so, we can get together."

Glancing at the clock on the wall, the mayor returned his gaze to concerned expressions moving around the table.

"We need to get ready for the meeting, be careful, and if you suspect something, please let me know or call Chief Evans. I plan on making this meeting as short as possible. Very little is on the agenda, so please follow my lead, and we can get home and unwind."

Leaving the conference room, each headed to the restroom to freshen up before meeting the public. Citizen participation had increased over the past few years since the recent crime spree had invaded the community. Counting the deaths of Walters and Bortel, seven individuals had their lives and careers ended senselessly.

One by one, the city commissioners and the mayor entered through the commission chambers' side door and took their respective chairs on the elevated stage. At Seven PM sharp, Mayor James motioned the videographer to begin the broadcast of the proceedings over the local cable provider's community channel.

A green light appeared above the door of the room,

housing the camera. Soon, the crack of a wooden gavel echoed throughout the commission chambers ending the muted chatter flowing throughout. Mayor James surveyed the near-capacity crowd and let out a cleansing sigh. At each entrance, the police presence eased the anxiety punishing him. Everything looked normal as the meeting began.

"Thank you for coming tonight. We appreciate your participation in making Oakmont a better place to live and work. Considering the recent deaths of Commissioner Walters and Commissioner-elect Bortel, we will have a moment of silence, followed by our opening prayer by Father Tim of St. Anthony's Catholic Church. Please stand."

As everyone stood and bowed their head, the lights dimmed as reverent and somber silence captivated the chamber.

"Thank you, and please remain standing."

As the chamber's lights returned to their usual intensity, Father Tim asked everyone to bow their heads once more. After a short prayer, "Amen" broke the solemn silence. As everyone returned to their seats, a few stragglers entered through the front entrance and sat near the video room in the rear of the chambers. Mayor James continued to scan the crowd returning his gaze to two men in the last row. While looking to his right, Commissioner Walters' vacant chair grabbed his soul like never before. He sighed and faced the audience.

"Citizens, considering Commissioner Walters' passing, we will have an abbreviated meeting tonight. The agenda is very light, and I apologize to those of you expecting more."

Grumbling filled the chambers. The sound of the gavel quickly silenced the audience.

"Based on the state constitution, the city commission met in a special session earlier today to discuss who will fill Bortel's seat."

Muted whispering filled the chambers as the audience looked at the three individuals being considered to replace Bortel.

"After careful consideration, and hearing from each person, Maggie Oliver will fill the seat of Commissioner-elect Bortel."

Immediately, loud applause followed, lasting a minute or so. As the applause faded away, the sound of the gavel regained control of the meeting.

"Maggie Oliver will be our first female commissioner breaking new ground."

Another round of approval filled the chambers.

"I've asked her to say a few words."

She took the podium off to the right of the stage. Thanking the current city commission, she promised always to keep the public's business a priority vowing to make Oakmont a better place to live, raise a family, and work. Another round of applause followed as she left the podium and returned to her chair.

After the applause had subsided, Mayor James called for adjournment. After a second by Commissioner Stewart, the gavel echoed off the walls. All in attendance slowly left the chambers through the front entrance. Within five minutes, the room was empty except the mayor and the commissioners.

Huddled up on the stage, Mayor James glanced around, ensuring no one else was in the chamber. He walked to the side door and locked it, then proceeded to the front entrance to secure it. After returning to the stage, bewilderment painted the faces of the three commissioners.

"Lester, what's going on?"

"Barry, the two men I spoke about earlier, they were in the audience tonight. I'm sure it."

"You're paranoid. Let's go home. It's been a long day."

"Barry, guys, hold on, it was them, so be careful, okay?"

After each acknowledged his advice, Barry unlocked the side door, and each commissioner promptly left the chambers leaving the mayor all to himself. They exited through the back entrance to the city hall, a freezing November night greeted them. Paying no attention to their surroundings, they walked together to their cars.

The last commissioner to pull out of the parking lot was Rich. Being the auto dealer tycoon in town, he cruised around in a red Corvette convertible. As it growled, he turned right onto Main Street, heading home. As the music blared inside, he was oblivious to a white sedan following him. Stopping at a well-lit intersection, he glanced in the rearview mirror seeing it. As muted light filled that vehicle, the driver sporting a dark beard glared at the Corvette. After the light turned green, Rich cautiously continued toward the interstate. The white sedan remained a safe distance behind him. Within a few minutes, the entrance ramp to the interstate came into view. After merging onto it, Rich watched the white sedan travel north out of the city.

# CHAPTER 25

Over a week had passed since Bortel and Walters' murders. Although Sherry's explanation of the forensic reports was interrupted by Angela and Preston's surprise visit, Carla and Bernie had a follow-up meeting with her at Ten AM today to finish reviewing her information. In the afternoon, they had a meeting with Mayor James and Chief Evans to continue their discussion from yesterday. Hopefully, everything will make sense at the end of the day.

Sitting at their workstations, they were reviewing the information from yesterday while Beth reviewed her cold case. Her current case was simply labeled Angel Hardesty, which was a twenty-year-old cold case. A cemetery employee found her body in a ditch at the rear of the cemetery. She was a loner, and all evidence indicated the cemetery was not the primary crime scene. All of her research and effort had yielded very little information. Although they had observed her for several days, they could tell her confident demeanor had morphed into one of frustration and disappointment.

At this point in their current case, they felt they hadn't needed Beth's help. However, it was becoming more apparent there wasn't any connection between the two deaths. Furthermore, Walters might have killed Bortel. And if so, proving that wouldn't be easy. Then the question was, who killed Walters and why. Hopefully, after meeting with Sherry this morning and the mayor this afternoon, answers to their questions will move their investigation in the right direction. As they silently pondered all the possibilities, several crashing sounds coming from Beth's desk shattered their thought-provoking silence.

"Beth, what's going on with you?"

"Ugh, this case is going nowhere, Carla. Every time I think I'm going to catch a break, it turns out to be a freaking dead end."

"Okay, I understand, but you need to control yourself. Do you need a break?"

"Sure. Parsons' Coffee Emporium okay with you?"

"Umm, not that type of break. I mean a break from your cold case."

"Maybe. What do you have in mind, Carla?"

"Let's go to the conference room."

Bernie's questionable eyes met Carla's smile as Beth nodded. Carla got up and moved around to meet Beth, who was already standing. As they walked a few steps toward the conference room, Beth turned around, glaring at Bernie, who was doodling on a notepad. She motioned him to follow her and Carla. Rising, he lumbered down the hallway. Catching up with them, Beth and Carla entered the conference room first, while Bernie followed and closed the door.

"What are we in here for, guys?"

"Beth, we need your help, right, Bernie?" Nodding, Bernie continued doodling on his notepad. "You know about our current case, well, we don't think both deaths, you know, are connected as it appears to be. We don't think Walters killed Bortel either. It just doesn't make sense."

"Beth, what Carla is trying to say, umm, is that the killers are not the same person. As it stands, we believe in some way they may be connected. However, we just don't know how or why, and as I said, we believe Walters is not a murderer."

"Okay, I can see that. How may I help?"

"We want you to begin investigating Bortel's death as a separate case. We need a new set of eyes to review the evidence and see where it leads."

"Umm, well, I do need a break, Bernie. I may never solve the Angel Hardesty case with the attitude I have right now."

"Great, here's the file on what evidence we have in Bortel's death. In about an hour, we will meet with Sherry for an update on the evidence."

As Bernie handed her the file, he smiled. Taking it, she immediately flipped it open and began reviewing the reports.

"See, Carla, I knew she'd jump right in. We'll leave you alone so you can be up to speed when we meet with Sherry in about forty minutes."

Nodding, Beth returned her gaze to the reports as they returned to their workstation to focus on Walters' death. After about twenty-five minutes of intense reading, Bernie glanced at Carla, who still had the report in front of her face.

"Hey, don't look now, but the chief is coming down the hallway."

Carla turned around; he was a few steps away. Stopping at her desk, he said, "What's Beth working on in the conference room?"

"Oh, that. Bernie and I need another set of eyes on the Bortel case. We don't think Walters killed him. Her cold case is going nowhere, and she is frustrated and needs a break."

"Okay, what makes you think Walters didn't kill Bortel?"

"Nothing makes any sense, does it, Bernie?"

"Nope, if Walters killed him, why commit it at his home and leave his body there? Makes no sense."

"Well, I hope you are right. By the way, Mayor James will be a few minutes late, but he said he will be here."

Chief Evans continued toward the common area while they returned to the conference room. Sitting across from Beth, she glanced in their direction.

"Well, Beth, what's your assessment on the Bortel case?"

"Carla, it doesn't make sense, which likely means two killers out there. The killers are not connected, which means the cases aren't connected, but someone wants us to thank that."

"Carla, see, I told you so."

"No, I told you so, dickhead."

"Hey, guys, does it matter?"

A sudden knock on the window drew their attention —Carla motioned Sherry inside the conference room. After entering, she closed the door. Sherry sat at the head of the table, which made her feel like a queen and in charge.

"Sherry, we invited Beth because Bernie and I don't think these cases are connected. Someone wants us to think that, so she is taking over the Bortel case."

"Wow, you think, Carla." Rolling her eyes, Carla threw Sherry a scowling smile with an invisible bird. "I concur. I was going to tell you that the other day before Mr. Hot Geronimo interrupted things, umm, the manner of death is completely different."

"How so?"

"Bernie, Bortel died when he crashed on that massive iron and glass table. Toxicology results found a high dosage of an old 'date rape' drug in his system. Someone slipped him several pills at some point before he died. Whomever that person is, stripped him of his clothes, wrote on his chest, and tossed him over the railing, at least that's my assumption. As I said yesterday, he'd had sex at some point before he died, not sure when, but he did. The female DNA found in the upstairs bedroom doesn't match the female DNA found on the rug on the upstairs landing. And thus far, their identities are still a mystery."

Although stunned by that last revelation, it more than likely confirmed the direction Carla and Bernie needed to take. Beth, unfazed by that information, knew she would be starting from scratch, which she would have anyway. With a little bit of information from Carla and Bernie, she would begin immediately. Sherry liked surprising Carla every time she could. Carla's eyes started wandering around the room, and she stood up.

"Sherry, I need a potty break. Why don't we all take about a ten-minute break, okay?"

# CHAPTER 26

Fifteen minutes later, everyone reconvened in the conference room, waiting for Sherry to reveal Commissioner Walters' cause of death. After the new revelation about Bortel's demise, Carla and Bernie were expecting the unexpected. In her usual queen-like demeanor, Sherry glanced at them as their stare zeroed in on her.

"So, about Commissioner Walters' death. Well, his untimely death was drowning." As mouths flew open, Sherry threw them an in-your-face smile, letting them absorb that revelation. "Yeah, he drowned. I'm sure you didn't expect that, did you?"

"Sherry, can we get right to it?"

"Sure, Kowalski. When did you discover his body? Oh, right, around eight, wasn't it?" Carla nodded. "Yeah, well, the time of death was maybe a couple of hours before you found him."

That was something they didn't expect, which meant the killer or killers might have been in the car, they saw leaving Lake Jackson. From what Bernie could recall, it was a light-colored sedan.

"What else is there? He didn't commit suicide, did he?"

"No, McBride. We found a needle prick on his neck. Toxicology reports indicate a potent tranquilizer paralyzed him. We haven't been able to identify it yet, but it resembles a sedative used to subdue large animals. That's all we have. The murky water destroyed any DNA on him."

While Carla and Bernie were speechless, Beth jumped in. "What's that perfume you're wearing, Sherry?"

"That's a weird question, but it's Umari Seduction by Shadé." A strange expression met Beth's curious eyes. "Yeah, I know. Angela and the mystery female wear it as well. Umm, that's all I have. Any further questions?"

"The photo I gave you yesterday, were you able to do anything with it?"

"Of course, McBride. Umm, it's not great, but I printed out what Angela's brother would possibly look like today." Handing a copy to each of them, she continued. "One with a beard, and one without. Anything else?"

"No, you've been a big help."

"Thank you, Bernie. I'll leave all of you alone to solve this intriguing puzzle. Good luck. You're going to need it."

Sherry left, leaving the three of them to brainstorm what was next in either investigation. Files and reports spread all over the table, including the projection of what Lenny might look like now. Carla pulled out her smartphone, pulling up the video from McGruder's. When it reached the place where the two men were, she paused it, staring at the image. Picking up the photo, she glanced back and forth at both images. While Bernie sat beside Carla, he viewed it at the same time. Handing the phone to Beth, she examined both for a moment before handing Carla her cellphone.

"Could be the same person, but that's your problem. As for the Bortel case, where do you suggest I start?"

"Start with Bobbi Tierney even though Bernie didn't see her as someone that could be a killer. She was very concerned about Commissioner Walters; she even thought he would be a good catch. Also, she mentioned his next-door neighbor, Clarissa. After hearing every-thing today, I have a gut feeling that one of those ladies might be involved. I'm not sure how or why, I just do. Right now, nothing makes any sense."

"Got it, but Carla, you always told me murder never makes any sense."

"Yeah, you're learning, gal. Uh, keep us informed, okay?"

"You bet. Now, if you don't need me any longer, I'm going to get started on solving Bortel's murder."

"Bernie, do we need her?"

"Nah, we can now focus on who killed Commissioner Walters and why. By the way, Beth, Bobbi works, so you'll have to contact her, say sixish or after."

Nodding, Beth left the conference room while Carla and Bernie remained to sort through all the information. While glancing at her smartphone again, the image seemed to stare back at her. She mouthed, "Who are you, mystery, man?" The morning had flown by as her phone indicated it was almost noon. Her stomach rumbled, reminding her it was almost lunchtime.

"Carla, was that your belly rumbling?"

"Yeah, McGruder's, okay?"

"Of course, why don't you eat something different today? It'll do you some good?"

"Bite me, dickhead. Why don't you, it'll do you some good, too?"

"Screw you, McBride."

Arriving at McGruder's, the lunch crowd was in full swing. Their favorite booth was still available, and they quickly grabbed it. As usual, Carla took the side where she could watch people coming or going and any individuals milling around outside. Sam was behind the bar, pouring beers and attending to those seated at the humongous u-shaped bar. Expecting Sam to wait on them, Mandy arrived.

"Detectives, what brings you here today?"

"Lunch, of course," Bernie exclaimed.

"The usual, I assume?"

"Nah, I'm getting the Reuben and fries today. Carla will have fish and chips. Iced tea with lemon and tell Sam to stop by when she is free."

"Seriously, are you just jerking my chain?"

"Of course not. It's time we changed it up a little."

"Hey, works for me."

Mandy left to place their orders. Behind the bar, Carla and Bernie noticed Mandy talking with Sam. With Carla and Bernie staring outside, Sam put iced tea in front of them. Carla immediately recognized the ring on the person's hand and looked up, smiling.

"Hey, guys, nice to see you here today. You guys have been here a lot lately, helping keep us open. Thank you. Mandy said you needed something? What is it?"

Carla unfolded a sheet of paper and handed it to Sam.

"Yeah, take a good look at this. Have you seen this guy in here before?"

"Umm, you know, it does look a lot like that guy, you know, Parker. Where did you get this?"

Bernie chimed in, meeting Carla's scowl across her face. "It's a prediction of what Angela Clark's brother might look like today."

"Wow, that's pretty cool. Anyway, uh, it could be him. What's going on, Bernie?"

"Hmm, not sure. Uh, here comes Mandy with lunch. Would you look at my delicious Rueben?"

"Bite me, dickhead."

"Here you go. Rueben, for you, sir, fish and chips for you, ma'am. Enjoy."

After an enjoyable lunch, they were back at the police station reviewing their notes from yesterday's interview with Mayor James. Now that they had the information needed to focus on Commissioner Walters' death, hopefully, they would get more helpful information from the mayor in their meeting with him this afternoon.

The big clock on the wall indicated they should finish their review as the mayor would arrive in fifteen minutes. Glancing toward the hallway leading to Chief Evans' office, a scowl came over Carla's face. Twenty seconds later, Chief Evans stopped at their workstation.

"Do we have Beth headed in the right direction?" Bernie nodded. "Good, now for some bad news. The mayor has canceled our meeting. Said something came up."

"Chief, you sound like you don't believe him."

"Don't know, Carla. He's acting strange, said he'd reschedule, didn't say when."

"Okay, then it's on to plan B. We're going to see if

Angela can see us for a few minutes and look at this." Carla handed him the projected photo of Lenny. He studied it and gave it back to her. "Chief, this guy looks a lot like the man in the video from McGruder's"

"Well, good luck. Maybe we'll catch a break."

Bernie called Angela, and she agreed to see them between appointments. Fifteen minutes later, they arrived at her business. After entering, the receptionist instructed them to sit in the lounge, and she would be right out. Within about five minutes, she walked out with a patient. While the patient took care of things with the reception-ist, Angela came over and sat in one of the chairs.

"Detectives, what did you want to see me about?"

"Angela, look at this, look at it very closely." Taking a photo from Carla, she studied it and started to hand it back to Carla. "Angela, now look at my phone." Taking it, she compared the pictures with curious eyes. "The photo is taken from the picture of Lenny we copied. Our forensic gurus used a program to determine what he would look like now. To us, the images look similar."

Handing the images back to Carla, Angela looked for calmness as tears surfaced on her cheeks. Wiping them away, she softly said, "It's him, I know it. I can see it in his eyes. What is he doing in Oakmont? What has my little brother gotten himself into, McBride?"

"Yeah, we're wondering the same thing."

# CHAPTER 27

Beth pulled into the driveway of Barbara Tierney's house hoping she was home. She cut the engine and exited the car. Walking onto the inviting porch, a swing at the far end looked relaxing. She imagined herself swinging in it with a glass of Pinot Grigio. After pushing the doorbell, melodic chimes rang out from within the house. Moving toward the front door, the familiar sound of heels on hardwood floors alerted her. Opening the door, Barbara Tierney stood behind the storm door. After she opened it, Beth identified herself. After giving Mrs. Tierney her business card, she examined it and returned it to her.

"Miss Pendergast, how may I help you?"

"Mrs. Tierney, may I come in?"

"Of course, but please call me Bobbi, okay."

"Sure, then Bobbi it is. Anyway, I'm working with Detectives McBride and Kowalski on the death investigations of Bryan Walters and Wilson Bortel. I want to ask you a few questions about Walters first. Then I'll get to Bortel. I won't take up much of your time, okay?"

"Of course, come in. What's a pretty, young gal like you, working at the police department?"

"Umm, I find police work fascinating. I graduated from the university, major in criminal justice, and a master's in psychology."

"You don't say. I'm a professor in the Department of Justice and Safety there. At least we have that in common."

"Yeah, we do. Cool, right?"

"Of course."

"Anyway, first things first, I need you to sign the paper on this clipboard to prove I was here, okay?"

"Well, yeah, they don't..."

"Nah, it's not that they don't trust me. It's just something new, you know, back everything up, dot every 'i,' cross every 't,' that kind of thing."

Handing the slick white plastic clipboard with a pen attached, Barbara took it, signed it, and returned it to her.

"Great, thank you. May we get started?"

"Umm, I'm ready when you are. Would you like a glass of wine?"

"Umm, why not. That would be nice, thank you."

While she headed to the kitchen, Beth surveyed the great room making mental notes of pictures and other things. As she heard footsteps, she turned in that direction. Carrying two glasses of wine, Bobbi handed one to her and motioned her to sit on the sofa.

"Thank you." Taking a sip, savoring the crisp and refreshing taste, she continued. "Pinot Grigio, Ecco Domani, right?"

"You know your Pinot Grigio. If you don't like it, I can get you a nice Mer Soleil Chardonnay."

"Nah, this is fine, thank you. Bobbi, how long have you known Bryan?"

"About a couple of years, ever since I moved back here. I wanted to get to know him better, but after his wife died, he needed time to grieve."

"I see. I know Detectives McBride and Kowalski asked you this, but I must ask again. Did you see anything suspicious that week he died? You know suspicious cars, activity, things like that."

"No, I'm not a nosey neighbor like that lady next door to him."

"What's her name?"

"Clarissa, I don't know her last name and don't care either. As I said, I keep to myself."

"Did you know Wilson Bortel?"

"Never heard of him before this awful situation."

"I see. You've seen his picture in the newspaper and on television, haven't you?"

"Umm, who hasn't these days."

"Right. Have you ever seen him in this neighborhood before?"

"No, as I said, I didn't know him, never seen him before."

"Okay, well, guess that'll do it. Thanks for the wine. I have other people to see in the neighborhood."

Rising from the sofa, Bobbi joined her and walked her to the door.

"Thank you, Bobbi, you've been a big help."

"You're welcome. If I can be of further assistance, feel free to contact me."

"Of course, you have a great evening, okay?"

Bobbi nodded and opened the door showing Beth out. As she walked off the porch, she heard the familiar sound of a deadbolt. Turning around, she noticed movement behind the window blinds. She got into her car, started it. After backing out of the driveway, her next stop was Carissa who lived next to Bryan Walters.

After pulling into the driveway of Clarissa's house, she exited the car. Walking up onto the porch, she promptly pushed the doorbell. Silence rang out from inside. Assuming it didn't work, she opened the storm door and used the doorknocker. Brass on brass echoed. Finally, a very shapely and attractive lady opened the door.

"Miss...."

"I'm Clarissa Morgan. How may I help you?" Handing Clarissa her business card, she studied it and returned it to her. "So, Miss Pendergast, you're with the police department. How may I help you?"

"I'm working with Detective McBride and Kowalski on the death investigations of Bryan Walters and Wilson Bortel. May I ask you a few questions?"

"What kind of questions?'

"Umm, I'm just getting information from Bryan's neighbors. May I come in?"

"Of course."

Beth entered surveying everything in sight. One picture on the mantel immediately caught her eye. Clarissa motioned her to sit on the sofa. Beth noticed a glass of red wine on the sofa table.

"Miss Pendergast, would you like a glass of wine?"

"Yeah, that sounds good. Umm, please call me Beth, if you like, more personable, you know."

"Of course, Beth, it is, red or white?"

"White, if you have it."

She walked to the kitchen and returned with a glass

of white wine. Handing it to Beth, she took a small sip. Right off, she knew it wasn't her favorite Pinot Grigio. Clarissa sat on the sofa beside her and took a long drink of her red wine.

"What kind of wine is this? Not sure I've tasted it before?"

"Mer Soleil Chardonnay, nice, a little expensive, but I say, why drink the cheap stuff, right?"

"Umm, yeah, I agree. Hey, the perfume you are wearing, what is it?"

"Umari Seduction, not sure who makes it, given to me as a gift, thought I would try it out."

"Oh, I'll have to check it out, as well. Anyway, I need you to sign this form that I was here. Yeah, it's kind of silly, but it's a requirement for new employees."

Handing the clipboard to Clarissa, she took it, signed by the "X," and returned it to Beth.

"Great, now how long have you known Bryan?"

"Let's see, probably about four years, that's when I moved here. While Bryan's wife was fighting cancer, we got to know each other very well. After her cancer progressed, he asked me to look in on her during the day, gave me a key. Come to think of it, I still have it. Anyway, after she died, we became closer. He just needed a friend, and we shared a glass of wine occasionally on the back patio. It was nothing more than just friendship, if you're wondering?"

"Umm, I wasn't. Over the past few weeks, did you notice any strange activity at his home?"

"Not really. I did notice what's-her-name across the street. I believe she goes by Bobbi. Anyway, she made a few trips over to see him, which I thought was strange."

"What was strange about that?"

"Uh, he said he didn't care for her. She's kind of snobbish, you know, stuck up. I kept my distance from her as well."

"What do you do for a living?"

"What's that got to do with Bryan?"

"Oh, nothing, just wondering."

"I'm a widow. My husband left me a huge insurance policy, big enough that I don't have to work anymore if I don't want to. Anyway, by profession, I'm a realtor."

"Lucky you, well, that should do it. You've, umm, been a big help."

Clarissa showed Beth out to the porch, where they said their goodbyes. Before walking off the porch, Beth turned around. "Umm, I forgot something. Did you know Wilson Bortel?"

"Who?"

"Wilson Bortel, the man found dead in Bryan's home."

"Oh, that guy. No, I never heard of him, never saw him before in my life until his picture was in The Daily Reporter. What a horrible thing that happened to him, right?"

"Yeah, anyway, thank you for being cooperative. Have a nice evening, okay?"

Clarissa nodded and quickly re-entered her house. Standing behind the storm door, she watched Beth walk off the porch to her car. Before Beth got into her car, she glanced at Bobbi's house, seeing movement behind the blinds once more. She entered her car, put the clipboard, pen, and business card in a large plastic bag, and sealed it. Backing out of the driveway, she proceeded to the police station dropping off two plastic bags containing a white plastic clipboard, an ink pen, and her business card.

# CHAPTER 28

Commissioner Rich Masterson's day began like any other. Breakfast with his gorgeous wife and two teenage daughters, both spitting images of his wife, Shelia. Although a powerful man in the city government, he had built his fortune in the auto business rather than following in his father's footsteps as a lawyer and now a Circuit Court Judge.

The Honorable William Howard Masterson had been on the bench for many years. Elected over thirty years ago, known as Judge Bill, he never had any serious challenges regarding his re-election bids. He always wanted his only child to follow in his footsteps, however, Rich was a rebel in many ways and didn't want anything to do with his father's profession.

As a youngster, Rich was a promising baseball player. While being a catcher, he controlled the game gaining valuable management experience. After a stellar senior year, the local university offered him a scholarship. Although Rich enrolled in college with a major in pre-law, he soon discovered that was not his calling. Ever since his dad bought him his first car, a Mustang convertible, his love for cars was born, and he changed his major to business management with a minor in marketing.

After hugging and kissing his wife, and two daughters, he walked to his four-car detached garage at the rear of his house. Entering the garage, he had his pick of three cars to drive to work. After surveying his possible rides for the day, he chose his shiny red Corvette convertible. A beautiful sunny day, temps close to fifty, it was the ideal ride to work. Life couldn't be any better for him and his family.

The Corvette growled as he drove it out of the garage. After coming to a rolling stop at the end of his driveway, he turned right and accelerated quickly, feeling the thrust and power of his pampered baby. The sounds of The Doobie Brothers filled the cabin as he passed through the security gates of Oak Ridge Commons. After coming to a complete stop at the intersection, he turned right onto Ritter Drive, rocking out to *Jesus Is Just Alright*. Knowing the lyrics all too well, he sang along, oblivious to his surroundings. He had several lights to go when a white sedan switched lanes, pulling up close behind him.

As the song ended and *Old Black Water* began, he glanced in the rearview mirror seeing the white sedan again. At first, he thought nothing of it. There were thousands of white sedans in the city. As the traffic signal turned green, the engine's power and thrust separated him from the vehicle. At the next traffic signal, the white sedan pulled up close behind him.

In the rearview mirror, the two men in the white sedan seemed fixated on him. While paying more attention to them, the light turned green. The driver honked, making a vulgar gesture at Rich. With a clear path ahead of him, the tires squealed, and he sped away. Initially, staying a safe distance behind Rich, the white sedan sped up, gaining on him.

Just ahead was the entrance to Masterson's Grand Auto Mall. As he moved to the left turn lane, the white sedan's left turn signal blinked. With oncoming traffic clear, he quickly turned into his auto kingdom. Keeping an eye out for the white sedan, he noticed it had just turned into the auto mall as well. As he continued down Masterson Way, the white sedan was no longer in the rearview mirror. Relieved, he continued to his office and thought no more about it.

The white sedan had turned right into the Chevrolet Dealership, heading for the used car lot. After driving down several rows of trucks, the car stopped. The two men got out and immediately began looking at several of the vehicles. Several minutes later, a salesman approached them.

"Good morning, guys. How may I help you? I'm Ted Lowery, and you are?"

The man in the beard replied, "Names are not important at this point. Uh, we're just looking. If we see something of interest, we'll let you know, okay?"

"Oh, yeah, I get it. Just take your time. If you find something you like, I'll be in the dealership."

After the man in the beard nodded, Ted walked away and entered the showroom. He watched as they continued to view several trucks. A few minutes later, they left the dealership, driving to the back of the auto mall. After reaching the building housing Rich's office, they began circling the parking lot.

His office had a row of windows giving him an unobstructed view of his kingdom and the white sedan. A few minutes later, the white sedan turned left on Masterson Way, and he breathed a sigh of relief. Calling around to each of his dealerships, he found out who had spoken to them. With the sun bright in the sky, the coolness of the morning had given away to its powerful warmth. Leaving the office building, he walked to the Chevrolet Dealership to speak with Ted. Finding him standing outside enjoying the day, Rich addressed him.

"Good morning, Ted. How are you?"

"Great, I think it's going to be a good day. Bill said you wanted to talk to me about something."

"Yeah, I did. Did you wait on the two men in a white sedan?"

"Oh, those guys, yeah, weren't all that friendly, didn't want me around, and made that very clear. They looked at several trucks, got in their car, and left. That's about it."

"Did you get any names? You know I'm a stickler about that."

"Yeah, I know, but those two guys weren't going to give me names and didn't want to be bothered. Not sure they were even serious about looking at vehicles. You know those types, right, boss?"

"Unfortunately, I do. I'm heading back to my office. If that white sedan shows back up, call the police, okay?"

"Yeah, of course, have a great day, boss."

Walking back to his office, he kept glancing over his shoulder, expecting the white sedan to appear. Fifteen minutes later, he entered the office building, promptly taking the steps to his second-floor office. His coffee had turned cold, just like his soul. Tossing the coffee in his bathroom sink, he walked to the coffee center and poured himself a fresh cup.

   Back at his desk, he pulled up the security video from the camera located on the front of the building. After entering the specific criteria, the video played. He watched the white sedan pull into the parking lot, circle around a couple of times, then turn left, heading down Masterson Way to the main highway.

   With the car still in view, he paused the video hoping to capture a still image of the license plate. After he did a screenshot of the still frame, he closed the video. The screenshot revealed a Missouri license plate. After copying the number down, he made a few calls and discovered the plate was reported stolen several months ago. Just the same, he would inform Chief Evans and the mayor about the incident.

**CHAPTER 29**

With Beth working later than usual yesterday, she awoke late the following day. Scott, her fiancée, had already left for work, and she relaxed with a cup of coffee in her favorite nightgown, one of Scott's long-sleeved dress shirts. Ever since they solved their differences in their relationship, they have been living together at her apartment. He finally realized he couldn't live without her and finally put a ring on her finger. With her position, she set her hours and took her time getting ready for work. Satisfied with her appearance, she started her day, checking her email and voicemail. Nothing needed her immediate attention, and she continued to relax with another cup of coffee.

Finally arriving at the station around eleven o'clock, Carla and Bernie were fixated on their monitors and didn't see her settle in at her workstation. After a few minutes of ignoring her, she coughed, getting their attention. Meeting Beth's gaze, Carla's scowling smile was greeted by a silent, "What?"

"Wish I could come in when I wanted to, right, Bernie?" His rolling eyes met Beth's nonchalant expression. "How did your fishing expedition go last night?"

"Well, Carla, in my opinion, both Bobbi and Clarissa seemed to be hiding something. They both seemed enamored with Bryan. So, neither is responsible for his death, of course, in my professional opinion."

"Uh, no shit." Again, Bernie's eyes met an even colder reception on Beth's face. "Tell us what we don't know, right, Carla?"

"What's got you two all riled up this morning? Silence hit her in the face. "Okay, be that way. Anyway, Clarissa had more than an interest in Bryan. They may have been physically intimate. She even has a key to his house. Supposedly, Bryan asked her to look in on his dying wife while he was at work. After his wife passed, they shared wine on the patio on many occasions, and who knows what else."

"Maybe it's her DNA from the upstairs bedroom."

"Could be, Carla. I'll get to that later. Now, for Bobbi, I'm just not sure. She's hard to read. Clarissa, on the other hand, wouldn't let anything stand in her way. She's the aggressive type."

"Hey, Bernie, maybe you should have interviewed her." An in-your-face bird met Carla's rolling eyes.

"Okay, you two, get your head out of the gutter. Anyway, neither of the ladies cared much for each other. I had them sign a form stating I interviewed them and told them it was a new procedure, especially for new employees like me. The form was on one of those new slick plastic clipboards, a fingerprint magnet, DNA, grease, etc. They each held my business card in their hand as well as a pen. Forensics has a clipboard, pen, and business card that each used. So, we wait for the results."

"You sly fox. You might eventually turn out to be a valuable member of our team, right, Bernie."

"I thought I already was." A chuckle met her ears. "Oh, I get it. April Fool's Day in November, funny. Get this, Clarissa wears…"

"Umari Seduction."

"Bingo, Carla. She's rich. Her husband left her a huge insurance policy. She is set for life and doesn't have to work unless she wants to. Not that it matters, but by profession, she's a realtor."

"How did he die, you know, Clarissa's husband?"

"Well, umm, I don't know, Bernie. I didn't ask, my bad." Feeling like a whipped puppy, she deflected their concerned eyes. "Yeah, I'll do my research. I'm sure something will come up. If I don't find anything, I'll pay her another visit. Oh, one other thing."

Bernie replied, "Yeah, what's that?"

"When I asked her about Wilson Bortel, her anxiety level went up a couple of notches, and her eyes showed it. How's your case going?"

"Bernie and I are waiting for Mayor James. He canceled yesterday. He's coming in this afternoon."

Feeling a little better, Beth opened Google on her computer and entered Clarissa Morgan. The search information confirmed she was a realtor in Columbus, Ohio. After moving on to the next search page, information about her real estate career loaded.

Quickly scanning the other information, she did a double take at the bottom of the search page. She clicked on the link titled *Local Bank Tycoon Dies in A Freak Accident*.

As she read the story about Thaddeus Edward Morgan, her mind began to wander. According to the article, he was worth millions. Reading further, a paragraph on his wife, Clarissa Antoinette Morgan, a successful realtor, indicated she was devastated by his death. Although the coroner ruled it an accident, the insurance company still investigated his death because of its suspicious nature and a huge insurance policy.

Because she was engrossed in her research and found such a revelation, she hadn't noticed Carla and Bernie glaring at her. Smiling at them, she returned her gaze to the monitor. Because of the story about Clarissa's husband, she had overlooked another one about Clarissa leaving her hometown of Columbus, Ohio.

Given her husband's philanthropic generosity, she embraced his numerous charities. He supported Habitat for Humanity, and she worked on several houses with him. However, after he died, it was too emotional for her to remain involved. She resigned from everything and made her intentions known to relocate to a much smaller community in Oakmont, Kentucky. The story gave no reason why she chose it. Needing a break, she scooted her chair out from her desk, leaned back in the chair, and let out a big sigh interrupting Carla and Bernie's muted conversation.

"Hey, Beth."

"Yeah, Carla."

"You look like you found something. You want to share it with us?"

"Clarissa's husband's name is Thaddeus Edward Morgan. He died of a freak accident at home in Columbus, Ohio. He was worth millions and had a five-million-dollar insurance policy as well, and the beneficiary was

Clarissa. Although the insurance company investigated the death because of its suspicious nature, in the end, they ruled it an accident paying out the full value of the policy to Clarissa. There you have it."

"Beth, how did the accident happen?"

"Bernie, the story said he fell off the second-floor balcony at home. It stated he had been drinking, stumbled on a throw-rug. Being a heavy man, hit the wooden railing and fell twenty feet to his death."

Carla chimed in, "Hmm, interesting."

"Guys, it's kind of far out that Clarissa or even Bobbi is responsible for Bortel's death. They had nothing to gain from it."

"Maybe not, but maybe you need to dig a little deeper. Maybe something was going on between Clarissa and Bobbi, and Bortel or, for that matter, Bryan, right, Carla?" she nodded. "Maybe jealousy, who knows why people go berserk in the heat of things and commit something they regret, something to check out, right, Beth?"

"Of course, I guess I'll be interviewing Bobbi and Clarissa again and making calls to people that know them and Bortel as well. Thanks for bringing me in. This is what I needed. It might give me a new perspective on the Angel Hardesty case after I solve this one." Carla and Bernie nodded. Glancing at the big clock, it was lunchtime. "Hey, guys, what time is Mayor James coming in?" In unison, they both said, one-thirty. "Great, that gives us time for lunch, my treat."

# CHAPTER 30

A t lunch, Carla and Bernie asked Beth to sit in on their discussion with Mayor James. Arriving at the police station, the receptionist told them the mayor was already in Chief Evans' office. While Carla notified the chief, Beth and Bernie entered the conference room and took their usual places. While waiting for them, mundane chatter flowed between them until Carla entered and sat down. A few minutes later, the mayor and chief entered. Mayor James sat across from the three of them while Chief Evans closed the door. After sitting at the head of the table, he opened his folder, and cleared his throat.

"Okay, Carla, where did we leave off the other day?"

"We had just talked about Parker Jarrell and Colt Lassiter, remember, mayor?" He nodded and mumbled under his breath. "Do you want to share that with us?"

"It was nothing, continue."

"Anyway, we were able to get a still photo from the video. Look at this, mayor."

After handing the photo to him, he never blinked as

his eyes glared at it. Glancing up at Carla, his eyes returned to the picture as he searched for calmness. Returning the photo, he tried to hide the anxiety taking over his body. With his pulse racing, he loosened his tie. As his respiration increased, his forehead began to glisten under the fluorescent lights.

"Who's that?"

"Parker Jarrell, or whoever he is. We searched, we got nothing. Look at this other photo." Handing him a photo of Angela's brother as a teenager, he recognized the young boy. "You do know who this is, right?"

"Lenny, right?"

Nodding, Carla handed him the photo forensic used to project what Lenny would look like today. A warming sensation covered his face. Feeling the warmth, he wiped the sweat from his brow. Holding the photo, everyone could see nervousness taking hold of him.

"Umm, what's, uh, who's this?"

"Mayor, we took Lenny's photo and had forensics use a program to predict what he would look like today. You're holding it. Here's the first photo we took off the video."

While sliding the photo over to him, his eyes moved back and forth, as bewilderment and fear punished his soul. He mouthed something under his breath. As he quickly stood up, silence took control of the table.

"What is it, Lester?"

"Uh, I need to get some fresh air, umm, and some water, okay?"

"Yeah, sure, guys, let's take ten."

Chief Evans motioned toward the door. Mayor James left the conference room, followed by him. While walking down the corridor toward the common area, silence accompanied them. Entering the common area, Chief Evans stopped by the coffee center, grabbing two bottles of water. Handing one to the mayor, he immediately opened it taking several big gulps before continuing through the main entrance.

Outside, the gloominess in the skies matched the mayor's demeanor. The mayor lit up a cigarette, surprising Chief Evans. While taking several quick puffs, he paced back and forth, mumbling under his breath. Scanning the entire parking lot, he took a final drag and extinguished the cigarette. Meeting the chief's questionable eyes, he let out a big relaxing sigh, mumbling again under his breath.

"Mayor, are you ready to go back inside?"

"Yeah, let's get it over."

"Lester, I didn't know you smoked."

"Well, sometimes, you know, I just need one to calm my nerves."

Without responding, Mayor James began walking to the main entrance and entered. Chief Evans, surprised by the mayor's abrupt departure, walked quickly to catch up with him. Walking together, they entered the conference room, where Beth, Carla, and Bernie sat patiently. Taking their respective places at the table, Carla continued.

"Mayor, we believe Lenny is in town using the alias, Parker Jarrell. Now, for the other guy, Colt Lassiter, we're not sure who he is. We searched, found nothing on him. Have you seen either of these men before?"

Nervousness immediately erupted in his body. Eyes randomly moving around the room, droplets of fear surfaced on his forehead. Wiping them away, he remained silent.

"Mayor, you look as though you have seen a ghost, talk to us, okay?"

"Uh, yeah, umm, the other day when I left here. Two men in a white sedan, maybe a Corolla or Sentra, followed me a few blocks and eventually turned right on Westover. One had a beard. That night at the city commission meeting, uh, those same two men entered the commission chambers just as the meeting began. Umm, they sat in the back, away from the cameras. Umm, so, you think the bearded one is Lenny?"

Bernie, sitting patiently while taking notes, chimed in, "Yeah, we do, and after seeing that photo forensics created, Angela does as well. However, we don't know why he is here, and neither does she. Anything else you want to tell us?"

"I got a call from Rich this morning. He told me that two men in a white sedan, one had a beard, followed him to his auto mall. He said they looked at a few trucks, didn't want to be bothered, and refused to give them their names." Taking a short pause and sighing heavily, he continued. "After that, Rich said they drove to the building housing his office. They circled the parking lot several times and then left. On their security camera, he got the license plate number. Rich made a few calls, pulled a few strings, and found out the owner reported the Missouri plate stolen several weeks ago."

"Mayor." Moving his eyes to Chief Evans. "I put out a BOLO, but I'm not sure it would do any good. If these guys stole one license plate, they've stolen several, making it harder to find them. We'll notify other law enforcement agencies in the area. Hopefully, we get a break. The bad thing is, we don't even know if they're involved."

Nods flew around the table as silence captivated the conference room. The mayor downed his remaining water, and his eyes began to wander around the table. However, he couldn't fight off Carla's curious eyes.

"Detective McBride, what is it?"

"Mayor, tell me about Bambi. The other day, you were noticeably bothered when we told you about her. The more we know, the better chance we have to find out what's going on and why Lenny suddenly resurfaced after thirty years or so."

"Look, Detective McBride, that was over thirty years ago. I just remember she was a wild child, and she had many partners. Uh, it was just a matter of time until she turned up pregnant."

"Mayor, did you have sex with her?"

Chief Evans chimed in, "McBride, tread lightly."

"Did you, mayor, did any of the Diamond Brotherhood have sex with her?"

"Uh, I don't remember. Maybe you should ask them."

"Don't worry, I plan to."

"As for me, no, I didn't. Heather, yeah, Heather Vass, as I recall, was the young lady I was dating back then. Besides, what does Lenny have to do with having sex with Bambi?"

"We don't know, but we're going to find out. You can count on that, mayor. Somehow, all of this is connected. I can feel it in my bones."

"Chief, detectives, I'm done with this conversation. No need to show me out. I know the way."

He left the conference room, rubbing his temples vigorously while mumbling four-letter profanities. After getting in his car, he started it and squealed the tires as he left the station.

Back inside, Carla exclaimed, "Dammit, chief, what's got him all riled up?"

"I don't know. I've never seen him act like this before."

Beth jumped in, "Guys, I don't know what's going on with him. But when you mentioned Bambi's name, his body language and his facial expression told me it scared the hell out of him."

# CHAPTER 31

P hilip Devaney worked very hard to have a
successful business and compete with the
national pharmacy chains and the host of super-
stores that sold everything. His company had been
successful because of their superior, family-oriented
customer service and his involvement in the community.
Not only was he a longtime city commissioner, being
president of the Chamber of Commerce and Rotary
exhibited his leadership qualities to help the community
grow. Native to Oakmont, he grew up in an affluent
household. His father, Greg Devaney, had just been
elected to the state senate when Philip was in high
school. Currently, Greg is still one of the most influential
senators in the commonwealth.

Philip, an excellent student, was also a natural
athlete playing every sport in high school. However,
baseball was what he did best. As a pitcher and first
baseman, he had many athletic scholarships to consider.
The Cincinnati Reds, Pittsburgh Pirates, and Atlanta
Braves were interested during his high school years. He

had everything going for him at the young age of seventeen.

Although his professional aspirations excited him and his parents, he knew most professional sports careers didn't last long. Wanting an education first, he elected to accept a full scholarship to the university in Oakmont to improve his skills. If he did well, the big leagues would be there when he graduated. However, that never panned out, as he threw his arm out in his junior year.

Being an excellent student, he majored in chemistry and biology in college. He also minored in business. Finally, in his senior year of college, pharmacy school became his calling. Readily being accepted into the University of Kentucky's pharmacy school, he had found his passion for owning his own business.

After graduating with honors, the national chains offered him a position, but he wanted to have his own business. Fortunately for him, an opportunity came along to join Oakmont Apothecary. For forty years or more, the family-owned pharmacy was a leader in the business community. It was still the place to enjoy an old-fashioned fountain drink and a hot dog.

Working tirelessly and saving money, he purchased the pharmacy achieving his lifelong dream without his father's help. He married his college sweetheart and had two teenage daughters. He couldn't think life could get any better. Recently, he won re-election, and by receiving the most votes of any city commissioner, he would keep his Mayor Pro Tem status.

Being the boss, he set his hours. Usually, he would manage the daytime hours. However, today he would cover the afternoon shift, giving his evening manager a night off. He believed in happy employees, and his night manager's daughter was in a school play she didn't want to miss. Arriving about a half-hour before the night manager was to leave, she brought Philip up to speed on the day's activities. With flu season in full swing, there had been a steady stream of people wanting shots and buying the usual remedies.

Philip knew most of the people in town and loved talking with them when they were in the store. Before his night manager, Emily Dawson left, she informed him about two men who came in that morning to see him. They said they were old high school buddies of his. She told them that Philip would be in later that afternoon. Wondering who they were, he looked forward to visiting with them should they return. The afternoon dragged on, but as soon as the workday ended for most of the city's citizens, foot traffic increased. Approaching seven o'clock, Mayor James entered the store and approached Philip.

"What brings you in here. I believe we just filled your prescriptions last week."

"Can we go back to your office, where we can talk in private?"

"Of course, follow me."

Walking through the store, the mayor seemed a little jittery. Reaching the pharmacy department, they entered his office, and Philip closed the door.

"Have a seat, Lester. You look a little, uh, flustered, have a bad day?"

"Yeah, but not at city hall."

"Really, in the doghouse, huh?"

"Not that. Besides, I stay in the doghouse all the time, if you know what I mean?" Nodding, Philip laughed. "What's so funny?"

"Nothing, lighten up, mayor. What's bothering you?"

"Uh, I met with Chief Evans and his detectives and the other younger gal. I believe her name is Beth. Anyway, umm, they believe Lenny, Angela's little brother, is in town using an alias."

"Really, why would he be using one?"

"Detective McBride believes he's connected to Bryan's death."

"No way, how, why?"

"They don't know. Anyway, they showed me a picture of what Lenny would look like today with a beard. It blew my mind, scared the shit out of me."

"I'm all ears."

"The other day, two men in a white sedan followed me for a couple of blocks after I left the police station."

"Now, you got my attention. Should I be concerned, are we in any danger?"

"Rich called me this morning, said a white sedan followed him into the auto mall, looked at a couple of trucks, then circled the parking lot back by his office, then left. He got the license plate number off the security camera. Turns out, uh, the plate was stolen."

"You didn't answer my question. Are we in danger?"

"What do you think? Yeah, not sure why, but it has something to do with Lenny and, get this, Bambi."

As Philip sighed, Mayor James' phone rang. Glancing at the caller ID, he motioned to Philip he needed to take the call and stepped outside his office. After a couple of minutes, he returned, where Philip showed signs of anxiety.

"Is everything okay?"

"Listen, I've got to go, the alarm at my house is going

off, police are on the way. We'll catch up tomorrow. Oh, and watch your back, okay?"

Nodding, he walked the mayor to the front of the store, and he left. The store was busier than usual, and he pitched in, easing the anxiety that overtook his body. Because he was so busy, he'd forgotten what Emily mentioned to him about the two men asking for him that morning. Time flew by, and closing time arrived.

After the last employee left, he turned off the unnecessary lights. He set the alarm, locked the front doors, and walked to his car, noticing his surroundings. Finally, reaching his car, he quickly unlocked it, got in, and immediately locked the doors. Starting it, the Miata purred. Putting the stick shift in reverse, he backed out. After glancing in the rearview mirror, he breathed a sigh of relief.

Suddenly, there was a tap on his window. His pulse raced as anxiety grabbed his soul. Quickly turning to his left, Darlene, one of his employees, stared at him. Seeing her face was a relief. After lowering the window, the night air felt good against his glistening forehead.

"Damn, Darlene, you scared the hell out of me?"

"Sorry to bother you, my car won't start. Would you give me a lift home?"

Breathing heavily as his pulse continued to race, "Uh, sure, get in."

Pulling out of the parking lot, the Miata turned right, heading toward the downtown area. After a couple of blocks, a white sedan caught up with him. Seeing the lights in the rearview mirror sent his pulse racing as adrenalin shot throughout him. Turning onto Main Street, the white sedan kept up with him.

Remembering what the mayor told him, he turned

right at the police station as the white sedan sped past him. Pulling into the parking lot, he needed time to collect his thoughts.

Bewilderment painted Darlene's face. "Is everything okay? Why did you pull in here?"

"It's nothing to be worried about. I'll have you home in about five minutes."

Turning around, he pulled out of the parking lot, heading toward downtown. Just before St. Anthony's Catholic Church, he turned right. A couple of minutes later, he pulled in front of Darlene's house. Twenty minutes later, he pulled into his garage. Entering his home, his wife, Judy, greeted him with a kiss on the cheek and a double shot of Four Roses Single Barrel bourbon. After taking a big sip, the amber liquid did its best to calm his rattled psyche.

# CHAPTER 32

**B**eth arrived at the station earlier than usual. The big clock on the wall read seven-thirty. After dropping off her purse at her workstation, she headed to the coffee center for her morning jolt of caffeine. Several minutes later, she was back at her workstation. Silence flowed throughout the common area pleasing her. Digging deeper into Bobbi Tierney and Clarissa Morgan's past was a huge priority for her. Waking up her MacPro, she chose Clarissa first because things didn't add up. A millionaire's wife doesn't move from a metropolitan area like Columbus, to a small community such as Oakmont without a reason. That was a big red flag, especially after her husband had passed and she inherited millions.

With her mind glued to the monitor, she was oblivious to anything in the common area. Muted chatter increased as more people arrived. She didn't mind as she was good at blocking out useless conversation. Engrossed in the information on Thaddeus and Clarissa, time moved by quickly. Hearing some disruptive commotion near her, Beth glanced in that direction seeing Bernie settling into his chair. He had this thing of finding the most comfortable position for his toosh. He was not obese by any means, however, he was useless at work until comfortable. Now, settled in, he smiled at her. Smiling back, she greeted him in her sweet way.

"Good morning to you as well. You're here early. What's going on?"

"Research on Clarissa, and Bobbi, I felt a little guilty yesterday. I thought I'd get an early start, see what I could dig up about them, especially Clarissa. You know, red flags are popping up everywhere. Where's Carla?"

"Who knows, she drives me crazy sometimes, anyway, red flags, like what?"

"Like Bortel, it appears he worked for her husband in Columbus."

"Okay, it could be something. What else?"

"Good morning, Bernie, Beth, what's going on? I heard something about Bortel. I can't believe you guys would start without me."

"We wouldn't do that, would we, Bernie?"

Nodding at Beth, he threw Carla his famous good morning smile followed by the look. A quick bird met his engaging eyes.

"Okay, guys, be nice to each other." Carla threw a scowling smile at Beth. "Okay, why don't you guys get some coffee and join me in the conference room. I'm going to refresh mine. See you in a few minutes."

After fixing herself another cup of joe, she entered the conference room sitting at the head of the table, waiting for them. Five minutes later, they arrived with their friendly banter. It was their way of getting serious and ready for the day. Sitting across from each other, they motioned Beth to begin.

"I found some intriguing information. When I interviewed Clarissa the other day, she told me she'd never met Bortel before. When I asked her that question, she seemed surprised by it. Anyway, I discovered that he once worked for her husband a long time ago. That's how he ended up in Oakmont. Thaddeus promoted him."

"Doesn't mean he knew Clarissa, does it, Carla?

"No, Bernie. What else do you have, Beth?"

"Okay, guys, how about this. I found where Clarissa and Bortel co-chaired one of Thaddeus' charity functions in Columbus."

Carla chimed in, "Now, we're talking. So, they knew each other a long time ago, and she moved here after her husband died, now that's a big red flag."

"Exactly, and Bortel was single. From the pictures in the Columbus newspaper, Thaddeus was obese, not all that handsome. Clarissa, on the other hand, well, she's, a Barbie Doll as Bernie would say."

"Watch it, Beth."

Ignoring his snide remark, she continued, "Maybe something was going on between them or happened long ago. Bortel was a decent-looking man, and as I mentioned, single."

"Yeah, maybe they have a romantic connection. What else do you have for us?"

"Well, Bernie, we know the Thaddeus' death was suspicious. I'll make some calls, see where that leads me. I'll be paying Clarissa another visit while I'm waiting for forensics to get back with me."

Carla remained silent, listening and taking notes. As

usual, she didn't let Bernie take control that often but was now fully awake and chimed in.

"Beth, anything new on Barbara?"

"You mean, Bobbi, right, Carla?"

"Look, Bernie, I know she gave you 'that look,' but let's keep it professional, okay?" An in-your-face bird flew at Carla's rolling eyes. Ignoring his raucous gesture, she continued, "Anything else, Beth?"

"Not really, just don't think she has anything to do with anything other than a secret fantasy of landing Bryan one day, and now he's gone."

"Okay, you focus on Clarissa and Bortel. Bernie and I will visit Freedom National Bank and see what we can find out from John Vickers, one of his VPs. You can take on Clarissa, rattle her a little bit, okay?"

"Of course."

"We're also going to revisit Angela. She knows more than she is telling us."

After getting up to leave the conference room, Chief Evans peeked his head in, motioning Carla and Bernie back to his office. Following him, they entered and took their usual seats. Closing the door, he settled in his chair with concern all over his face. They had seen that expression way too many times.

"Chief, whatever it is, it's Bernie's fault."

"Calm down, you two. I received a call from Mayor James a few minutes ago. It seems Philip Devaney was followed by this white sedan last night. That can't be a coincidence. Somehow, we have to find this car before something terrible happens."

Suddenly, the phone rang. The caller ID was familiar. After placing it on the speaker, an agitated voice filled the room.

"Mayor, calm down. I've got you on speaker, and Carla and Bernie are in my office. Go ahead and begin."

"I just received a call from Rich. A white sedan followed him yesterday morning. You guys need to find these guys. This situation is not good."

"Calm down, mayor. We can't stop every white Corolla or Sentra or whatever make it is. We'll get to the bottom of this, okay?"

"You better, or you know what."

An annoying dial tone blared from the speaker and quickly ended as the room grew silent. A warming sensation began to invade Chief Evans' forehead. They had seen him like this before. Sometimes, his expression was louder than words, and there was no need for him to say anything further to them. They knew finding the two men in the white sedan was at the top of their to-do list.

# CHAPTER 33

While Beth was on her way to Clarissa's home, Carla and Bernie called Freedom National Bank, making an appointment with John Vickers, senior VP. With the death of Bortel, corporate had elevated John as interim CEO. Since he couldn't meet with them until one-thirty, they headed for lunch at McGruder's. Meanwhile, Beth took a chance that Clarissa was at home. After being cleared by security, she slowly drove down Mahogany Way. Reaching her house, Beth pulled into the driveway and cut the engine. For a moment, she remained in her car, observing the front porch and home. Exiting her car, she took the four steps up onto the porch. From her first visit, she knew the doorbell didn't work and used the old-fashioned doorknocker. After a minute or so, the door swung open. Clarissa, still in her sleep attire, opened the storm door and greeted her.

"Mrs. Morgan, do you have time to answer a few more questions? I won't take much of your time. May I come in?"

Showing hesitancy, she pondered her request. "Didn't I answer everything the other day? What else do you want to know?"

"Well, a few new things have surfaced that I need to clear up with you."

"What things?"

"Mrs. Morgan, may I come in?"

"Sorry, call me Clarissa, okay?"

"Right, Clarissa, it is."

Motioning Beth in, she entered and sat in a chair across from the sofa. Sitting there gave her the best view of Clarissa's demeanor and body language as she answered her questions.

"May I get you anything to drink?"

"Nah, I'm okay. Shall we begin?" Nodding, Beth continued. "The other day, you said you became good friends with Bryan and eluded that it wasn't what I thought it was."

"Yeah, if you want to know whether we were romantically, sexually involved, that answer is no. I wouldn't do that to him. He wasn't ready. It's not that I didn't want him. He was so vulnerable, and it wouldn't have been right. I'm not like that."

"I see. Okay, are you seeing anyone? Being new in the community makes it hard to meet people. You're still young enough to find love again."

"Well, I've had a few dates, got to know a few men through the church, just casual dating, that kind of thing."

"Good, do you think Mrs. Tierney ever hooked up with Bryan? You said she went over there at odd times."

"I wouldn't know, but I wouldn't put it past her."

"Right. Now, the other day, you said you didn't know

of Bortel until he ended up dead, ironically, next door of all places."

"Yeah, that's what I said. What are you getting at?"

"Clarissa, you know it's my job to investigate anyone connected with this case, right?" Nodding, she began to show signs of anxiety. "So, I did some digging and found out Bortel worked with your husband about twenty years ago." As her eyes wandered around the room, she deflected Beth's intense stare. "Clarissa, do you remember that? You even co-chaired a charity event with him."

"Oh, yeah, I'd forgotten about that. That's not a crime, is it?"

"Of course not. Let's cut the bullshit. You knew Bortel before the other day, didn't you?"

"Okay, okay! Umm, we had a few dates, but nothing serious, dinner and drinks, nothing else. Seriously, you think I had something to do with his death?" Hesitating for a moment, Beth looked around the great room as she became more agitated. "Beth, do you?"

"Oh, of course not. So, you have a few dates with him, big deal. Is he the only person you've dated?"

"Hmm, no, there's been others."

"Okay, your perfume is different today. What was it called?"

"That's another strange question. Anyway, I'm trying a new one, not sure what it's called. I can get the bottle if you really need to know."

"Nah, that's okay. Well, that should do it. If I have any more questions, I'll be in touch."

After showing Beth out to the porch, Clarissa watched her enter her car and back out of the driveway.

Beth stared at Clarissa on the porch; deep concern painted her otherwise radiant complexion.

While Beth was on her way back to the station, Carla and Bernie had finished lunch and walked the two blocks to Freedom National Bank. Entering and approaching the receptionist, they flashed their badges. John Vickers, who was standing outside his office, immediately walked toward them. After exchanging pleasantries, he led them back to his office. Once inside and seated, John closed the door.

"Detectives, how may I help you today? You said earlier you wanted to ask me a few questions about Bortel, shoot."

At lunch, they decided Bernie would ask the questions while Carla observed.

"Mr. Vickers, thank you for seeing us on short notice." Nodding, Bernie continued. "Being Bortel's number one guy, you probably knew about his personal life. Carla knows all about mine. What can you tell us?"

"Oh, yeah, we were pretty close, had a few drinks after work, that kind of thing. Sometimes, Bortel's lady friend would join my wife and me at Pascali's."

"Umm, yeah, Pascali's, nice restaurant."

"One of my favorites. Anyway, yeah, I think he was getting serious with this lady."

"Name, please?"

"Of course, sorry, Clarissa, Clarissa Morgan."

"Did she come in here a lot?"

"Yeah, this is where she banks."

"Right, did you know she inherited a ton of money from her husband? He died in a freak accident four years ago."

"Yeah, Bortel told me about that. He said it was millions. What does this have to do with his death?"

"I don't know, maybe nothing, but we have to check everything out."

"Of course. Anything else I can help you with?"

"Has she been back in since he died?"

"Umm, not while I've been here, which is most days. Why?"

"No, reason. Hey, that should do it. Thanks, we'll show ourselves out."

Walking back to Bernie's car, they remained silent, observing people coming and going. Reaching his car, a big white ticket on his windshield irked him. He grabbed it as Carla broke out laughing, pointing at the two-hour limit on the sign. Grumbling under his breath, Bernie unlocked the car, and Carla got in, still laughing under her breath.

Fifteen minutes later, they were back at the police station where Beth was waiting for them. She motioned them to the conference room to discuss her interview with Clarissa. After discussing all the information presented, they agreed she knew more. Waiting for her DNA and fingerprint results was frustrating because that information may validate that she could be a person of interest in Bortel's death. The DNA results would help them more than Clarissa's fingerprints. She had a key to the Walters' house, and her fingerprints were likely everywhere.

Complicating matters, two men in a white sedan appeared to be stalking the four remaining city commission members. This case was beginning to resemble a deadly cat and mouse game. Who might be the next man up, and why? Who were the two men, and why were they allegedly terrorizing them? If Chase Ballard was Colt Lassiter, and that was a big if, the only person who might have those answers was Chase's grandmother, Karen Ballard, living in Jellico, Tennessee.

# CHAPTER 34

**K**aren Ballard had recently lost her husband, George. He finally succumbed to lung cancer a few months ago. They left Oakmont over thirty-five years ago, allegedly because of the shame their daughter, Joni, put them through when she non-surprisingly turned up pregnant. George, a pharmaceutical sales associate, could live anywhere in his region. Jellico seemed the right fit for them, and Interstate 75 ran right through it. George had been a good husband and provided for his family, although he wasn't rich by any means. In his marriage, he controlled everything. He was old-fashioned in many ways. He believed a wife's job was being a housewife and nothing more.

Just over the Kentucky state line, Jellico was about a ninety-minute drive from Oakmont. Ever since The Black Rose case, Carla was more open to Bernie driving even though he was a stickler of obeying posted speed limits. Their appointment with Karen was at ten-thirty AM. Traveling south on the interstate was always an adventure. However, the traffic was light this morning, hopefully giving them the best opportunity for an uneventful drive. Most of the autumn vistas were past their peak, making their trip much more boring. Other than music coming from the speaker, silence provided a relaxing respite from each other.

As one particular song filled the cabin, their ears perked up. Knowing the lyrics by heart, they sang along with Tim McGraw as he belted out his megahit, *Live Like You Are Dying*. Sometimes their version of car karaoke went awry, but never with this song. As the lyrics faded away, Bernie muted the volume.

"What did you do that for, dickhead?"

"Uh, no reason. Are you and Chris going to tie the knot someday?"

"That's personal."

"Are you? You two have been at it hot and heavy lately, don't you think it's about time?"

"We've sort of talked about it, and things are going very well, and we're both happy with our situation. Hey, our exit is coming up. I hope this is not a useless fishing trip."

"I always say these types of visits are never a waste of time. We'll learn something about Chase that may help us decide if he is involved or not. That's why we are here, right?"

Nodding, Bernie took the exit ramp into Jellico. The navigation had them turning right, then heading to the old residential part of town. Within about twelve minutes, they turned left on the street to Karen's house. Most were old craftsman-style houses. Given her husband was in pharmaceutical sales, Carla expected something a little more upscale.

Pulling over to the curb in front of the house, a for-sale sign graced the small yard. In Carla's conversation with Karen, she didn't mention the house being for sale. Parked under the carport was a white sedan with Tennessee plates. Further down the street was another white sedan. Carla couldn't quite make out the plates, but she knew it wasn't Kentucky or Tennessee. As they sat looking at the old house, it needed some updating. According to Karen, they had lived in this house ever since relocating to Jellico. A University of Kentucky flag hung proudly on the porch while the house next door donned a white flag with a big orange "T."

Bernie, the jokester that he was, nudged Carla pointing at the two flags. "See, I told you not every Kentucky fan hates everyone from Tennessee." Carla rolled her eyes in his direction before shooting him an in-your-face bird. "Are you ready, partner?"

"Yeah, remember we agreed I would conduct this interview, woman to woman, right?"

Bernie nodded as she exited the car and stood on the sidewalk in front of the house, waiting for him. Finally, getting out of the car, he lumbered around it, eventually standing next to her. A small concrete stoop made the house look old and drab. Approaching the front door, Carla took one step and knocked on the door while Bernie waited patiently behind her.

Hearing soft footsteps, Karen opened the front door staring at Carla. She flashed her badge identifying herself and introduced Bernie as he flashed his badge. Satisfied with their credentials, she welcomed them into a small but comfortable living room. Motioning them to sit on the sofa, they settled in while Karen sat in her favorite lounger with the television's best viewing angle. Her eyes moved back and forth at them.

"You must be thirsty after that boring drive down the interstate. May I get you both a glass of sweet tea? I just made it." Appreciating Karen's generosity and a tradition of southern hospitality, they nodded. "Great, I'll get three glasses of ice and the pitcher of tea, be back in an instant. Lemon, anyone?" Again, Bernie nodded quickly.

While she entered the kitchen, Carla rose from the sofa to explore the room, looking for pictures of Chase. After noticing a photo on the mantel, an old family picture of George, Karen, and Chase grabbed her curious eyes. Hearing footsteps, she quickly returned to the sofa just as Karen, carrying a tray, entered the room. Setting the tray down, she poured the sweet tea into the glasses filled with ice. The sound of the warm tea flowing over the ice broke the silence in the room.

"There you go, detectives, enjoy."

Bernie nodded as Karen took her glass with a lemon and sat back in the lounger. Meanwhile, Bernie squeezed the lemon in his glass, mixing it with the long-stemmed spoon. Taking a sip, he let out a big sigh. Carla bypassed the lemon, took a long drink, and put her glass on the coffee table. As Carla's eyes met Karen's weathered smile, she broke the silence between them.

"What do you want to know about Chase, and why?"

Wanting to ease Karen's apparent anxiety, Carla replied, "First of all, we're sorry about your husband's passing." Karen nodded as she sipped on her iced tea. "Anyway, just tell us about Chase, you know, growing up with you and George. Hmm, just start there, okay? Start with the picture on the mantel. When was that taken?"

"Oh, that one. Yeah, it was back in junior high school. We were so proud of him back then. You know, he was a pretty good athlete. Not sure where he got his natural ability. He wouldn't have gotten it from his mother, Joni; she had two left feet. It must have been from Chase's father, whoever he is. You know, Joni would never tell us who the father was. I guess she had her reasons, and we let it be."

"Karen, I'm glad you mentioned your daughter, Joni. If you don't mind, tell us about her, what was she like growing up, then we can get back to Chase, okay?"

Although thirty-five years had passed since Joni unexpectedly died after giving birth, tears still flowed from Karen's heartstrings.

"Do either of you have children?"

"Hmm, no, I'm single, just never had time for marriage or children. Bernie, on the other hand, has two grown sons."

"I see, well, umm, whoever said that time heals everything hasn't lost a child. I still think about her every day, uh, my little angel."

As Karen wiped the remnants of years of heartache off her cheeks, Bernie knew what she meant. He swallowed hard, keeping his emotions at bay. Rising from her lounger, she replenished their glasses, then grabbed her drink, and filled it to the brim. Setting it on the table by the lounger, she walked over to an antique bookcase and took out a scrapbook. Walking back to the sofa, she placed it on the coffee table. Reading her mind, they made room for her on the couch.

# CHAPTER 35

Sitting between them put Karen at ease. It's what Carla wanted so that she would open up more about Joni and Chase. After about thirty minutes and three glasses of tea, bittersweet tears flowed from Karen. Reliving her daughter's short life through pictures touched everyone. Noticing all the empty glasses, Karen gathered them up and headed for the kitchen. A few minutes later, she returned with the glasses full of ice. Replenishing each glass, she picked up the scrapbook and returned it to the bookcase. Pulling out another one, she returned to her lounger. While sitting with it on her lap, she dried the remnants of sadness off her cheeks. As her eyes met the seriousness in Carla's determined eyes, she continued, "Now, what do you want to know about Chase?"

"First of all, thank you for sharing Joni's life with us. She was a beautiful child, just like her mother. I'm truly sorry that you didn't get to spend more time with her. But I'm sure raising Chase you got to see parts of her in him helping you cope with your loss."

"Umm, yeah, it did make it easier for me. However, she was a daddy's girl. Not sure George ever got over losing her. I know I haven't."

"I see. When you are ready, tell us about Chase, okay?"

Rising out of the lounger, she joined them on the sofa, placing the scrapbook on the coffee table. Opening it up, an innocent newborn picture of Chase began to tell the story of his young life. While leafing through the pages, her heartstrings began to describe her experience of raising him. After flipping the last page over, the innocent newborn pictured on the first page morphed into a handsome young man receiving his high school diploma. Karen's southern sweet tea had run its course. Rising off the sofa, she returned the scrapbook to the bookcase. Instead of sitting in her lounge chair, she gathered up the glasses and an empty pitcher of tea, placed them on the old-fashioned tray, and returned to the kitchen.

"Let's get to Chase. I'm getting kind of hungry."

"Listen, dickhead, all of this was to get her prepared to open up about him, and it's working. Just keep your pants on while I handle it, okay?"

He reluctantly nodded as Karen returned from the kitchen with a tray of sandwiches. Putting them down on the coffee table, she returned to the kitchen. A couple of minutes later, she returned with another tray containing a new pitcher of tea and three glasses of ice. Taking one of the sandwich plates and a glass of tea, she placed them on the table beside the lounger and sat down.

"You two, grab a sandwich and eat while I answer your questions about Chase, okay?"

"You didn't have to do this, you know?"

"Yeah, but I made a fresh batch of my southern

pimento cheese spread, and it's too much for me to eat, so enjoy. Now, what do you want to know about Chase?"

"The last picture you showed us was at his high school graduation. What did he do after that?"

"As I said earlier, he was a natural athlete and received a scholarship to play baseball at a small college here in Tennessee. After he graduated from college, he said he wanted to travel out west for some reason. He ended up in Oregon. I think Portland. He said he would fit in better there."

"What do you mean?"

"Joni, if she were alive, would have never thought her son would be different."

"Karen, do you mean gay?" As she nodded, her eyes glistened. She wiped the disappointment off her cheeks. "Okay, go on."

As more tears flowed, she wiped them away. "That's it, he stayed out there, hardly ever came home. We'd talk occasionally, but he wanted to live his life on his terms."

"I'm sorry."

"Hmm, that's okay. Chase did make it home before George died. They spent a lot of time talking, not sure what they discussed. Anyway, he brought a friend with him, he was older, but Chase didn't care. I assumed they were a couple. He got a little testy with me when I made them sleep in separate bedrooms. Guess I'm old fashioned, just didn't seem right."

Pulling out her smartphone, Carla pulled up the picture of Parker Jarrell. "The other man, could this be him?" Taking Carla's phone, she studied it and returned it.

"Hmm, maybe it's hard to tell with the beard."

"Why is that?"

"Chase's friend didn't have one, but the eyes and nose look the same."

"What kind of car did they come in?"

"Just like mine."

"When they left, do you know where they were going?"

"Didn't say. Why do you ask?"

Pulling up another picture on her smartphone, she handed it to her. While studying it very closely, a tear surfaced in the corner of her eye. Wiping it away, she gave the phone back to Carla.

"Karen, is that Chase?" Seeing his picture on a police detective's phone made her uneasy and speechless, and she just nodded. "Okay, do you know how Chase and…"

"Parker Jarrell was his name."

"So, how did they meet?"

"Chase said they met at a rehab house somewhere in Missouri. I believe he said it was called The Last Chance. I don't know how they got there. I asked, and Chase pretty much said it wasn't any of my business."

"Why is your house up for sale?"

Surprised, her eyes glistened once more, wiping the tears away. She took a deep breath and a long drink of sweet tea. Finally, making eye contact again with Carla, she replied, "I don't have any choice, can't make the payments anymore. Social Security checks barely cover the necessities."

"I don't understand. You lived here for over thirty-five years, wouldn't your house…be?"

"You don't understand. George was not the best money manager and took out a second mortgage. He was a heavy drinker, gambled, and spent the extra money foolishly."

"Extra money, where did it come from?"

"George said it was none of my business and told me not to worry about it. Whenever I would bring it up, he'd get mean, never hit me or anything like that, just mean, he was a mean drunk."

"How long has the money been coming?"

"Hmm, I believe the first check came right after we moved."

"Really, for over thirty-five years, hmm."

Nodding, Karen continued, "Then it came every month after that. After George passed, the checks stopped. No explanation, no notification. I just don't get it."

"Do you have something you can show us, maybe tell us who sent them?"

Rising from the lounger, she went over to an old-fashioned rolltop desk, pulled open a drawer, and grabbed a white envelope. Walking back, she handed it to Carla. After looking at the return address, a scowl crossed her face. Giving it to Bernie, he shook his head.

"Keep it. Maybe you can find out what is going on, why the checks stopped. Anything you can do that will help me stay in this house is appreciated."

"Of course, but it's not much to go on. Would you have a copy of the check?" Shaking her head. "Okay, what about a bank statement? It might show the name."

"I'll have to find them. I still have to go through George's stuff, and that will take some time."

"Okay, you can look after we leave. Call us if you get a name, okay? Now, you said earlier that Chase talked with George a lot. Any ideas on what they talked about?"

"Nah, all I know is the last time before George died, Chase came out of his bedroom with fire in his eyes. I heard him mumble something under his breath like I'll take care of it, or something like that. George died later that evening. After the funeral, they left the next day. I haven't heard from him since. Is he in any trouble?"

Glancing at her phone several times, Carla knew it was time to head back to Oakmont. Karen got out of her lounger and took the tray containing the plates and empty glasses to the kitchen. She returned with two large Styrofoam cups filled with her southern sweet tea.

"I see you need to leave. Here's something for the road." Handing the tea to them, they walked toward the door. Opening the door, Carla turned around, seeing a woman wondering what was next for her and her only grandson. "Detectives, if you find him, please let me know, okay?"

"Of course, thank you for being so open. You take care, now."

# CHAPTER 36

Returning to the police station, Carla and Bernie sat at their workstation wondering about the checks. They knew a standard white business envelope with a post office box wasn't much help. Tracking down the owner in Charleston, West Virginia, was a difficult problem and would take time. Maybe time they didn't have if any of the other city commissioners were in danger.

While glancing at Carla and Bernie, frustration met Beth's curious eyes. Silence flowed back and forth until Beth commented, "Rough trip?"

With a scowling expression, Bernie replied, "I'd say it was more like a frustrating one, right, Carla?"

"Yeah, we found out that Colt Lassiter is Chase because he brought his partner, Parker Jarrell, home for his grandfather's funeral. Given that premise, Parker Jarrell is Lenny Clark."

"How did they meet?"

"Drug rehab and halfway house in Missouri."

"All of that's good news, right? So, why the gloomy disposition?"

Bernie replied, "George and Karen Ballard had received a monthly check from someone ever since they left Oakmont, some thirty-five years ago. All we have is a standard business-size envelope with a post office box number as a return address in Charleston, West Virginia. Nothing else."

"Okay, I know the owner of post office boxes is hard to track down, but you said had?"

"Yeah, I did. Hmm, the checks stopped coming about a month after George died. And complicating matters, Karen may be tossed out on the street. She had to put her house up for sale to make ends meet."

"Umm, that's terrible. You know, maybe it's not a coincidence that Walters' death occurred right after George died and the checks stopped."

Carla chimed in, "Sort of, maybe they are tied together, but why? We've got a post office box that may hold the answers to all our questions. Anyway, anything new with you?"

"Nah, just waiting for the DNA results like everyone else is. I checked with Sherry. She's hoping we'll have them tomorrow. I'm waiting for a call back from the insurance company that paid the settlement to Clarissa. How about you guys? What's your next move?"

"Bernie will contact the rehab house in Missouri where Lenny and Chase met. Maybe we get lucky, talk to someone that remembered them. I'm going to try to find the owner of the post office box."

"Good luck with that, Carla. While I'm waiting for the insurance company to return my call, I'm revisiting

Clarissa. She has been lying all along about knowing Bortel."

"Yeah, Beth, we could all use some good luck, right, Bernie?"

As Bernie nodded, Beth left, heading to see Clarissa while her cohorts tackled their respective assignments. Dialing the phone number for The Last Chance rehab and halfway house in Missouri, Bernie listened to annoying menu options on the other end. Deciding none of them fit his purpose, he pushed zero.

As he waited for the person to pick up his call, Carla's smartphone rang. Answering it, she threw Bernie a crooked smile. Jotting down some information, she gave Bernie a thumbs-up gesture. Ending the call, she put her smartphone on her desk and turned her attention to Bernie, still on hold.

Finally, a smile crossed Bernie's face, and he spoke. Carla gave him the signal to place the call on speaker so that she could listen in. Instantly, Carla heard a woman's voice while Bernie put two fingers to his lips, hushing her.

"Miss Jacobi, I'm Detective Bernie Kowalski with the Oakmont Police Department in Kentucky. I'm trying to find someone that can tell me about two men that were there for treatment."

"Detective, you know that is confidential information." Silence met her ear. "Anything else I may help you with?"

"Well, if you change your mind, give me a call."

An annoying dial tone filled their workspace for a few seconds, and then silence took over. Bernie knew finding information would be difficult where privacy concerns were paramount everywhere.

"Carla, who called you?"

"Karen, the envelope belongs to an accounting firm, Capital City Accounting in Charleston, West Virginia. That's all that was on a check stub she found in an old shoebox George had hidden in a closet. We will see where that leads us."

The remainder of the day, they reviewed Bernie's notes from their visit with Karen. They knew it didn't take a rocket scientist to figure out the monthly payments had to be hush money or blackmail. Furthermore, why it had gone on for thirty-five years might be the key to cracking this case. The big clock on the wall was pushing five o'clock, almost quitting time.

"Hey, partner, you want to get a drink?"

"Only if you are buying, Bernie." A thumbs-up gesture met her smile. As they were walking out of the police station, Carla's smartphone rang.

"Hey, Beth, why don't you join us at McGruder's, then you can tell us what you found out from revisiting Clarissa?"

Fifteen minutes later, Beth joined them in their favorite booth. Carla had already ordered drinks and munchies. After sliding in beside Carla, Sam arrived with their drinks and assorted munchies. All were holding their glasses up, and a well-deserved cheer filled the booth. Christening it, each savored their adult beverage— Pinot Grigio for Beth, Jameson for Carla, and a Yuengling for Bernie. As all eyes moved around the booth, Beth could see she had the floor.

"Okay, guys, Clarissa opened up about her relation- ship with Bortel. They had been a couple for a long time. She even had a brief fling while working on her husband's charity event. Not to bore you with every little detail, she chose Oakmont because of her relationship with him. Anyway, it's kind of funny. She hasn't shown any remorse about his death. Something happened in their relationship. Maybe when I hear from the insurance company, we'll know more. How about you two?"

"Bernie struck out, but I got the name of the company that sent the checks to George. Let's hope tomorrow we get a real break."

Glasses met in the middle of the table as another cheer set the tone for another round of drinks. The evening flew by, and with drinks finished, each went home to the love of their life.

# CHAPTER 37

**T**he most powerful lawyer in Oakmont, Barry
Stewart, began his day by working out in his
home gym. After he finished and showered, a
light breakfast with his wife, Lynda, would put him in the
best frame of mind to begin his day. Having the premier
law firm in town, his leadership on the city commission
was also instrumental in bringing high-profile companies
to the Oakmont Industrial Complex.

He was a blessed man for many reasons. His father,
Harry, started the firm over thirty-five years ago. In many
ways, Barry's dad paved the way for his success. Harry
was once a city commissioner helping shape Oakmont
into the city it is today. He was well respected back in the
day. He built his firm based on honesty, integrity, and
fairness and expected his son to follow those attributes.
Anything different would be an embarrassment to the
family name.

Barry was a gifted individual and a natural athlete.
Playing all sports as a teenager, he was best suited for

baseball. With his blazing speed, he could steal any base. Out of his centerfield position, he could run down any fly ball. An excellent hitter, he could handle any pitch with power. Professional scouts were drooling over his potential. He had numerous college scholarship offers to consider, as well. He had his whole life in front of him if he didn't screw it up.

Like Philip Devaney, Barry knew a professional contract was exciting and enticing. Anyone that was any good in baseball dreamed of making it to the big leagues. He was no different. During his senior year, the Cleveland Indians were chomping at the bits to draft him. Harry Stewart was very proud of his son's athletic accomplishments. However, he wanted his son to follow in his footsteps, and he continuously reminded him of that.

Ultimately, Barry decided that being a lawyer was his calling and chose to attend the University of Kentucky on a full baseball scholarship. After a stellar baseball career with the Wildcats, the University of Kentucky Law School accepted him. He would follow in his father's footsteps making his dad proud.

After graduating and passing the bar exam, he joined his father's firm and worked his way up the chain, eventually becoming a full partner.

Harry Stewart was a gentleman and a very generous man. However, making money was more important to Barry, and he and his father often argued over his generosity. After his father's passing several months ago, Barry took over the firm and hired an independent accounting firm to audit the company. He wanted to make the company lean and mean. Recommendations were made to reduce unnecessary expenses and operating overhead. He implemented those recommendations, and immediately, profit increased, and life was good.

Today, he was hoping to land a big job representing a new industrial firm moving to Oakmont. Securing it would take his business to a whole new level. After a healthy breakfast, he was energized and confident he would be successful. Kissing his wife goodbye, he entered his detached garage looking at his options for his commute today.

Sporting a black suit, white shirt, and a red tie, he felt powerful and chose the black Cadillac Escalade. Backing out of the garage, he maneuvered the exquisite and luxurious machine down the driveway. Turning left, his SUV commanded the street in his upper-class subdivision.

Passing through the security gate, he turned left onto the by-pass toward Oakmont. Enjoying this pleasant November morning, he listened to public radio. He felt it was essential to stay informed about the state, national, and worldly news. While glancing in his driver's side mirror, the car behind him looked familiar.

A better view was in his rearview mirror. He had seen the car before on his way home the other day. As the car stayed a safe distance behind him, he remembered what the mayor had told them that night after the city commission meeting. He knew seeing this white sedan twice in the last few days was not a coincidence. Trying not to panic, he took several deep breaths keeping an eye on the car. Not taking any chances, he hit his hands-free button on the steering wheel. Barking out his command, he waited for Chief Evans to answer.

"Barry, what's up?"

"A white sedan has been following me the last couple of blocks. The driver has a dark beard. I believe Lester mentioned this in his meeting with you the other day."

"Are they still following you?"

After looking in the rearview mirror, the white sedan made a right turn onto Locust Street. Breathing a sigh of relief, he replied, "Not any longer. The car just turned onto Locust Street."

"Okay, I will alert any units in the area to be on the lookout for it. Relax, and have a good day, okay?"

"Yeah, thanks."

Barry ended the call, and NPR resumed talking about the current state of the economy. Continuing to his office downtown, he pulled into his dedicated parking spot behind his office building. Exiting his vehicle, he turned around, surveying the area. Relieved that everything looked normal, he entered the building, greeting employees on the way to his office.

Once inside his office, he took care of the usual morning housecleaning items. The first order was a cup of strong coffee from the firm's small breakroom, where a full pot was always ready. Before he left his office, he opened his laptop and entered his password. Reaching the breakroom, he poured the steaming hot coffee into his UK mug. Smelling its robust aroma, he took a small sip. Returning to his office, he was ready for the day.

Sitting in his comfortable leather chair, he reviewed his schedule for the day. The most critical item on his agenda was this afternoon's meeting with the new industrial firm. Otherwise, his day was mostly open. Quickly reviewing his email, nothing of importance caught his eye.

When he left his office earlier, his voicemail light

was dark. Grabbing his coffee, he took several sips before putting it back down. Out of the corner of his eye, the voicemail light flashed. Placing the phone on the speaker, he pushed the voicemail button.

Immediately, the mayor's distinctive voice filled the room. Lowering the volume, the mayor had left him a message he wanted to meet with him, Philip, and Rich as soon as possible. Since it was not about the city commission, they would meet at the mayor's home. Ending the message, he immediately hit the mayor's speed dial button and put it on the speaker.

"Barry, how's your day going?"

"Great, what's this meeting all about?"

"I'd rather not discuss it on the phone. Can you meet with us tomorrow evening at my house, say seven o'clock?"

"Yeah, I suppose so.

"Great, see you then."

Before Barry could respond, the call ended, leaving the annoying dial tone filling the room. As Barry silenced the phone, he sat contemplating why Lester wanted to meet, and by the tone of his voice, something serious was worrying him. Knowing it did not involve city business, his mind began wondering.

The one thing that kept arising was the two men in the white sedan. They were present at McGruder's just before Commissioner Walters died, and now, he, along with Lester, Philip, and Rich, had an unwanted encounter with them. The entire city commission belonged to the Diamond Brotherhood thirty-five years ago; thus, whatever it had to do with, it had to be something regarding their past.

Later that afternoon, Barry received a call from Chief

Evans regarding the white sedan that followed him for a short while this morning. A police cruiser in the area spotted a white sedan parked on Locust Street. The patrolman ran the license plate, false alarm. It belonged to James Goodwin, a squeaky-clean citizen.

# CHAPTER 38

Arriving at the police station, Beth was determined to get to the bottom of Bortel's death and his relationship with Clarissa. In her mind, something wasn't right with his death. It was eerie similar to Clarissa's husband's unfortunate death. Many things hadn't made sense from the beginning. In her eyes, whoever killed Bortel wanted to make it look like Walters killed him in a fit of anger, or perhaps he did murder Bortel before someone killed him. At this point, both possibilities were on the table until otherwise proved differently.

Carla and Bernie had arrived earlier and were meeting with Chief Evans about Walters' death. Beth knew the only person of interest was Angela Clark. However, Beth's concern was investigating Bortel's death. After getting settled at her workstation, her illuminated voicemail button grabbed her attention. Picking up the receiver, she pushed the button, and Jason Everett's voice from American Life and Annuity sent a smile across her face. Taking a few minutes to gather her notes, she moved to the conference room for privacy. After placing the phone on speaker, she dialed the number and waited. Within seconds, his voice lit up her face.

"Mr. Everett, this is Beth Pendergast. Thank you for calling me back."

"Of course, your message said you have a few questions regarding our death benefit paid to Clarissa Morgan, wife of Thaddeus Morgan. What kind of questions?"

"We're investigating the suspicious death of Wilson Bortel. He and Clarissa had a history when they both lived in Columbus, and he worked for her husband. Anyway, in my research of Mr. Morgan's death, the story mentioned that his death was suspicious, and American Life and Annuity investigated the accident. Can you tell me why? What was suspicious?"

"With any large policy like this one, we investigate and inspect the accident site. Our initial inspection and investigation revealed some issues with their second-floor railing. Let's just say it appeared loose, perhaps intentionally. When Mr. Morgan crashed into it, the force of his weight broke it from the wall."

"So, the entire railing landed on the floor below with him, right?"

"No, it just gave way enough for him to tumble over or around it. Then the carpet he tripped on looked brand new, and the wood underneath was the same shade as the rest of the flooring in the balcony. Usually, wood flooring covered by a rug will not fade over time. That was a red flag to us."

"I see, so why pay out the settlement?"

"Well, the evidence just wasn't definitive, and she had the best lawyer money could buy. The coroner ruled it an unfortunate accident. When local law enforcement chose not to pursue any charges, we had no choice but to pay her the full value of the policy."

"I sense you think something else might have happened, am I right?"

"Uh, the toxicology reports indicated an extremely high level of a sedative. I don't recall the name, but that spelled disaster along with an extremely high alcohol level. Mr. Morgan was a smart and successful man. He wouldn't combine a strong sedative with excessive drinking. It just didn't make sense."

"I see. Would it be possible to get a copy of the toxicology report and any other information regarding your investigation, fingerprints, DNA sample, that kind of thing?"

"I guess. Why?"

"Well, in our death investigation here, we have a similar situation. It might benefit us both to compare them. I'm sure if you could prove it wasn't an accident, you would try and recover the money, or what is left of it, right?"

"Well, of course. Give me your email address, and I'll send everything we have."

After giving him her email address, Beth ended the call. She returned to her workstation, where Carla and Bernie were involved in a meaningless but entertaining bantering. It was part of their love-hate relationship, which made them the formidable team they had become.

Catching Beth's beaming smile, Carla asked, "Uh, you look like you have good news, do you?"

"I think so. I'll know more after getting the toxicology reports and other information from the Thaddeus Morgan death investigation. It seems he had a powerful sedative in his blood, along with an extremely high alcohol reading, sound familiar?"

"Yeah, so you think Clarissa caused Bortel's death?"

"Right, Carla, and maybe even her husband's death. I've got some more digging to do before I can be certain. What about you two?"

"Okay, unless something else happens, and I hope it doesn't, Carla and I have Angela as our only person of interest. We don't have enough to arrest her, but we're going to bring her back in for more questioning, probably this evening. She knows more, I'm sure of it."

"Well, good luck. I've got to see Sherry about getting Bortel's bank records, and if she has the DNA results from the clipboard, pen, and business card. That could help us at least solve Bortel's death."

At that moment, Beth's phone rang. Answering it, she kept nodding her head, then ended the call. Smiling at them, she gave them a thumbs-up gesture. With eyes glued on her, Bernie said, "You going to keep us in suspense?"

"Sherry will meet with us in the conference room in about fifteen minutes. She has a surprise for us. Maybe we'll get a real break, now."

"Yeah, we could use one, right, Carla?"

Nodding at Bernie, Carla called Angela and arranged up a meeting for around seven that evening. The big clock on the wall indicated it was time to meet with Sherry. Seeing her enter the conference room, each gathered up their file folders and joined her. As usual, Sherry was in her "queen bee" seat at the head of the table. After all, she loved being in charge, especially when it involved Carla.

"Okay, guys, here's what we've got. From what Beth

gave me, DNA from clipboard number one matches the DNA found in the upstairs bedroom. It belongs to Barbara Tierney."

"Carla, I told you she looked like she was hot-to-trot." Bernie's eyes felt the wrath of Carla's scowl. "So, Sherry, what else did we learn about Mrs. Tierney?"

"That's it, she had sex with Walters sometime before he died, maybe even before he met Angela."

Sherry enjoyed seeing Carla and Bernie's wide-open eyes wandering around the room, knowing their thoughts were in motion.

"Now, for the DNA off clipboard number two, which was Clarissa Morgan. Well, we did find semen on a throw rug on the upstairs landing. That belonged to Bortel. We also found several hairs. Hmm, drumroll, please."

"Shit, Sherry, just get to it, right, Bernie?" While nodding, Bernie's scowl met Sherry's wandering eyes.

"Okay, sourpusses, you're no fun. Anyway, they belong to Clarissa Morgan."

All around the table, awe-and-shock expressions glared back at her. Sherry loved every minute of it. Her smile expressed her superiority, which Carla hated.

In her most sarcastic tone, Sherry continued, "See, Beth, I told you I had a surprise, didn't expect that, did you?"

"No, I didn't. So, it appears Clarissa and Bortel had sex on that balcony rug. That's what you are indicating, right?"

"Yeah, it's the only plausible explanation."

"Hmm, Clarissa, I'm about to get you. Sherry, I need you to dig into Bortel's financial footprint, everything, okay?"

"On it, Beth."

With the meeting over, Sherry left to secure Bortel's financial life. Carla and Bernie returned to their workstation with even more questions than answers. Beth left with a hunch, and if it panned out, it could return up to five million dollars to American Life and Annuity.

# CHAPTER 39

**A**ngela and Preston arrived right on time. Meeting them at the receptionist's desk, Carla led them to the conference room where Bernie and Chief Evans were waiting. As usual, Chief Evans manned the head of the table. With Bernie already sitting to the chief's left, Angela and Preston took their seats to the chief's right, while Carla sat beside Bernie.

The inquisition of Angela was solely Carla's responsibility. While observing, Bernie would take notes. Chief Evans attended because of his relationship with Mayor James and the city commissioners. But specifically, the mayor because he sometimes was difficult to deal with because of the recent violent crime spree.

Not sure how long this interview would last, Carla had already made sure water, coffee, or sodas were plentiful should they need a break. Carla and Bernie needed more information to break this case wide open, or more lives may be in jeopardy. At least they assumed the mayor and the remaining city commissioners were in danger.

"Okay, Angela, let's begin." Placing her smartphone on the table, she pushed the record button. "As you can see, I'm recording this interview. You know, at any time you can leave. You are here of your own volition. You do know that, right?"

"Yes, of course, I have nothing to hide."

"Great. Now for the record, please state your name."

"Angela Clark."

"Have you ever seen or know of Clarissa Morgan pictured on my phone?"

Showing her the picture, she studied it closely and handed it back to Carla.

"I've only seen this lady once, and I didn't know her name. She was at Bortel's victory party. Why is this important? Does she have something to do with Bryan's death?"

"We're not sure." Pulling up Barbara Tierney's picture, she continued. "Do you know, or have you ever seen this lady before?"

Again, studying the picture, she replied. "I don't know the name, and I have never seen that lady before. Does she have anything to do with Bryan's death?" After pausing, curious looks bounced around the table. "Well, does she?"

"We're not sure."

"Are you sure of anything, Detective McBride?"

As anger exploded in Carla's eyes, Angela's disposition felt the wrath of her Irish heritage. "Yeah, we do know one thing for sure, Barbara Tierney was in his upstairs bedroom at some point. Not sure when, but before your sexual interlude with Bryan."

Showing no reaction to that, Angela replied, "We weren't lovers or a couple. He could screw anyone, and it wouldn't bother me. What do either of those questions have to do with me or Bryan's death?" Silence pounded the room. "That's it. Umm, you all don't have a clue, do you?"

"We're not showing all of our cards."

"Umm, so, this is a game. Okay, I can play games. Detective McBride, is that what you want? You know, I took some acting classes in college, even starred in a few plays, so I'm pretty good at playing games, you know, fooling and deceiving people."

"No games, Angela. Anyway, I assume you know your uncle, George Ballard, died a couple of months ago."

"Yeah, what's that got to do with me?"

"We're not sure. How did you know about George's passing?"

"Karen called me, but I was unable to attend the funeral. I plan to visit her soon."

"Well, you better hurry. When we visited her, a for-sale sign was in the yard."

"She never mentioned it. Probably too embarrassed. She's a proud woman. Did she say why?"

Pausing for a moment, Carla grabbed her water, taking a thirst-quenching swig. As her eyes bored into Angela's soul, she showed signs of anxiety.

"Yeah, I'm glad you asked that question. Karen told us George had received a monthly check ever since they moved from Oakmont thirty-five years ago. They moved because Joni became pregnant. Do you have any idea who was sending this money or why? I can only assume it was hush money."

As anxiety seized Angela, she glanced around the room, wondering how to answer or whether to answer at all. Whispering something in Geronimo's ear, she found Carla's intenseness glaring down on her.

"May we take a five-minute break, then I'll tell you what I know, okay?"

Nodding and stopping the recording, everyone left. Five minutes later, everyone reconvened in the conference room. Pushing the record button on her smartphone, Carla resumed the interview.

"Angela, tell us what you know about this hush money."

While letting out a big sigh, a few tears surfaced from the corner of her eye. She wiped them away. Taking a deep breath, she sighed and met eye contact with Carla.

"I guess after my father died in an auto accident, my mom began to open up about her past. It wasn't long after my dad died she was diagnosed with stage-four pancreatic cancer. She didn't have long to live, and I guess, umm, she wanted to cleanse her soul of past sins and guilt. That was over two years ago. After she passed, I had no reason to stay in California and moved back here. Not sure why. It just felt right."

Pausing, Angela took several deep breaths before wiping away the tears streaming down her cheeks. Taking a drink of water, she put the bottle down and continued.

"While I was growing up in Oakmont, my mom took a job in Alex Walters' campaign headquarters. That's Bryan's dad. At that time, Alex, a state senator, was running for re-election. My mom was always enamored with politics, and when he came calling, she grabbed it with all her might. My mom spent a lot of time with him. Working late nights were the norm. My dad didn't mind.

He didn't make much money. Although he was a proud man, what she made, uh, made it easier on him."

Pausing, she took another drink of water. Wiping a few more tears away, she met Carla's probing gaze.

"Angela, I know this is not easy, so if you need another break, please let me know, okay?"

"Thank you, but I'm fine. It wasn't soon after my mom turned up pregnant, she abruptly quit. She said she didn't want to work while carrying her son, Lenny."

"Are you sure you don't want to take a break?"

Nodding, Angela finished her bottle of water, then opened another one. Taking a drink, she put it down.

"After graduating from high school, we moved to California. Anyway, life went on. We were one happy family, or so I thought. After Joni passed, my mom traveled back home for the funeral. I had to stay home and take care of Lenny."

Carla wanted to keep this flowing because she believed she was going to find out crucial information. However, this was very painful for Angela, and Carla called for another five-minute break.

# CHAPTER 40

While Chief Evans accompanied Angela and Geronimo outside, Carla and Bernie checked their voicemail. After hitting the restroom, they returned to the conference room, waiting for the three of them to return. Although they were a few minutes late, Carla didn't mind. Angela was opening up and hopefully helping them get closer to solving Bryan's death. With everyone back, Carla continued her probing inquisition.

"So, Angela, you were telling us what you and your mom talked about before she passed. Let's begin there, okay?"

After glancing around the room, her eyes ended up fixated on Carla. Taking a deep sigh, she nodded.

"Of course. She told me when she went to Joni's funeral, she and George went out to one of their old watering holes. Well, my mom said she had too much to drink and spilled her guts, her deepest and dark secrets, to him."

Pausing for a moment, Angela grabbed a drink of

water. With her eyes glistening again, Geronimo handed her a tissue. After drying her eyes, she sighed once more.

"One night, when she was alone with Alex at his campaign headquarters, he opened a bottle of wine to relax after a long day. Anyway, after two glasses of wine, my mom began to get woozy. She normally could handle that many drinks without any problems. However, that night something was different, like, uh, maybe, he slipped her a pill. Anyway, umm, he forced himself on her. He was a strong man. My mom was a small person and couldn't fight him off. She told him to stop, but he wouldn't listen."

As tears streamed from her eyes, she patted them away and sighed. After taking a long drink of water, all eyes focused on her as she continued.

"My mom just laid there, letting him take advantage of her. She just wanted it to end. That son-of-a-bitch raped her several times that night. Uh, once she got home, even a hot shower couldn't wash away the dirtiness she felt inside her soul. She even blamed herself for it happening. So, yeah, at that moment, if Alex would've been alive, I would've hunted him down like a hungry lion. Umm, sorry for losing my composure. Uh, I guess I shouldn't have said that."

Silence captivated the room at such a revelation. Angela's heartstrings exploded. Geronimo squeezed her hand, offering words of encouragement.

"Angela, I'm so sorry, are you okay? Why didn't she go to the police?" No response, as Angela's emotions were in control of her soul. "I know this is not easy. We can take another break if you want?"

"No, I need to get, uh, all of this off my chest." Nodding, Carla reached over to show compassion. "Alex was powerful, running for re-election for the state senate. She was a nobody. She didn't want to go through the humiliation in public. I'm sure you understand."

Carla nodded and offered comforting words. Angela sighed and took another drink of water.

"When she ended up pregnant, she knew my dad was not the father of that baby. She did the math and realized my father was working out of town."

"So, Alex is Lenny's biological father, right?" Nodding, Carla continued, "Then that means Lenny is Bryan's half-brother. Could Bryan have known that?" Shrugging her shoulders, Angela deflected Carla's determined demeanor. "Did your dad know?"

"My mom thought he suspected it. Lenny didn't look like either of them, however, my dad accepted that it was his boy. Every man wants a son, and Lenny became his son and he loved him unconditionally. Furthermore, my dad knew my mom would never cheat on him."

"Does Lenny know he is Alex Walters' son?"

"As far as I know, he doesn't unless someone other than my mom told him. She wanted to take it to her grave."

"Okay, did Alex know about Lenny?"

"As far as Alex knowing that, umm, my mom never divulged that to me."

"Okay, Karen said that Chase brought a friend with him to see George before he died. Karen told us his name was Parker Jarrell. Remember the picture I showed you of what Lenny would look like today? You seemed certain it was Lenny. What if George told Chase, then Chase told Parker, or I guess Lenny?"

"Maybe, but Lenny will still be my brother regardless of this. What other questions do you have?"

"Did you kill Bryan out of revenge since you couldn't go after his dad?"

"No, I didn't. That's ludicrous. What good would that do? I know you think I killed him based on all the evidence you have collected and what I said earlier. I know it looks bad, but I'm not your killer. I tried to warn him, remember?"

"Yeah, I remember."

"Detectives, Chief Evans, we are done, Angela came of her own volition, spilled her guts, and now you're accusing her of murder, let's leave Angela. We'll show ourselves out."

Geronimo stood up, pulled Angela's chair away from the table. She stood, staring at Carla, in an attempt to rattle her, but to no avail. Wiping her tears away, they left the conference room.

Carla zeroed in on her boss, "What's your gut feeling chief, is she guilty of murder?"

"Guys, I'm just not sure. She seemed sincere, but I've seen that before from others. And she's had some acting experience, and she is a psychologist. I could see in a fit of rage that she could've done it. Her DNA, fingerprints, and perfume tie her to him and the crime scene. She was the last person we know of that saw him alive. Now, we have a possible motive, pent-up revenge knowing her brother is only a half-brother born out of rape. I'll talk to the district attorney and get back to you. I don't think any of us expected these new revelations."

"Right, we didn't. However, what we learned might tell us why George received a monthly check from Capital City Accounting. Blackmail. Alex Walters is running for state senate. If it got out that he raped Angela's mom and fathered a child, it would have destroyed his life, political aspirations, his marriage, and family. He would've lost his chance at being governor. Maybe that's why it went on for years since Alex was a two-term governor. The question is, why did the blackmail payments suddenly stop? Was it tied to Bryan's death or something else we don't know yet? Many questions still need to be answered."

"Carla, if you are right, proving it will be difficult with both of them dead."

"Yeah, Bernie, unless we get a confession from Angela, we may never know the answers to all of our questions."

# CHAPTER 41

As Chief Evans left the conference room, Carla mulled over Bernie's notes in dead silence. They now had more questions than answers. There was no doubt in their minds Angela was bitter and held revengeful thoughts in her subconscious world. Although circumstantial evidence might be enough to get an arrest warrant for her, the motive was unclear and on shaky ground.

They struggled with that and couldn't dismiss Barbara Tierney's connection to Bryan or as a person of interest in his death. From their conversation, she led them to believe there was nothing between them. DNA results said otherwise, meaning another visit with her was necessary. Knowing anything was possible in this crazy world, maybe Bobbi could be responsible for his death. The burning question they had to answer was why.

As late as it was, they couldn't pull themselves away from this bizarre and twisted case. Typically, Carla or Bernie would make an appointment instead of just showing up to talk to a person of interest, but tonight was different. Twenty minutes later, they stopped at the security gate of Camelot Estates. With the code memorized, Bernie keyed it in, and the gate opened, allowing them access. Traveling down Mahogany Way, the street appeared very peaceful under the amber backdrop created by the antique-style lighting. Reaching Bobbi's house, they pulled into her driveway. Cutting the engine, they immediately exited the car.

Before walking up on her porch, they turned around, looking at the crime scene across the street. The unsightly yellow tape irked Bernie. Surprised that it was still there for no reason at all, he quickly walked across the street and removed it. Returning with the wadded-up ball of yellow tape, he opened the rear driver-side door tossing it in. He joined Carla at the bottom of the steps leading up to the dimly lit but inviting porch.

Finally, standing on the porch, Bernie pushed the doorbell. Chimes emanated from the foyer. Thirty seconds later, Bobbi appeared. Dressed in a pale-yellow lounging ensemble, she opened the storm door, greeting them. No need to flash badges. She knew them but wondered what prompted them to visit her this late.

Bernie, who never thought she was sinister enough to be involved in anything illegal, had a different perception after the DNA results confirmed she had been in the upstairs bedroom. After flipping a coin, Bernie won the rights to grill Bobbi.

"Mrs. Tierney, we apologize for not calling you, but we have an urgent matter to clear up in the death investigation of Bryan Walters. May we come in?"

"Of course, detectives, please come in."

Entering her house, she motioned them to sit on the sofa. Carla immediately noticed a bottle of Caymus

Zinfandel. On a table beside her favorite chair, a half-filled glass of wine and a James Patterson novel described her loneliness. Gas logs created a comforting atmosphere of warmth and peacefulness. After sitting on the sofa, Bernie's gaze met Bobbi's questionable eyes.

"Detectives, so how may I help you? Hmm, you said you had something you wanted to ask me about Bryan's death?"

As Bernie's curious eyes bored through her soul, she tasted the sexiness of the Caymus Zinfandel. While rolling her eyes, a flirtatious gesture met the seriousness painting Bernie's face.

"Well, Detective Kowalski, let's get to it."

"Okay, it's late, and I'm tired. It's been a long day. Anyway, uh, after collecting every shred of evidence from Bryan's house, forensics found your DNA on the bedsheets in the upstairs bedroom."

Bobbi repositioned herself in the chair, trying to deflect Carla's glaring expression. "Well, uh, how do you know it was mine? I never submitted a DNA sample that I'm aware of?"

"That's not important. Furthermore, forensics found your fingerprints on a wineglass in the upstairs bedroom. How do you explain that? You made no mention of a relationship with him the first time we spoke."

"Umm, how did you get my fingerprints? I don't recall submitting to that either?"

"Doesn't matter. Would you like to explain how your DNA and fingerprints ended up in that bedroom? You know, Bobbi, we can do it here or at the station. If you wish to have a lawyer present, just say so, and we'll see you both at the station. What will it be?"

After a taste of wine, her eyes wandered around the

room. With the gas logs blazing, the atmosphere in the room grew warmer and uncomfortable. Quickly picking up the remote, the dancing flames in the fireplace vanished. As she hit the remote for the elegant ceiling fan, the air began to ease the anxiety invading her soul. Returning her gaze to them, she sighed.

"Okay, Bryan and I began a relationship several months ago. One day, a package for him was delivered to my house by mistake. After taking it over, he invited me in and offered me a glass of wine. He looked lonely and just needed a friend other than the bourbon in his hand. One drink led to another, then several more. We were, umm, just having a good time unwinding."

"Okay, hmm, go on."

Finally, Bobbi showed signs of cracking; tears surfaced on her rosy cheeks. Wiping them away, she sighed.

"Uh, I purposely wore a revealing blouse, and umm, I caught his eyes devouring me from head to toe. I smiled. I think he was a little embarrassed, you know, like a teenager."

She sighed heavily and finished the remainder of her wine. After replenishing her glass, she took another long sip. Setting the glass down, she took a deep, cleansing breath.

"You know, umm, it just happened. I wanted him, and I sensed he wanted me. I put my wine down and took his bourbon from him. After setting it on the table, I leaned in to kiss him. At first, he backed away. Uh, the next thing I knew, his lips met mine. As we searched for more passion, my breasts responded to his tender touch." Pausing, she tasted the spiciness of the Caymus Zinfandel and returned it to the table. "I stood up and took his hand, leading him to what I assumed was the master bedroom. But he stopped me and motioned me upstairs. Guess he wasn't ready to kick his wife's memory out of the master bedroom."

"Okay, we get it. What happened after that?"

"Uh, we enjoyed each other's company almost every night. At first, you know, it was just a physical relationship. However, the longer it went on, I thought we were falling for each other until election night."

"Why is that?"

"Hmm, I knew he lost the election, and I was watching for him to come home. I knew I could erase his disappointment. Finally, I saw a Beamer pull into the driveway. The lady who got out blew me away. I thought his wife had returned from the dead."

"Umm, Angela."

"Who's Angela?"

"Doesn't matter, go on."

"I called him that night, said I had a package for him. He blew me off. Well, the next day before I left for work, I confronted him. He told me to screw myself. That was the last time I spoke to him and saw him. I was so mad at him, you know, I could've kicked..."

"Could've what?"

"Oh, never mind. Do you have any further questions?"

"Yeah, did he ever take you to his houseboat on Lake Jackson?"

"Sort of, he showed me where it was when we took a Sunday drive, but he never took me on board. Anything else?"

"Nah, thank you, you've been a big help. We'll show ourselves out."

After they left, Bobbi sat in front of the gas logs finishing her wine. She pondered what could have been between her and Bryan. On their ride back to the station, Carla and Bernie wondered if this scorned lover might have taken matters into her hands.

# CHAPTER 42

Examining Bortel's financial footprint revealed a man deep in debt and no plausible way out. As Beth, Carla, and Bernie listened to Sherry explain Bortel's financial history, Beth could only think of Clarissa Morgan. As she suspected, plenty of evidence suggested that they possibly had been having an affair for a long time. Credit card statements showed he stayed at a Cincinnati hotel almost every weekend over the past twenty years. Also, receipts from various restaurants in the Cincinnati area filled his credit card statements.

One unexplainable thing was his checking account showed miscellaneous monthly transfers from within Freedom National Bank. Only a bunch of numbers and letters described the manual transfers, which started about four years ago.

"Okay, folks, there you have it. Bortel was almost broke and close to bankruptcy. Any other questions?"

"Not from me. I'm going to make some calls to the hotel and see what I can find out. With Bortel staying there about every weekend for like twenty years, someone will know him and maybe someone else, like Clarissa. Thanks, Sherry."

"You're welcome. Beth. How about you two?"

"Yeah, Sherry. We were wondering about the evidence collected at Walters' houseboat."

"Uh, what about it, Bernie?"

"Is it possible something got missed, you know, got overlooked?"

"Like what?"

"I don't know?"

"Well, Bernie, if you don't know, I can't help you."

"Are you sure you only found one female DNA there?"

"Yeah, Bernie, I am. Do you think otherwise?"

"Umm, just a hunch. We interviewed Barbara Tierney last night, and she knew where the houseboat was. Maybe she went there and saw them. He dissed her for Angela. Based on what I saw last night, she could be revengeful. Umm, what's that saying?"

"Hell hath no fury like a woman scorned."

"Right, Carla. Anyway, do you mind rechecking it?"

"Bernie, of course not, just for you, okay?"

"Thank you."

Nodding, Sherry glared at Carla. "What about you, McBride?"

"Nah, I think you covered everything. We are going to the houseboat. See what we can find."

Sherry's infamous "screw-you-bird" smacked Carla's warming face. She left, leaving them to mull over her findings.

"Carla, I didn't know we were going to that houseboat again."

"Me neither, but when forensics missed something as

they did in the Black Rose case, maybe they missed something at the houseboat."

"Umm, I don't know. It's been over ten days since they pulled the body out of the water."

"We're going, or at least I am. What about you, dickhead?"

About twenty minutes later, they turned down the gravel road to the houseboat. Cutting the engine, they exited Bernie's car and began walking around the parking area, looking for anything. Moving down the gravel walkway to the boat, they carefully examined the wooden railing. Halfway down the path, the gravel appeared as though someone had slipped there and grabbed ahold of the railing. It seemed to have a small, jagged piece missing as though someone had used the railing to keep their balance. While examining the ground below, nestled in the grass, was a small piece of wood.

After putting on plastic gloves, Carla picked up the sliver of wood and placed it in a plastic evidence bag. While continuing down the path, nothing caught their eyes. As they crossed the gangplank to the boat, eyes searched the water in every direction; nothing caught their fancy. Walking around the port side of the boat, nothing strange caught their eye. After entering the living quarters, everything looked the same.

Moving onto the starboard side, where they found Commissioner Walters's body, they noticed something dried on the outside walls. Examining it closely, they couldn't determine what it was. Taking a DNA swab out, Carla rubbed it as hard as she could, hoping whatever it was would leave enough particles on the swab to determine whether it was human or animal or something else.

Placing the swab in a plastic evidence bag, she tucked it inside her pocket.

After peering over the side of the boat, a syringe floating next to the hull seized their attention. Bernie walked back to his car, getting the large Styrofoam cup Karen gave them the other day. Returning to the houseboat, he scooped the syringe out of the water. Placing it in a plastic bag, he put it in the Styrofoam cup to avoid sticking himself.

A half-hour later, they were in forensics, logging in these items. They knew the items could yield nothing or might be the thing needed to identify Commissioner Walters' killer. Based on the interviews of Angela and Bobbi, both had plausible motives. The question is which one, or it could be the two men in the white sedan. When Carla and Bernie returned to the common area, a beaming smile emanated from Beth's beautiful complexion. Seeing them approach her, that beaming smile could cheer anyone up.

"Beth, what's that shit-eating grin about?"

"Oh, nothing, Carla. Have you guys had lunch?"

"No, we were just about to head to McGruder's."

"Sounds great. Let's go, and when we get there, I'll share my news."

"What news?"

"Sorry, let's go, I'm hungry, and Bernie's buying today."

With the lunch crowd nearly gone, McGruder's provided the right atmosphere to discuss each other's new developments. Like most times, their favorite booth was open, and they quickly grabbed it. Within a minute, Sam greeted them. After taking the usual lunch orders, she left and placed them. As muted chatter filled the pub,

Sam returned with their iced teas with lemon. After each had quenched their thirst, Bernie broke their mundane bantering.

"Beth, you go first."

"Yeah, I was right. I called the hotel Bortel stayed at, and immediately, the day manager recognized the name. Said the hotel seemed like a second home to Bortel. I asked if he ever saw him with a lady friend. He indicated he had, so I sent him a picture of Clarissa Morgan. He immediately responded, identifying her as Bradley Compton. Anyway, I did a little recon on Clarissa. Her maiden name is Bradley. Bingo, as you would say. Now, I just need to tie everything together. I'm visiting with John Vickers this afternoon at the bank to see if I can find out more about those transfers. How about you guys, any good news or developments?"

"Well, sort of, Carla and I visited Commissioner Walters' houseboat and brought back some new evidence, we hope. Now we just wait to see if it is helpful or whether it was just a waste of time."

Their conversation was interrupted by the smell of Reubens, fries, and fish and chips. Sam refilled their glasses and left them to enjoy a well-deserved lunch.

# CHAPTER 43

While standing in his office, Mayor James viewed Main Street, watching people moving about. Two men leaving Parsons' Coffee Emporium caught his eye. As he watched them, he could only wonder what their motives were. He asked himself why they were intentionally stalking him, Barry, Philip, and Rich. Watching them continue toward Third Street, they turned right, heading toward Water Street. He called Chief Evans, and the conversation was short and sweet.

Mayor James wasn't one to consume alcohol on city property, however, seeing those two men in his city, he poured himself a shot of Wild Turkey Bourbon. Neat, or straight up, was how he liked to savor its amber elegance. While tasting its nuances, he watched a white sedan travel north on Main Street. Although he couldn't make out the license plate, he knew it wasn't a Kentucky plate. Watching it disappear out of his sight, he glanced down at the street, seeing someone else from his past. Angela and Geronimo were entering Parsons' Coffee Emporium.

Seeing her took him back to his high school years. Although he and Angela were not good friends in high school, he could only wonder why she decided to return to Oakmont after thirty-five years. Sitting in a chair by the windows, he enjoyed Wild Turkey, savoring its nuances before experiencing its smoothness as it went down.

He began reminiscing about growing up when life was simple and carefree. In high school, he was a good baseball player and outfielder that hit with power. Of course, back then, he aspired to give the big leagues a try. However, he just wasn't good enough. As he sipped on Wild Turkey, more of his past flashed in his subconscious.

His father, Eugene, was a member of the Diamond Brotherhood in his high school years. He had been a three-term mayor of Oakmont before being elected to the state legislature. Mayor James thought how ironic it was that Bryan, Rich, Barry, and Philip's fathers were also members of the Diamond Brotherhood at the same time as his father, Eugene.

Staring at his empty glass, he rose and absorbed the appealing streetscape. The city's vintage streetlights cast their amber glow on the historical buildings, making Oakmont the charming town it was. Walking over to the credenza, he blessed his glass with another shot of Wild Turkey. After returning to his chair, the darkness consumed Main Street. Even though Oakmont was thriving, it had a black cloud hanging over it because of the recent violent murders. And now, he and the remaining city commissioners were presumably being stalked for something from their past.

Swallowing the remainder of the bourbon, a knock on

the door startled him, causing him to choke on the bourbon. Coughing restored his labored respiration as his face grew warm. Walking to the door, he opened it. Facing him, his lovely wife, Lynn, leaned in, laying a friendly kiss on his cheek. She was his college sweetheart, and they married in their senior year.

"Honey, are you okay?"

"Yeah, uh, why do you ask?"

"You going to let me in?"

After the door swung open, she sat in one of the chairs at the window. He walked to the credenza and poured her a shot of bourbon. Opening the dorm-size fridge, he put a few ice cubes in it. Joining her by the window, after a light-hearted toast, silence surrounded them.

"I asked if you were okay, your face is flushed, and you are sweating."

"Oh, bourbon went down the wrong way. What are you doing here?"

"Geez, what a question to ask your wife. Don't you remember our dinner date with Barry and Adele tonight at the country club?"

"Oh yeah, guess I forgot. What time is our reservation?"

"Uh, now. Remember, you reserved the Sunroom."

"Right, then, we better go."

A ten-minute drive away, Avondale Country Club was the place for the movers and shakers in town. Arriving right on time, Lester could see that Barry and Adele were already seated. A bottle of wine and four glasses graced the table. After being seated by Carrie, the Stewarts were already enjoying the Caymus Cabernet Sauvignon Reserve.

"Mayor James, may I pour you and Lynn a glass of this elegant wine?"

"Absolutely. Carrie, how are you tonight?"

"Great, I'll leave you all alone to enjoy the wine while catching up with each other, then I'll be back to take your orders."

Everyone nodded, and she left. As they glanced at each other, silence grabbed their souls. Within minutes, muted chatter filled the Sunroom as the last ounces of the wine replenished their glasses. Carrie returned, taking their orders. After placing them, she returned with salads and another bottle of cabernet.

As they enjoyed each other's company in the Sunroom, time flew by. Since all of them were native to Oakmont, reminiscing about old times was fun. Laughing and even a few tears reminded them of simpler times. Their entrées arrived, and more wine was flowing. Life was good for all of them, or at least tonight it was.

Lynn and Adele were cheerleaders back in the day. They each worked hard to keep their cheerleading bodies in mint condition. Lynn and Adele were having a separate conversation about running into Angela Clark at Parsons' Coffee Emporium. Lester, who had been eavesdropping, heard Angela's name mentioned.

Lynn broke the men's silence. "Guys, do you remember Angela Clark?" Lester decided to use his selective hearing skill, ignoring Lynn's question. Barry, on the other hand, didn't want to be rude and nodded. "Well, Adele and I ran into her earlier today at the coffee shop. You know, at first, we didn't recognize her. She's changed from her high school days, and she looks a lot like Cynthia Walters."

Lester replied, "Really, like how?"

Adele responded, "Well, let's just say, uh, we're glad we snagged you a long time ago. She's, well, hot, never would've imagined that. Anyway, she sent her regards."

Barry and Lester nodded and remained silent as their wives continued their monotonous chatter. Barry and Lester showed signs of anxiety as they both took a long drink of water. Dinner and wine finished, a night of friendliness gave Barry and Lester a break from the demons trying to steal their souls. As they all walked out of the country club, the coolness of the night felt good on Barry and Lester's flushed faces. Saying their goodbyes, Barry and Adele walked to their car. Lester and Lynn remained on the side porch as they drove away.

While walking arm-in-arm to the car, Lynn's left breast teased his hormones. Opening the door for her, she settled in the passenger seat. As Lester walked around the car, he scanned the parking lot, then sighed. Opening the door, Lynn's tantalizing legs and curves grabbed his lustful soul. After settling behind the wheel, he placed his right hand on her thigh. Lynn smiled and leaned toward him. As their lips met, she tasted his alcohol-induced lust for her. Wanting to get home and finish this prelude of things to come, he backed off and immediately hit the start button. Driving out to the country club's main entrance, he turned right and headed for a night of passion and heat.

Although his hormones were burning inside his soul, he kept glancing at the rearview mirror. As the darkness of the night met his gaze, he sighed once more. After passing Westover Drive, a car pulled out onto Main Street. The reflection in the rearview mirror inched up closer to him. Reaching the next traffic light, it was red.

The car behind him pulled to a stop imposing itself on his psyche.

The street lighting illuminated the car casting its light on the two men inside. He had seen them before. Turning right onto Avery Boulevard, the white sedan also turned, following a safe distance behind him. Silence in the car was eerie as he kept glancing in the rearview mirror. While merging into the turning lane, the white sedan sped past them. Sitting there for a moment, trying to remain calm and not alarming Lynn, he finally turned left into Oakmont Commons, breathing a big sigh of relief. He quickly pulled into the garage and lowered the door. After entering the house, anxiety and paranoia replaced his lustful hormones. As Lynn went to fix the nightcaps, he entered the master bedroom. Moments later, she entered with two glasses of wine, ready to quench her raging hormones. Disgusted by Lester's alcohol-induced snoring, she left to cool her disappointment.

# CHAPTER 44

**B**eth was determined to nail Clarissa to the wall. In her mind, she was somehow responsible for Bortel's death. All the evidence pointed to a showdown with her. After meeting with John Vickers of Freedom National Bank, she found out Bortel was embezzling from Clarissa's account over the past four years.

After researching Clarissa's social world, two ladies who worked with her on several charity events stood out. Using the department's resources, she tracked them down. Conversations with them revealed a whole new side to Clarissa. She was a vindictive person, and she and Thaddeus were having big marital problems. Although he never served her with divorce papers, he was on the verge of following through with that threat when he died.

Beth also found out that she had been active in Habitat for Humanity in the Columbus area. She was handy with tools and knew her way around the construction of houses. Meeting with Chief Evans, Carla, and

Bernie, she presented all the evidence collected along with these new revelations regarding a possible divorce. After a lengthy discussion, Beth wanted to bring Clarissa in for further questioning.

Beth informed her new evidence surfaced in Bortel's death investigation. She convinced her to come in that afternoon. Also, she explained that Freedom National Bank's interim CEO, John Vickers, would be present to explain a few irregularities with her account. Before ending the call, Beth informed her she might want her lawyer present. With everything set, Beth hoped she would cooperate.

At half-past two in the afternoon, Clarissa entered the police station with a man at her side. Meeting them at the receptionist's desk, Clarissa introduced her lawyer, Dale Edmundson. After exchanging pleasantries, Beth escorted them to an interrogation room. She left them alone while she gathered her files and let them stew for a few minutes. Five minutes had passed before the door swung open, and Beth entered with a folder. Chief Evans, Carla, and Bernie would watch from behind the mirrored window. Sitting across from Clarissa, Beth's lioness glare met Clarissa's tenuous demeanor.

"Clarissa, thank you for coming in. As always, I'm recording this interview. Let the record show you have brought Dale Edmundson, your lawyer. For the record, please state your full legal name."

"Clarissa Antoinette Morgan."

"Clarissa, you did come of your own volition today, is that correct?"

"Yes."

"Okay, John Vickers had to cancel unexpectedly. Are

you okay with that?" Clarissa glanced at Dale, then nodded. "Great. After corporate completed an internal audit of the bank, he came to us. Anyway, uh, the audit discovered internal deposits to Bortel's checking account. Following the paper trail, the deposits came from your savings account. But you already know that don't you?"

"Don't answer that."

"Isn't it true your deceased husband was close to serving you with divorce papers?"

"Don't answer that."

"Isn't it true you and Bortel were having an affair for a very long time? His bank records indicated he stayed in the same Cincinnati hotel just about every weekend. I called and talked to the day manager. I sent him a picture of you, and he identified you as the lady meeting him there. He said you used the name Bradley Compton. Bradley is your maiden name, correct?"

"Clarissa, don't…"

"Dale, it's okay. I'll answer the question. Yes, that is my maiden name. I was having an affair with Bortel, and we met in Cincinnati. That's not a crime, is it?"

"Of course not, but murder is."

"Listen, I didn't murder him. I loved him."

"Did you murder your husband?"

"Don't answer that."

"Clarissa, Thaddeus was going to divorce you, and that would mean no inheritance. He knew about your affair, didn't he? I'm surprised he didn't fire Bortel."

"Don't answer that."

"Miss Pendergast, Thaddeus tried to fire him. I convinced him not to do that. I promised him I would end the affair, and I did. That's the truth."

"Okay, back to the money Bortel illegally transferred

from your account to his. You eventually found out, didn't you? And you confronted him, isn't that right?"

"Don't answer that."

"Okay, isn't it true you have a key to Commissioner Walters' house?"

"You already know that. Yes, he gave me one to check on his ill wife when she got worse."

"Right. Where was his wife when you always checked on her?"

"In the master bedroom. She was too weak to be anywhere else in the house."

"Okay, did you ever go upstairs anytime you looked in on her?"

"Of course not. I'm not a snooper."

"Right. In collecting evidence at the crime scene, forensics discovered female DNA on the upstairs landing. A national database identified that DNA as yours."

Dale Edmundson exclaimed, "Don't answer that. How did you get her DNA?"

"The authorities in Columbus sent it to us. Your client submitted her DNA and fingerprints to them during the death investigation of her husband."

"Okay, okay. What if I did go up there a few times to get his wife some things? Yeah, that's likely how it got there."

"Okay, when did Cynthia die?"

"About two years ago, you know that."

"Yeah, but did you know Commissioner Walters was a stickler about cleanliness and had cleaning service come in weekly?"

"Don't answer that. Clarissa, I'm advising you to end this interrogation." Nodding at Dale, tears surfaced on Clarissa's cheeks. "Okay, either arrest her, or we're leaving." Questionable eyes flew at the mirrored window briefly and returned to the seriousness in Dale's eyes. "That's what I thought. Let's go, Clarissa. This ambush is over."

Beth got up, opened the door, and Clarissa and Dale immediately left. Grabbing her file, she slammed it on the table as frustration exploded in her soul. While facing the mirrored window, dejection glared back. A minute later, Carla, Bernie, and Chief Evans joined her in the room.

"Dammit, chief, she's guilty as hell. I can feel it."

"Hold on, sister. Slow down and get ahold of yourself, okay?"

After sighing, she continued, "Sorry, chief. She pushed Bortel over that railing just like she did her husband. We've got her DNA on the balcony, and she…"

"Beth, please…slow…down. We get it."

"Uh, sorry, chief. Here's what I think. Somehow, Bortel knew Clarissa was responsible for Thaddeus' death. He started embezzling money from her, like blackmail. When she confronted him, he told her he would turn her in. We have enough to get an arrest warrant for her. The sooner, the better, before she bolts with all of her money."

Stepping out of the room, Chief Evans called the district attorney. Inside the room, anticipation painted Beth's face. Ten minutes seemed like twenty. Suddenly, the door swung open as Chief Evans appeared. He was not one to show a great deal of emotion unless he had a burr up his ass, or Carla and Bernie had pissed him off.

Giddy with anticipation, Beth met the chief's stoic expression. "Well, do we?"

"Your arrest warrant will be ready in a few hours, and then you guys can go pick her up. I hope you're right."

"Wasn't I right in the last case?"

Chief Evans made no response and left. Glancing at Carla and Bernie, Beth's eyes met smiles, big smiles. Within seconds, high fives echoed off the walls.

# CHAPTER 45

hree hours later, Beth, Carla, and Bernie arrived at Clarissa's home. While pulling into the driveway, amber lights emanated through the window blinds. Within a minute, they walked up on the porch. After Beth used the brass doorknocker, they waited as silence filled the air. Impatience began to control Beth's demeanor as she reached for the doorknocker once more. Suddenly, the door opened. Clarissa showed remnants of anguish as her eyes glared at the document in Beth's hand. Handing her the warrant, she glanced at it briefly and gave it back to her. Clarissa's blank expression was as cold as steel.

"Clarissa, please step outside." While stepping out onto the porch, her blank and cold demeanor never changed. "Clarissa Morgan, you are under arrest for the murder of Wilson Bortel."

At that moment, the local television station's mobile newsroom pulled up in front of the house. Bernie immediately approached them, keeping them away from the porch.

"Please don't cuff me. I'm not going to flee. Please call my lawyer. Here's his card."

Glancing toward Carla for direction, she nodded at Beth. While Beth read her the Miranda Rights, Carla called Dale Edmundson, explaining the arrest warrant's details.

"Yeah, I know my rights. Can we go now? Will you keep the news vultures away from me?"

With Beth on one arm and Carla on the other, they walked her off the porch to Beth's car. Clarissa could see Kiersten St. Clair extending her mic toward her. Seeing the cameraman zeroing in on her, Carla released her grip on Clarissa's arm, allowing her to shield her face as much as possible.

As Carla opened the rear passenger door, Kiersten St. Clair's distinctive voice blared in the background. Beth helped her into the backseat while Carla walked around the car and slid in beside her. With Clarissa safely inside the car, Beth closed the door. Tinted windows masked Clarissa's stoic, cold complexion. After Bernie joined them in the car, Beth backed out of the driveway and pulled away from the media circus.

A few minutes later, Beth left Mahogany Way, heading for the county detention center. It would be Clarissa's home until her arraignment. As she drove to the detention center, silence smothered the cabin of the car. While visibly upset, Clarissa watched her freedom zip past her. Arriving at the detention center, Dale Edmundson greeted Clarissa, instructing her to remain silent. Beth presented the arrest warrant to him, he quickly read it, showing no emotion.

With Beth's job finished, pride exploded in her soul. After glancing at the clock, she turned her gaze to Carla and Bernie. Smiles painted their faces as thumbs-up gestures met her glowing face. Knowing what a day it had been, a celebratory drink at their favorite watering hole was ahead of them. Twenty minutes later, they entered McGruder's taking their favorite booth.

Pinot Grigio for Beth, Jameson for Carla, Yuengling for Bernie with house chips and pretzels blessed their celebration. While glasses clinked together, Beth's smile lit up the whole place. From their favorite booth, Carla liked watching people. Every time the main doors made a swooshing sound, her gaze gravitated in that direction. While scanning the pub, several men caught her attention. As she savored her Jameson, she kept a careful eye on them. With their drinks finished, Beth ordered another round.

Returning her gaze at the men, Carla kept her eye on them until a man and woman entering the pub grabbed her attention. Angela and Geronimo did not see her because they immediately walked to the other side of the pub. Glancing back at the men, the second round of drinks arrived. Blessing her lips with Jameson's nuances once more, Carla's gaze drifted back to Angela and Geronimo. They appeared to be having a friendly conversation rather than a professional one. Carla rose and walked toward the men. Approaching them, she faced their table.

"Mayor, commissioners, what's the score of the game you're watching?"

"Who cares? May we help you, Detective McBride?"

"Nah, I'm headed to john, have a good evening."

After visiting the john, she took the long way back to her booth. Passing by Angela and Geronimo, they ignored her friendly gesture. Returning to the booth, she slid in beside Beth. Several minutes later, Mayor James, Barry, Philip, and Rich passed by their booth on their way out. Watching them as they left, her gaze returned to Angela and Geronimo. After seeing her reaching for his hand, she knew this meeting was more of a date than a work session.

Working its magic, Jameson was easing Carla's anxiety as her mind drifted to Commissioner Walters' death investigation. As she watched Angela in action, she could only wonder about her involvement. She was still their primary person of interest. Then there was Bobbi Tierney's involvement. She was devastated when Commissioner Walters blew her off, which ended their relationship. She could've gone off the deep end and killed him in a fit of jealous rage. Anything was possible. Plus, the two men, presumably Lenny Clark and Chase Ballard, were now on their radar screen after following the mayor and the remaining city commissioners for the past week. They had not broken the law, now or in the past, throwing a monkey wrench in this whodunit mystery.

As the night grew old, Beth, Carla, and Bernie began to wither down as well. Angela and Geronimo had ended their evening, whatever it was. Maybe they were an item now, or perhaps it was just business. Solving a case always gave Beth, Carla, and Bernie an immediate high. Still, as they celebrated, that high morphed into the cold reality that Walters' death investigation was now, front and center. The clues to solving it, more than likely, were right in front of them tonight. And, hopefully, in the next few days, the new evidence found at the houseboat will help solve this mystery. Leaving McGruder's, the cold winds of uncertainty grabbed their weary souls with all its might.

# CHAPTER 46

As expected, Clarissa pleaded not guilty at her arraignment. Because of her flight risk possibilities, the judge denied bail. Although she had no previous criminal record, she had plenty of money that allowed her the ability to disappear to a foreign country. Given she likely caused her husband's death four years ago and is now arrested for allegedly killing her lover, the district attorney and judge couldn't take that chance.

She would remain in the women's detention center until her trial date. After spending several nights in a jail cell, she began to consider her options. She thought if she cooperated with the authorities, she might be able to negotiate a lighter sentence or convince everyone Bortel's death was an accident, or self-defense. However, complicating matters, she intentionally took Bortel inside Walters' home, eliminating any self-defense options. Realizing her only option was a plea deal, she instructed her lawyer to arrange a meeting with District Attorney Marv Barnett. After lengthy discussions with him, he was receptive to such a quick solution to this homicide investigation.

The following morning, Clarissa arrived at the police station, accompanied by her lawyer. Cuffed and shackled, dressed in an orange jumpsuit, she shuffled through the common area on her way to one of the interrogation rooms. Upon entering, Carla motioned her to sit at the head of the table. Her lawyer sat to her left, while Carla, Beth, Bernie and District Attorney Barnett sat opposite them.

"Marv, thank you for meeting with us today and considering the possibility of a plea deal. My client will tell you everything for a lesser charge and sentence."

"Counselor let's hear her story, then we'll decide if a plea deal is possible. Based on the information I have, your client drugged him and took him to Commissioner Walters' home with the intent of killing him. None of this makes any sense, so let's hear her story, and we'll go from there."

"Please give me a few minutes alone with my client, okay?"

After five minutes, everyone returned to the interrogation room, taking their previous seats around the table. With eyes glistening, Clarissa took a deep breath before telling her story.

"Listen, everyone. I didn't mean to cause his death. It was an unfortunate accident. I know that is hard to believe since his death occurred in his political rival's home. I'm sure you are wondering why we were there in the first place."

"Yeah, let's get that out of the way."

"Beth, let her tell her story, okay?

"Sorry, chief. Clarissa, please continue."

"All the time I helped Bryan with his wife, I thought we were starting to hit it off. After his wife died, I comforted him, we drank wine together, he just needed a friend, and I was there for him. At first, our relationship was friendly. However, it moved to a sexual one as time went by. After several months of that, I began to fall for him, and I believe he was starting to feel the same."

"So, what changed?"

"Well, Miss Pendergast, I started noticing that the lady across the street was visiting him a lot."

"You mean Bobbi, right?"

"Yeah. Anyway, one day UPS delivered a package of his to my house. So that evening, after Bryan got home from work, I decided to take it to him. Since I had a key, I entered through the back door and went into the great room. I didn't see him and called out his name. Within a few minutes, he appeared on the upstairs landing wearing his boxers. It wasn't long before Bobbi appeared in sexy lingerie. I stormed out, didn't even close the back door. I felt betrayed because I was so close to having him."

"Okay, so you're upset. What happened next?"

"Miss Pendergast, I called him and asked him why it wasn't me he wanted. He told me it was none of my business and never to call him again. Then I started seeing Wilson again, but our relationship was just sex. I would never love that pompous asshole after I found out he was embezzling from me. Anyway, when Bryan lost to Wilson, and I saw Bryan threaten him that night, I thought I would get even with him."

"How so?"

"By having sex on the upstairs landing in his home hoping he would come home and find us getting it on.

Anyway, Wilson was drunk, and acting crazy. He was out it."

"Right. He had evidence of a 'date rape drug' in his system. How do you explain that?"

"I can't. I didn't put anything in his drink. You have to believe me. Anyway, I took him to Bryan's house and entered through the back door. We went up to the upstairs bedroom where Bryan and Bobbi had sex. After we had sex in the shower, I thought I heard something, hoping it was Bryan. Both naked, we walked out to the balcony. We didn't see anything or hear anything. The next thing I knew, Wilson grabbed my hair, pulling my head down toward his penis. I told him no. He wouldn't take no for an answer. I just lost it and shoved him. Next thing I know, he went over the railing, landing on the glass table."

"Why didn't you call the police?"

"I don't know, scared, that's why I wrote "cheater" on his chest and left the note. He was dead after hitting the glass table the way he did. I thought his death would implicate Bryan. I would be out of the picture and free from Wilson's embezzling. That's it. It was an unfortunate accident, and that is the truth."

"Really, what about the loose railing on the balcony? You loosened it, didn't you? Then you drugged him, lured him over there, then shoved him over after having sex. That's premeditated murder, and you could get the death penalty if convicted."

"Beth, that's enough, okay?"

"Sorry, Carla."

In tears, a deputy sheriff transported Clarissa back to the detention center. Now, it was up to the district attorney to decide if it was an accident. If not, he had to determine whether a plea deal was possible.

Beth had done her job and returned to her previous case involving Angel Hardesty while Carla and Bernie waited for the result of the evidence found at the houseboat.

# CHAPTER 47

A week had passed since Clarissa, and her lawyer met with the district attorney. Nothing had changed, nor was any deal made. Taking Beth's notes of her investigation into the death of Clarissa's husband, the district attorney requested more information from Columbus authorities and American Life and Annuity.

Carla and Bernie were still waiting for the DNA results they collected at Commissioner Walters' houseboat. And as far as everyone knew, Mayor James, Rich, Philip, or Barry hadn't had any further encounters with the two men in the white sedan. In other words, the death investigation of Walters stood at a standstill. Angela was their primary person of interest. However, Bobbi remained on their radar, pending the DNA results from the houseboat.

As a lull continued in the case, Carla had been taking advantage of the slow period. While arriving later than usual, Bernie's stern scowl met her smile as she settled in at her workstation. While her laptop booted up, she visited the coffee center for a cup of coffee. As she approached it, the smell of old coffee hit her in the face. Given that the coffee would taste as bad as it smelled, she chose a medium roast K-cup and used the Keurig instead.

Several minutes later, she sat staring at her laptop, hoping good news would help her impatient disposition. After sipping on her coffee, she murmured under her breath. Bernie watching her lips move, smiled at her. While rolling her eyes in his direction, her stoic expression returned to her laptop. Bernie liked the downtime as much as Carla, however, his patience drove her crazy. As he read her lips, their eyes met.

"What, dickhead?"

"Oh, nothing. It's funny to watch you talk to your laptop, thinking it will answer you, has it?"

Rolling her eyes again, a quick bird flew in his face. He was used to her antics and just smiled, which also drove her up the wall. While holding her coffee with both hands, a shit-eating grin lit up her face.

"Yeah, it just did. Sherry wants to meet with us in a half-hour. She didn't indicate what it was about, but it has to be the DNA results, and it's about time."

"That, it is. What do you think we're going to find out?"

"I'm not sure. If the DNA on the piece of wood belongs to Bobbi, we have a problem. If it belongs to Angela, it may clear things up, and we can move on with an arrest warrant. If it's something new, then we might be up the creek without a paddle, or maybe even the boat."

"Interesting analogy, McBride."

"Bite me, dickhead."

Scanning through the rest of her emails, one caught her eyes. Clicking on the email, it loaded. Someone from

Capital City Accounting had responded to her emails. She had called the company several times but always had to leave a voicemail message. Finally, her email inquiry received a reply. Although the email didn't divulge who was sending the checks to George Ballard, the last name at the bottom of the email piqued her interest. Larry Stewart had replied that the information she requested was confidential.

While murmuring under her breath, her expression met Bernie's curious eyes. "What did you just say? Just spit it out, McBride."

"I finally got a reply from Capital City Accounting about the checks George Ballard received. Larry Stewart said that it was confidential information and left it at that."

"Who's he?"

"The owner, I assume. Umm, Stewart rings a bell."

"How so?"

"I don't know, like…"

While glancing at the time on the laptop screen, she noticed Bernie's head nodding toward the hallway. Turning around, Sherry had just entered the conference room.

"Guess Larry Stewart will have to wait. Let's go find out where our case stands."

Leaving their workstations and entering the conference room, Sherry sat at the head of the table with superiority glowing from her face. Carla hated that and ignored her queen-like pose as she sat to Sherry's left. Bernie sat to Sherry's right, grinning at Carla's fuming eyes. Catching his smirky gesture, she kicked him under the table, which brought a scowl on his face. A folder in front of Sherry graced the table. While Carla's eyes attempted to wipe Sherry's expression off her face, she opened the file. Taking one sheet of paper out of the folder, she began.

"Okay, guys. Let's start with the piece of wood you found. It had DNA embedded in it, and the results are quite interesting."

"Listen, Sherry; we don't have to time to dick around here. Just tell us whose DNA it is, okay?"

"Wow, just calm down, McBride." An in-your-face bird met Sherry's eyes. "Okay, I get it. Not sure why you always have to be a bitch, but it belongs to Barbara Tierney."

"Are you sure?"

"There you go again, McBride, questioning me. Yeah, I ran it twice."

"Shit, what else you got?"

"The substance on the outside wall of the boat is from an unidentified male."

"Damn, does it get any better?"

"The syringe being in the water for a long time compromised any DNA left. However, we did find traces of a powerful sedative in it. And get this…"

"Dammit, Sherry, just tell us, okay?"

"Wow, McBride, what's got your panties in a wad today? Anyway, it matched the sedative in Walters' toxicology report. That's it, any questions?"

"Not me, Bernie. You have any?"

Shaking his head, Sherry handed them copies of the results and left the conference room. Commissioner Walters' death investigation got a little muddier. Given that the piece of wood had Barbara Tierney's DNA on it, they now had to consider her as a person of interest.

Returning to their workstations, Carla woke up her

laptop and keyed in Larry Stewart. After the search pages loaded, she began reviewing them. Although the history was limited, information at the end of the search results lit up her face.

"Hey, I know that look. What do you have?"

"Well, partner, Larry Stewart is from Oakmont."

"So, what good is that?"

"His cousin is Barry Stewart."

"And how does that help us?"

"Not sure, but why would Barry's cousin's accounting company be sending checks to George Ballard all these years? Someone has some dirty skeletons in their closet. I can feel it."

"So, did he say why he stopped sending the checks?"

"No, said it was confidential."

"Of course, what's next, partner?"

"Let's go see Chief Evans."

"I can see his door is open. He's pushing papers and probably needs a break."

Walking down the corridor, Chief Evans glanced at them, approaching his office. Waving them in, they sat across from his curious eyes.

"What brings you two here this early in the day?"

"Bernie, why don't you tell him what's going on?"

"Of course, well, we just met with Sherry on the DNA we found at Walters's houseboat, and—"

"Bernie cut to the chase, okay?"

"Yeah, Barbara Tierney's DNA was on a piece of the railing while DNA from an unidentified male was on a wall outside the boat. The DNA on the syringe was compromised. However, traces of a powerful sedative inside matched Walters' toxicology report. We are back to square one."

"What's next, McBride?"

"Well, chief, we'll interview Angela Clark and Barbara Tierney again and see where that points us. We don't have enough on either to get an arrest warrant. Hopefully, we have a clearer direction after interviewing them again."

"Great, keep me informed, okay?"

"Of course. On another subject, have you ever heard of Larry Stewart?"

"Nah, who's he?"

"Barry Stewart's cousin and he owns the firm that sent checks to George Ballard until he died."

"And how does that help?"

"I don't know. We're going to visit Barry after lunch and see what turns up."

"Okay, keep me posted."

# CHAPTER 48

While at McGruder's, Carla and Bernie decided on a strategy for Angela and Bobbi. Interviews would take place at the same time but in different rooms. As far as they knew, Angela and Bobbi had never met. However, they couldn't dismiss how they ended up back in Oakmont, their hometown, about the same time. Coincident or not, they needed to find out more about Bobbi's past.

Back at the station, since Beth had contacted Bobbi before, Carla let her make Bobbi's arrangements while Bernie made them with Angela. Both were informed that new information had surfaced in Walters' death investigation. They agreed to come in at Seven PM and to bring their legal counsel if they chose to.

With those meetings set up, they turned their attention to Barry Stewart. His cousin's accounting firm was responsible for the checks sent to George Ballard. Barry's cousin also knew the reason they stopped. Although Carla was uncertain whether this had anything to do with Walters' death, she still needed to answer that nagging question. With Barry's law office near the police station, they dropped in unannounced. Unfortunately, Barry was in court for the remainder of the day.

Hoping to catch him during a recess, they headed for the Hall of Justice. After finding a parking spot, they found the courtroom where he was. Slipping into the courtroom, they sat in the last pew. Unsure what the case was about, they observed one of the most influential lawyers in town performing at his best. Even though they knew this courtroom well, they viewed it differently since they didn't have a dog in this fight.

The judge's gavel echoed off the walls; the court was in recess for ten minutes. Stepping outside the courtroom, they waited for Barry. As predicted, he came out of the courtroom within a few minutes. After noticing Carla and Bernie, curious expressions crossed his face. They immediately approached him. After exchanging pleasantries, Barry walked with them to a recess room. Entering, Barry closed the door.

"What can I do for you detectives?"

"Your cousin, Larry's firm, has been sending checks to George Ballard for a very long time, do you know why?"

"Who's George Ballard, Detective McBride?"

"Do you remember a girl from high school? I believe she went by the name of Bambi?"

Immediately Barry's pulse skyrocketed, a warming sensation flowed throughout his face. After breaking eye contact, his eyes wandered around the room as his forehead glistened under the buzzing fluorescent lights. He was instinctively stalling to eat up the time before he would have to be back in the courtroom.

Breaking his intentional deflection of the question at

hand, Carla became agitated, "Mr. Stewart, answer the damn question, do you remember Bambi, yes or no?"

"Sorry, yeah, I remember her. What's this about?"

"Bambi's father was George Ballard, but you already knew that, right?"

Glancing at his watch, he smiled. "Yeah, is this what that's all about?"

"Do you know why your cousin's accounting firm was sending the checks?"

"Look, detectives, why don't you call my office and set up an appointment where we can continue this discussion?"

"Just answer my question."

A knock on the door was like being saved by the bell. Recess was over, and Barry was off the hook for now. As they left the room, Carla told Barry they would set up an appointment for tomorrow. After calling Barry's office, they returned to the police station.

While having several hours to kill until Angela and Bobbi arrived, Carla woke up her laptop. After performing a search on Barbara Tierney, the most recent information loaded first. She'd seen that movie before and quickly moved through the numerous search pages. She found out that Bobbi attended St. Anthony's Catholic School until she graduated from high school. Bobbi played softball but was also a cheerleader. Carla knew that Angela had attended public schools growing up in Oakmont, and nothing connected the two. Bernie had done the same thing with Angela. However, because Angela was practically a "plain Jane gal" in high school, there wasn't much information, and it was unlikely, Angela and Bobbi knew each other back then.

Switching gears, Carla took a chance and followed up

with Capital City Accounting, hoping to catch Larry Stewart off-guard. Keying in the number on her smartphone, she crossed her fingers. Luck was on her side today as a man answered. Quickly she put it on speaker.

"Mr. Stewart, I'm Detective Carla McBride. Will you answer a few questions for me?"

"Didn't you receive my email?"

"Yeah, but…"

"What's in the email is all that I can tell you."

"Yeah, I get that, but just tell me why you stopped sending the checks."

"I received an email to end the checks. That's all you are going to get."

"By whom?"

An annoying dial tone blared off the walls. Quickly silencing it, they glared at each other with curious eyes. Noticing Bobbi and a lady they hadn't met entering the police station broke their stoic expression. Carla went over to greet them, asking them to follow her to interrogation room number one. As they passed Bernie's workstation, Angela and Geronimo checked in with the receptionist.

Carla glanced in their direction as Bernie lumbered over to greet them. As he led them to interrogation room number two, Carla, Bobbi, and her lawyer entered room number one and closed the door. Passing by the interrogation room window, Angela recognized the lady with Carla. After reaching interrogation room number two, Bernie, Angela, and Geronimo entered and closed the door.

After an hour, ironically, both doors to the interrogation rooms opened, and everyone stood in the hallway staring at each other for a moment. Awkwardness filled the corridor as Bobbi stared at Angela. Then Bobbi and her lawyer were escorted out of the station by Carla. Moments later, Angela and Geronimo showed themselves out.

Beth, assigned to view both interviews from the monitors in the conference room, waited on Carla and Bernie to join her. After hearing Beth's comments, they left with only one viable person of interest. Now, they had to convince Chief Evans to pursue an arrest warrant.

# CHAPTER 49

As Barry Stewart left the Hall of Justice after a lengthy day in court, his thoughts weren't on what transpired in the courtroom. The visit by Carla and Bernie was foremost on his mind causing him uncontrollable anxiety. Parking in the back of his office building, he quickly unlocked the door and entered. Securing the door, he quickly walked to his office. Sitting at his desk, he wondered how Detectives McBride and Kowalski knew about the checks, so, he called his cousin. Larry informed him Carla had contacted him about the checks, but he didn't give her any specific information hoping she would drop her inquiry. That seemed to reassure him. With his wife out of town, he was in no hurry to go home.

Walking to the credenza on the far wall, he pulled out his Waterford Crystal whiskey decanter. Smelling the aroma emanating from it, a three-finger pour of Pappy Van Winkle Reserve swirled around the bottom of his rock glass. Drinking it Neat, he sat in a lounge chair sipping the history of this unique bourbon.

After about an hour, the effects of the bourbon warmed his soul. He knew if he finished the three-fingered pour, it would not be safe to drive home. However, it tasted so good, and he needed its comfort after his long day. Calling the Oakmont Courier Service, he arranged a ride home. He continued enjoying all the characteristics Pappy Van Winkle had to offer as he chilled out. For times like this, he kept food in the refrigerator in the breakroom.

After walking to it, he grabbed his leftover Reuben from the fridge. It was only a day old, and he knew it would still be safe to eat. This wasn't his first rodeo with a Reuben and his microwave. Slowly warming it up, he took it. After separating it, he knew by the steam rising from the corned beef it was ready. He grabbed a bag of kettle chips and headed back to his office.

While enjoying the Reuben and Pappy Van Winkle, his mind drifted back to his high school days and Bambi. He never really dated her. He had been dating another girl from the catholic school, a cheerleader who also played softball. After graduation from high school, they separated ways amicably. He remembered the good times they had, especially when they both lost their virginity at his father's lake house during their junior year of high school.

With the Reuben finished and Pappy Van Winkle put away until such time warranted tasting its luxurious life once more, he closed his office door and walked to the front lobby waiting for his ride home. Five minutes, he received a text on his smartphone. After opening the door, his ride arrived. Seeing a white sedan sent his pulse racing. Peering into the car, he checked his text, which had a picture of his driver. Satisfied it matched, he opened the rear passenger door and got in.

As his pulse returned to a normal rhythm, the white sedan pulled away from the curb. Taking Main Street toward the interstate, he kept looking in the driver's side mirror. What appeared to be another white sedan was following them. Stopping at the next traffic signal, he could see that car was still behind them. Turning around to look at the car, he could see two men in the car, and one had a beard.

With his pulse now racing, he instructed the driver to make a U-turn and drive to the police station they had just passed. He told the driver he'd forgotten to drop off some papers. When the light turned green, the driver made a U-turn heading toward the police station. The white sedan turned left onto the by-pass and merged onto the interstate.

After reaching the police station, he got out and told the driver to wait. Five minutes later, Barry was back in the car. Twenty minutes later, the driver stopped at the guardhouse, where Barry spoke to the attendant, and the security gate opened. Another ten minutes, Barry was safe inside his home. The anxiety he experienced on the way home needed calming. Visiting the bar, Pappy Van Winkle graced his favorite bourbon glass, an etched rock glass from Avondale Country Club, an award for winning Senior Player of the Year for the second year in a row.

After pointing the remote at the gas logs, flames danced erratically, warming the great room and his soul. Walking over to the mantel, a picture of him and his wife made him smile. Taking a seat in a lounger to the left of the fireplace, he pulled out his smartphone and pushed the number for his wife. Within seconds, she picked up the call easing his anxiety. Adele always had a way of relaxing his worried mind. As he sipped on Pappy, her voice put him at ease.

After ending the call, the dancing flames mesmerized him and his thoughts. Suddenly, he thought he heard a noise coming from the breezeway leading to the garage. Walking over to the bar, he put his glass down. Opening a drawer, he grabbed his nine-millimeter. After loading it, he moved slowly through the kitchen toward the breeze-way. After flipping on the light, the breezeway illumi-nated. Nothing caught his eye. He turned on the lights outside the garage seeing only the light rain coming down. Satisfied that it was probably just the wind or something else, he returned to the great room to finish Pappy in front of the dancing flames in the fireplace.

With his gun in hand, he grabbed Pappy and retreated to the master bedroom. After placing the gun and bourbon on the nightstand, he visited the bathroom to take care of every night's pre-sleep necessities. Returning to the bedroom, he finished off Pappy. Lying in bed, he turned on the television to catch the last of the news. As his alcohol-induced world spun around him, blurriness crept in, and he closed his eyes, willing the spinning to stop. Several minutes later, he succumbed to too much Pappy and the anxiety invading his soul.

A half-hour later, a lightning bolt and a thunderous boom rocked the walls. He awoke to a shadow in the doorway.

"Who's there?"

Silence flowed off the walls. While fumbling for his gun, his bourbon glass fell to the floor, shattering. His hand found the barrel of his nine-millimeter, feeling around for the handle, it crashed to the floor as well. He squinted at the doorway, but the shadow had disappeared. Closing his eyes momentarily, they grew weaker and weaker until the effects of the alcohol took control of his mind and body.

# CHAPTER 50

C onvincing Chief Evans to secure an arrest warrant for Angela Clark was a dog fight, however, it was their only choice. And feeling the pressure from Mayor James, Chief Evans took a chance, whether it was right or wrong. He told them convincing the district attorney took patience and fortitude. Then the right judge would need to bless it, and that would take time.

While waiting for the warrant, they dropped in to see Barry Stewart. After entering the law firm, they sat in the lobby, waiting for him. Ten minutes later, he greeted them. Following him to his office, they sat in well-appointed chairs as he closed the door. Silence took hold of the room as they observed a different demeanor from him. He appeared a little hungover and aloof. Clearing his throat, Bernie chased the silence away. As Carla watched Barry, worrisome eyes wandered back and forth at them.

"Okay, detectives, what does Bambi or my cousin have to do with the checks sent to George Ballard?"

"Mr. Stewart, Carla, and I want to know that answer as well. Why don't you tell us? Carla spoke to your cousin Larry yesterday and found out everything about this situation is confidential, umm, but we think you know. So, why don't you quit giving us bullshit that you don't know anything?"

While deflecting Bernie's cold stare, his eyes moved around the room, searching for the proper response. As the fluorescent lights glowed from the ceiling, his forehead began glistening. Feeling the warmth on his face, he grabbed a tissue out of the dispenser, wiping the anxiety off his brow.

"Mr. Stewart, Bernie asked you a question. I suggest you answer it now."

"Or you will do…"

"Listen, something is going on, and we are not leaving today without getting some answers."

"Okay…okay, I get it. When my dad died, I took control of the company. The first thing I did was hire an independent auditing firm. That's when they discovered an expense from Capital City Accounting. My cousin's firm was sending checks to a George Ballard."

"Now, we're getting somewhere. Do you know why?"

"No, my cousin said it was confidential, and unless my dad gave him permission, he protected the client confidentiality, and he wouldn't budge even though my dad was dead."

"Who was the client?"

"He wouldn't tell me, so I located George Ballard, but he was on his death bed. His wife knew about the checks, but George told her not to worry about them."

"So, what happened?"

"After I found out George died, I instructed my cousin to stop sending the checks, which he did. That's all I know."

"You're aware of the reason Bambi moved away her senior year, aren't you?"

"Mayor James said she ended up pregnant, and her parents moved because of the shame on the family."

"Did you have something to do with that?"

"Detective McBride, I take offense to that. This meeting is over, please leave, or I'll call Chief Evans."

Anger filled Barry's voice and face; he was enraged by such a question. As Carla's eyes bored into his soul, her smartphone dinged. Glancing at it, she read the message and placed her smartphone back into her pocket. Meanwhile, Bernie was anxiously waiting for Carla to let him know the contents of the text.

"Mr. Stewart, we have other matters to attend to, but we will be back. Thank you for your time. We'll show ourselves out."

Once outside, Bernie's patience had run its course. "Carla, what the hell is going on?"

"Partner, it's showtime. We got our arrest warrant. Let's go bring in Angela Clark."

After a quick stop at the police station, they arrived at Angela's house to serve the arrest warrant. Pulling up in front of her house, they exited and approached the front door as the last patient of the day was leaving. Entering the practice, Angela was chatting with her receptionist. Hearing the door close, Angela turned around, seeing Carla carrying a blue document in her hand. All color drained from her face, and she knew what was coming next.

"Angela Clark, we have a warrant for your arrest in

the murder of Bryan A. Walters. Please put your hands behind you."

Turning to her receptionist, Angela instructed her to call Preston Geronimo. Returning her gaze to Carla, she said, "Are the cuffs necessary, Detective McBride? I didn't kill him. I will go with you without incident. Besides, we don't want that Kiersten bitch here, do we?"

As Carla put her cuffs away, Bernie stated the Miranda Rights. All the time, she confessed her innocence. Before escorting her out of her house, she instructed her receptionist to cancel all appointments indefinitely. After a quiet ride to the police station, Geronimo met Angela and comforted her as best he could. While being processed, she continued to express her innocence to no avail.

After being grilled for several hours, she finally realized she couldn't convince anyone of her innocence and knew she would spend the night in the women's detention center until bail could be set at her arraignment the next day. After a sleepless night, Angela appeared in front of the judge that signed her arrest warrant. Although her appointed public defender did his best to convince the judge that she wasn't a flight risk, he set her bail extremely high hoping no one would step forward and pay it. Fortunately for Angela, Geronimo had the means and paid the bail. He would be responsible for her throughout the whole process.

Rumors of an arrest in Commissioner Walters' death were running rampant in the community. As Geronimo led her out of the Hall of Justice, Kiersten St. Clair was on the scene with the local television station's mobile newsroom. Reaching the bottom steps, Kiersten St. Clair had her claws out.

"Angela Clark, can we get a statement?" Geronimo deflected her mic. "Did you kill Commissioner Walters?" Again, Geronimo shielded Angela from Kiersten St. Clair's ferocious demeanor. As Geronimo led Angela away, Kiersten St. Clair faced the camera, "There you have it, Angela Clark, a behavioral psychologist, was arrested today for allegedly killing City Commissioner Bryan Walters. Reporting from the Hall of Justice, this is Kiersten St. Clair. As more develops in this case, we will bring it to you, and as always, visit our online newsroom for updates. Now, back to your local programming."

After watching this spectacle unfold, Carla and Bernie left to continue their discussion with Barry Stewart. With his office near the police station, it didn't take long to arrive there. Parking in front of the office building, they entered and were promptly greeted by the receptionist. Unfortunately, she informed them he had not arrived yet, but she expected him any minute.

Deciding to hang around, they waited patiently in the lobby area. After about a half-hour, the receptionist called his cell, the call went straight to voicemail, and they left without any more answers. Although disgusted they didn't get to meet with Barry again; today had been a good day for them, nonetheless. Unless the district attorney offered Angela Clark a plea deal and accepted it, she would go on trial for the murder of City Commissioner Bryan Walters.

# CHAPTER 51

ater that afternoon, Carla and Bernie reveled in the fact that the death investigations of Bortel, and hopefully, Walters, were over. While at McGruder's, Jameson for Carla, Pinot Grigio for Beth, and a Yuengling for Bernie got the celebration started. And as usual, two baskets of fried banana peppers graced the table along with the necessary condiments. Friendly bantering flew around the booth as their well-deserved celebration continued.

Although still relatively new, Beth held her own with these two seasoned veterans. Based on the past several cases, they were building a formidable team. With one round of drinks down, Carla held her glass toward Sam. Within minutes, she delivered another round. Sitting in their regular booth, they had the best view of watching people come and go. Today it was just ordinary people unwinding.

They also had the best view of the television above the bar. As another celebratory cheer rang out, breaking news flashed on the screen. Immediately, Kiersten St.

Clair's stunning looks grabbed Carla's attention. While getting Sam's attention, Carla motioned Sam to turn up the volume. As Beth and Bernie focused on the television, the alluring and distinctive voice of Kiersten St. Clair filled the pub. While she glanced around the pub, the breaking news blared from every television.

"This is Kiersten St. Clair reporting from the home of City Commissioner Barry Stewart. His wife, Adele, just returned home from a business trip to find her husband hanging from the second-floor balcony. Although details are sketchy, it appears it was not suicide. Our sources overheard that he was naked and had something written on his chest and back. That's all we have at this time. As more becomes available, we will bring it to you..."

As Kiersten St. Clair's voice faded away, Carla's smartphone rang. Answering it immediately, she quickly ended it. After downing their drinks, Carla, Beth, and Bernie headed out the door. Within twenty-five minutes, Carla flashed her badge at the security gate of Barry Stewart's gated neighborhood. Bernie jumped out to question the security guard while Carla continued toward Barry Stewart's home.

Carla pulled in front of his house; yellow tape secured the crime scene. After getting out, Carla and Beth ducked under the tape and walked up onto the porch. Once inside, they found DJ Franklin, county coroner, examining the body while forensics gathered every shred of evidence. The outline of Barry Stewart's naked body lay under a white sheet.

"Time of death, DJ?"

"Carla, based on everything, I'd say, eighteen hours ago."

"Umm, that would put the time of death last night, eightish, wouldn't you say?"

"Sounds about right."

"Cause of death?"

"Once he went over the balcony rail, his neck snapped, that did him in."

"Suicide?"

"Don't think so. There's a needle prick on his neck."

"Okay, a news report said something about words written on his chest and back."

"Yeah, take a look."

After pulling the sheet away, his chest displayed the word, "who's." Turning the body over, the words "on deck" stared at them while a recognizable odor smacked Carla in the face.

"Carla, what do you think that means?"

"Well, DJ. I'd say Angela Clark didn't personally kill Commissioner Walters. However, I have a gut feeling that his death and Stewart's death are connected, and it involves her somehow. That odor, do you recognize it?"

"Should I?"

"Yeah, that's Angela's perfume, Umari Seduction. It was present at Walters' house, in his car, and his houseboat."

Questioning eyes met Carla's stoic expression. "Shit, that does complicate things."

"Yeah DJ, but what's more concerning is the message the killer left for us. 'Who's on deck' means the killing isn't over. There will be more."

As DJ shook his head, Carla scanned the room, spotting Barry's wife in the kitchen being interviewed by Officer Pete Wiesmann. Seeing Carla and Beth approach him, he met them just outside the kitchen.

"Mrs. Stewart is pretty shaken up. She talked with her husband around six last night. She said he seemed fine and was still at his office. That's all I could get out of her. I think she is just as shocked as we are. I called Mrs. Stewart's sister, and she is on her way over here. She will stay with her sister indefinitely."

"Yeah, probably a good idea. Beth, why don't you stay with her until her sister arrives?"

"Of course."

"Pete, where's Sherry?"

Motioning toward the second-floor balcony, Carla met her gaze. Walking up the stairs, they exchanged strained pleasantries. That's just how their relationship was.

"Sherry, what can you tell me?"

"Umm, not much. We're collecting what evidence there is. However, it appears, whoever killed him was either let in or came in with him."

"That's not much to go on, is it? Does this house have security cameras?"

"Didn't find any. Maybe the security guard can shed some light on this one."

"Yeah, Bernie is checking that out."

Sherry pointed in the direction of the front door where Bernie stood staring at them. Walking down the steps, Carla met him at the front door as Beth joined them.

"What did you find out from the guard?"

"Terry, the security guard, told me Mr. Stewart stopped at the gate around sevenish, and he let him through, said he seemed a little nervous. Terry noticed a man in the passenger seat. I asked him if anyone was in the back seat, and he said he couldn't tell through the dark tinted windows. Terry pulled up the video, which showed a man in the passenger seat, and that's it. I got a copy of it, but it's not much to go on."

"Did he have a beard?" Bernie shook his head. "Dammit."

"Did you expect the man to have one?"

"No, yeah, maybe. I don't know."

"You're not making any sense."

"Yeah, Beth, none of this makes any sense. Bernie, did the guard see the man or a white sedan leave?"

"Nope, and video footage validates that."

"Shit, let's take a hike through the woods behind the house."

Leaving the house and walking towards the woods, a gravel path led them into the dark thickness. The trail ended three hundred yards later at a county road. All that was left were compromised footprints and tire tracks, making any mold useless.

# CHAPTER 52

After returning to the police station, Carla, Beth, and Bernie arranged a meeting with Chief Evans and District Attorney Barnett to discuss Angela Clark's status. Being in the detention center certainly gave her a concrete alibi in Stewart's death, but not for Walters. It was going to be a long night as their meeting would take place in about an hour. They all agreed Carla would handle Angela's questioning, while Beth and Bernie, along with the district attorney, would observe from another room. Although there were still many questions regarding a possible motive in either death, Carla was sure Angela knew more.

Two county deputy sheriffs escorted Angela to the police station. Her overnight stay in a jail cell failed to dampen her spirits. Although hand-cuffed and dressed in her orange prison attire, she was still stunning. The only difference was the absence of her seductive scent of Umari Seduction. After being led to the interrogation room, she sat across from Carla. Angela's blank expression showed her calmness waiting for Geronimo to arrive.

Five minutes later, Geronimo arrived and sat to the left of Angela. Chief Evans was at the head of the table. Dumbfounded, Angela sat quietly, wondering why Carla brought her in again. She was not aware that another death had occurred. Another member of the Diamond Brotherhood had struck out. Carla had never taken her eyes off Angela, and for that matter, Angela was equally focused on Carla, waiting for her to end the silence.

"Angela, you may not be aware of this, but Barry Stewart's wife found him hanging from the second-floor balcony this morning. According to the coroner, his death occurred last night, so we know you didn't personally kill him. However, the scent of your perfume exuded from his body. That's troubling to us."

"So, a lot of women wear it, probably even some gay men as well. I'm sorry to hear Barry is dead. Please give the family my condolences, will you?"

Nodding, Carla continued, "I want to ask you some questions about your relationship with him during your high school years."

"I only knew of him. He was a star in everything, you know, part of the Diamond Brotherhood. I was not their type."

"What was their type?"

"Cheerleaders, majorettes, and the wild ones."

"Umm, like Bambi, your cousin, right?"

Quickly nodding, "Where's this going? I didn't kill Bryan. I didn't kill Barry. I don't know what's going on or who's involved."

"Angela, you told us you thought your brother Lenny

might be in trouble. Who knows, he might be the person committing these crimes. Do you still believe that?"

"I don't know, maybe."

"Forensics is still examining the evidence while the body is on its way to Frankfort for an autopsy. However, we know that he had a needle puncture on his neck, just like Bryan. It appears the same person or persons committed both murders, too many similarities to think differently."

"Then, why are you still holding me?"

"Are you working with your brother, you know, masterminding all this, manipulating him and Chase to commit these murders for you and get revenge on the Diamond Brotherhood?"

Geronimo interjected, "Detective McBride, that's enough. Angela was not involved, nor did she commit either murder. Let's move on, or we're leaving."

"Angela, tell us about your high school days and the Diamond Brotherhood? We did a little checking, and that special club disbanded the year after you graduated. Did you know that?"

"I had heard that, too. What's that got to do with any of this, or me?"

"Maybe something bad happened, maybe to you, did it?"

"As I said before, I wasn't their type."

"What about Bambi? Was she, you know, their type?" Nodding, Carla continued, "Did something happen to her? She did get pregnant, you know. Do you know who the father was?"

"No! Although we were cousins and very close, I didn't know her darkest secrets."

"Did you hear any rumors about anything regarding

Bambi and the Diamond Brotherhood?" Angela's eyes moved around the room while her expression said she was hiding something. "Angela, what do you know?"

"Okay, Detective McBride, I'm not your killer. I will help you, but I get released today. Do we have a deal?"

"That's not how it works. Tell us what you know, and then we will go from there."

Silence captured the room as Angela whispered to Geronimo. "Will you give me a minute? Nodding, everyone left the room. Five minutes later, Geronimo stepped outside the interrogation room, motioning everyone to return.

After everyone was seated, Angela continued, "There was this party at a cabin in the county. Bambi, as well as her best friend, Jody, attended. I understand things went down that night, not sure what happened, but I heard things got wild. You could ask Jody. However, she died in an auto accident that fall."

"Who is Jody?"

"Umm, Jody Dennis. I always thought the accident was suspicious. From what I remember, she swerved to miss an oncoming car, hit a big oak tree, died at the scene. Things didn't add up."

"What do you mean?"

"She mentioned to me one time she knew stuff."

"What kind of stuff?"

"I don't know. It died with her. Listen, you should talk to Mayor James, Philip, or Rich. They were at that party. They might know what she knew. I believe Rich was dating her at the time she died."

"Yeah, we'll do that. What else are you not telling us? What other girls, you know that type, were at that cabin?"

"I don't know. It was a long time ago. I don't remember everything about that night."

"So, you were there?"

"Umm, no… I misspoke, sorry."

"Angela, you were there, weren't you?

"Umm, did I say that? Mmm, sorry. I meant to say, Jody told me about that night, you know, that's when she mentioned she knew stuff. Stuff that could get a lot of people in trouble and destroy their careers. As I said, whatever she knew, died when she did. Like I said, ask Rich?"

"I will, and then I'll…"

A knock on the door startled everyone. Chief Evans opened the door, and after stepping outside, he closed the door. A couple of minutes later, he opened the door and motioned Carla outside. Five minutes later, she returned to the room. Returning to her seat, she locked eyes with Angela staring deep into her soul.

"Well, are you going to release me?"

"The district attorney has…"

The door opened once more, and Chief Evans motioned Carla out again. About a minute later, she re-entered the room. Her face was stoic and stone cold.

"Everyone, Rich Masterson, died in an auto accident a few hours ago. Details are sketchy, but it appears another car deliberately ran him off the road. After hitting a large oak tree, his Corvette burst into flames, and he died instantly. His remains are burned beyond recognition."

As silence grabbed the room, Carla glared at Angela and sighed. Carla returned to her chair across from Angela. Locking eyes with her, Angela remained cool and calm, testing Carla's patience.

"Don't play games with me, Angela. Did you have anything to do with this?"

"Detective McBride, that's enough!"

"Geronimo, it's okay. No, I didn't. I'm sorry to hear Rich is dead. Please give my condolences to the family."

# CHAPTER 53

A fter returning to the women's detention center, Angela was a free woman. As she exited the building, the twilight of the moon hit her glistening eyes. Standing beside his Porsche, Geronimo waited to comfort her. Angela's radiant beauty glowed under the amber streetlights. As his open arms tugged on her heartstrings, she latched onto him. After embracing each other, a passionate, tender kiss eased her anxiety.

Sitting in her car across the street, Carla and Bernie observed their passionate display of affection. For whatever reason, their friendship was more than just business. However, she didn't care about that. What mattered to her was how Angela was involved. She had hired Geronimo to find her brother after being estranged for thirty-five years, but why. She had arrived in Oakmont two years ago, and now three members of the final edition of the Diamond Brotherhood had had their last at-bat in life. Bryan, Barry, and Rich had struck out. Now, "who's next" meant the killing wasn't over.

As the pearl-white Porsche zipped away, they

followed them from a safe distance to Angela's house. Parking on the street, Geronimo exited and walked around the car, opening the door for her. After a quick push on the key fob, the Porsche beeped. Within a minute, they disappeared inside the house, and the first floor illuminated. Seconds later, an amber glow appeared in the upstairs window, and the first level gave way to darkness.

They left, heading for the crash site. When they arrived, the mangled and charred Corvette was on the wrecker's bed. As the tow truck pulled away, the cold darkness of the night swarmed them with questions. Although it appeared to be an unfortunate accident, Carla wondered if it was more than that. After all, a white sedan had followed each Diamond Brotherhood member in the past several weeks. Could they have been stalking each man, planning all of this, Carla wondered? And, if so, why?

The following morning, Carla and Bernie returned to the crash site. Remnants of death were all around, burnt grass and charred tree bark. The first thing they noticed was the absence of skid marks. It appeared maybe he didn't hit the brakes, or perhaps he did, and there were none.

While scanning the immediate area, only a few houses were visible from the road. Across the street, two white frame houses set back about fifty yards from the road. One driveway led to both homes, which were about one hundred yards apart. About halfway down the driveway, it split. Parked under the carport next to the house on the right was a white Corolla sedan. Parked in front of the other home was a blue Chevy Colorado.

Driving down the long driveway, the sight of a

white sedan sent their pulses racing. Choosing the house on their right, they pulled in behind the white sedan. Carla immediately took a picture of the license plate and sent it to Sherry with instructions. Before exiting the car, her phone dinged. The vehicle belonged to a Beulah Scarberry. After breathing a sigh of relief, they exited the car. A porch spanned the entire front of the house. A swing at one end of it had seen its day, while the outdoor furniture was covered for the winter months.

After Bernie pushed the doorbell, chimes rang out from inside the house. Within a minute, a lady, presumably Beulah Scarberry, opened the door and stood behind a storm door. Flashing their badges, the lady lowered the glass panel.

"Beulah Scarberry?"

"Yes."

"I'm Detective Kowalski, and my partner is Detective McBride. I wanted to ask you a few questions about the horrible accident last night. May we come in?" Opening the door wider, they entered. Motioning them to take a seat on the sofa, she sat across from them.

"What do you want to know, Detective Kowalski? That was a terrible accident last night. Is the driver, okay?"

"No, he didn't survive."

"Oh, I'm sorry, prayers for the family. May I get you some coffee? I have a fresh pot."

"Thank you, but we'll pass. Did you see anything last night?"

Shaking her head, "When I heard the sirens coming, I stepped out on the porch and saw the flames. I wasn't sure what was going on. I watched for a few minutes, then went back in to read the Bible and pray for that person. That's about it."

"What about before you heard the sirens, you know, did you look the window anytime, you know, some people do that?"

"No, I read in my bedroom. Do you have any other questions?"

"Do you live alone?"

"That's an odd question, Detective Kowalski. My husband, Paul, died last year. We were married for fifty years. Now it's just me and old Sparky. I imagine he's on his last leg, though."

"I'm sorry, Mrs. Scarberry, we will show ourselves out."

Arriving at the house next door, they pulled in behind the Chevy truck. Carla snapped a picture of the license plate and sent it to Sherry. Within a couple of minutes, she received a response, and they could safely proceed. Roscoe Franklin was the registered owner. As with the house next door, a porch spanned the front of the house. Once upon the porch, Bernie pushed the doorbell, silence rang out inside. He tried it again, the same result. After knocking a few times, they could hear a dog barking, and then Roscoe appeared behind the storm door. Flashing their badges and identifying themselves, Roscoe stepped outside with his dog.

"How can I help you, detectives? Are you here about the accident last night?"

Both nodding, Carla replied, "Yeah, what can you tell us?"

"Well, Detective McBride, you know I'm the person who called the accident in, anyway, I never saw anything like it."

"How so."

"Umm, I let old Brandy out to do her nightly routine. She's going on twelve, and well, she must have her time outside. Anyway, I saw headlights coming down the highway. I'd say around sixty miles per hour. The next thing I know, headlights appeared out of nowhere, heading straight at that car. Also, I could see a red light reflect off the windshield. That's when the Corvette swerved hard and crashed through the fence. The funny thing is, I never saw the brake lights illuminate. The next thing I saw, flames lit up the sky. I told the police all of this last night."

Bernie interjected, "What happened to the other car?"

"Well, that was kind of strange, too. As soon as the Corvette swerved, the lights on the other car went out."

Bernie continued, "Any idea what kind of car?"

"Best I could tell, a white, tan, or gray sedan. I know that's not much, but that's the best I can do."

"Hey, that's okay."

"You got it. Brandy, it's time to go in, finish your business, okay. Whose car is that?"

"Mine, why?

"Sorry, Detective McBride, Brandy loves to bless the tires, as you can see."

"Yeah, she's not first and won't be the last. If you can think of anything else, please give me a call. Here's my card. Thank you, Mr. Franklin."

Inside Carla's car, silence grabbed them for a moment. "Doesn't sound like an accident to me, it sounds like murder. What about you, partner?"

"Yeah. Chief Evans and the mayor aren't going to like this one bit. I wonder who's next?"

"I don't know, Bernie. We've got a fifty-fifty chance of being right."

# CHAPTER 54

A ngela was ecstatic to be out of the women's detention center. Her time inside was frightening enough, and she never wanted to experience it again. Waking up in Geronimo's arms was like paradise. As she yawned and stretched in the bed, the aroma of her favorite coffee brought a smile to her face. While staring at the ceiling, her thoughts drifted to her brother. She wondered where he was and whether he could be involved in any of these deaths. Before she knew it, Geronimo delivered a cup of coffee to the bedside table. Taking a sip and putting it down, she grabbed the remote, turning on the television.

Kiersten St. Clair appeared on the screen; behind her was the accident scene where Rich Masterson lost his life. Not only would the community feel his loss as a city commissioner, but he also owned many auto dealerships. He was also very generous, supporting many worthy causes, with his favorite being Habitat for Humanity. Working on many builds, his network of friends was many. As they listened to her report, she thought about the commissioner's family and prayed for them. She knew the pain firsthand as her father died in an auto accident. Watching and listening to Kiersten, a man entered the screen. His name flashed on the screen, and Angela turned up the volume.

"Mr. Franklin, I understand you witnessed the accident. Would you tell our viewers what you saw from your porch?"

"Well, I had let out old Brandy for her nightly ritual, you know, she takes her time. Anyway, uh, I saw headlights moving quickly towards town. I heard the distinctive sound, you know, of a Corvette, love that sound. Suddenly, headlights appeared out of nowhere on a head-on collision course with the Corvette. I saw a red light reflect off the Corvette's windshield. That's when the Corvette swerved, crashing through the fence, uh, then flames lit up the sky. I immediately called nine-one-one."

"A red light, you mean like a laser."

"Yeah, I had one, and it drove old Simba crazy when he was alive."

"Right, thank you, Mr. Franklin."

"Well, based on that, it appears Commissioner Masterson's death was more than an unfortunate accident. That will do it from the mobile newsroom, back to you guys."

After the television went blank, a stoic but concerning expression grabbed Angela's rosy complexion attracting Geronimo's gaze.

"Hey babe, what are you thinking about?"

"My brother, if he's involved, then why after all these years?"

"Do you think he is behind all of this?"

"I don't know, but we need to find him somehow. If it's him, Mayor James and Philip are in danger."

Nodding, he took her lukewarm coffee and replenished it, and popped it into the microwave. Returning to the bedroom, the bed was empty. Hearing the shower running, he entered the bathroom seeing a sexy silhouette behind the steamed shower doors. Placing the coffee cup on the vanity, he removed his boxers and joined her in the shower.

After a wet interlude of passion, Angela put on a comfortable and silky jogging ensemble. Already dressed in his classic khakis, Geronimo was in the kitchen, whipping up breakfast. After entering the kitchen, bacon and eggs pleased her senses.

"Looks good. How long before we eat?"

"Five minutes, okay?"

"Yeah, I'm going downstairs and check things out. I'll get the mail and the newspaper while I'm there."

Nodding, he continued preparing breakfast. With everything on the table, he hollered at Angela. A few minutes later, she returned to the upstairs living quarters. Carrying the newspaper along with the mail, she tossed them on the sofa table. With everything on the dining table, they sat down for a relaxing breakfast.

Thirty minutes later, she picked up the mail and started going through it, while Geronimo began with the newspaper. As expected, news of Commissioner Masterson's death was front news. A short sidebar mentioned the release of Angela Clark. Geronimo liked to devour the newspaper and was oblivious to Angela's blank stare. One envelope was mysterious. Finally catching her disturbing gaze, he put the newspaper down.

"What's wrong, Angela?" Staring at the envelope, she

turned it over. After pulling out a piece of paper, she gasped. Her silky and rosy complexion quickly vanished.

"Angela, what's going on?"

As her pulse began to race, she handed the note to him. After reading it to himself, he handed it back to her.

"What does 'two more to go' mean?"

"Uh, Mayor James and Philip Devaney are definitely in danger."

"Why?"

"My guess, umm, something terrible happened thirty-five years ago, and someone wants revenge. If it's my brother, I don't understand why. If it's Chase, I don't have a clue. All I know is that every member of the Diamond Brotherhood is dead now except them, and if we don't warn them, they will die."

"What's 'guess who's on deck' about?"

"I'm not sure. We need to inform Detective McBride and Kowalski about this note before it's too late."

Twenty minutes later, Angela and Geronimo arrived at the police station. Carla greeted them and led them to an interrogation room. Within a few minutes, Beth, Bernie, and Chief Evans arrived. As stares bounced around the table, Angela pulled out the envelope she received this morning, and she took the note out.

"This was with my mail. It's not addressed to anyone, but it's for me. It reads – two more to go, guess who's on deck. Mayor James and Philip Devaney are in danger. I can feel it. We need to talk with them now, Chief Evans. Can you make this happen before it's too late?"

Handing the note to Carla, the scent and handwriting was familiar. Passing it around the table, it ended up with Chief Evans. Without saying a word, he stepped outside the interrogation room. Inside the room, silence and a sense of urgency captivated everyone.

"Angela, who is behind this? Are you? The handwriting and scent on it are familiar."

"Detective McBride, no. My guess, it's my brother, and my nephew, Chase. I'm not sure why, but I believe something terrible happened thirty-five years ago, and someone wants revenge."

"What could have happened?"

"I'm hoping Mayor James and…"

At that moment, Chief Evans returned to the room. "Mayor James will be here in ten minutes. However, Philip didn't answer his cell, went straight to voicemail. I called the pharmacy, and he hasn't been in yet."

# CHAPTER 55

Everyone remained in the interrogation room, waiting for Mayor James to arrive. Anticipation, tension, and a sense of urgency smothered the room. Chief Evans left the room while Carla grabbed bottles of water from a dorm-sized fridge and passed them around the table. Within five minutes, Chief Evans returned with Mayor James. The mayor sat at the far end of the table facing everyone, while Chief Evans sat at the opposite end.

"Chief Evans said you needed to talk to me. What about?"

Angela passed the sheet of paper down to him. As he read it, his reddish complexion gave way to a pure white emptiness. Feeling everyone's eyes on him, he massaged his temples. Somewhat composed, the eyes glaring at him wanted answers.

"What's this, Detective McBride?"

"Angela received this. She thinks you're in danger, and Philip, too."

"Why?"

"She thinks you have the answer, so if you want us to help save your life, and hopefully, Philip's, it's time to let the skeletons out of the closet, don't you think?"

Silence grabbed Mayor James as his pulse skyrocketed. Rubbing his temples, then his eyes, the silence became deafening as he caught everyone's gaze and their collective power.

"Okay, after we won the state high school baseball championship, we celebrated at Greg Devaney's cabin at Lake Jackson. It was wild, drinking everything, smoking weed, and all. At first, it was just the Diamond Brotherhood celebrating until Bambi showed up with a few of her friends. They began celebrating with us, and we were all dancing, just acting crazy, having a good time. The next thing I knew, Barry led Bambi to one of the bedrooms."

"Dammit, I knew it. Bambi just makes sense now."

Carla said, "What do you mean, Angela?"

Angela directed her gaze at Mayor James. "Tell them, mayor, tell them the whole story."

"Anyway, about ten minutes later, Barry returned with a huge smile on his face and then yelled, next man up. Barry held a handful of condoms up. Rich, Haywood, Moseley, and Philip grabbed one. Bryan and I knew better and chose not to participate. Barry began to taunt us on how good she was. I'm not sure who went next. Barry said she was out of it."

Carla continued, "So, they took advantage of an incapacitated young girl. That's rape, you know. Then she ends up pregnant. Are you sure everyone used a condom?"

"I don't remember. And then there was…"

"Was…what?"

"Uh, I can't recall…"

"Mayor, what aren't you telling us? You know Philip is not answering his phone, so what is it?"

"Uh, Philip's father, Greg, umm…"

"Dammit, mayor, it's time to let the skeleton out of the closet, don't you think?"

While massaging his temples, his eyes wandered around the room. Unexpectedly, Carla's anger smacked him in the face.

"Dammit mayor, answer me now!"

Carla's in-your-face Irish temper burned his face. After rubbing his eyes, he replied, "As Bryan went into one of the other bedrooms, Philip's father, Greg, arrived to check on us. Greg was feeling it already, and he grabbed a beer, chugging it. Philip had just returned from the bedroom with a shit-eating grin on his face. I remember Philip telling his dad he had just lost his virginity with Bambi. Greg hugged him and grabbed two beers, and they toasted the occasion."

"Anything else, mayor?"

"Hell, no!"

"Your face tells me otherwise. Why did Bryan go to the other bedroom?"

"Listen, I don't remember, too long ago. Anyway, umm, next thing I know, Greg entered the bedroom where Bambi was. Later, he came out smiling. That's about all I remember. It was a wild night."

"Yeah. Umm, Greg Devaney, that piece of shit. Chief, try Philip's number again." He stepped outside the room. Within a minute, he returned, shaking his head. Carla met his gaze, then continued, "Shit. Mayor, where does Philip live?"

"Across from the country club, the last house on the left, Banfield Lane, his father, Greg, lives with him now."

"Damn, we need to go there now. Mayor, keep your ass here. It's the safest place to keep you alive for now." Everyone got up to leave, including Angela and Geronimo. "Angela, you need to stay here as well as Geronimo. You can keep the mayor company reminiscing about old times and that night."

"Detective McBride, if it's my brother and Chase, then they're eliminating everyone that had sex with Bambi that night. It just makes sense. You may need me."

"Angela, let's say that's true, but why now after thirty-five years?"

"I don't know."

"Damn, the checks, maybe that's it. George Ballard had been receiving a check from Capital City Accounting up until the time he died. After that, the checks stopped. Barry Stewart's cousin, Larry, owns the company.

"And?"

Without answering her, Carla found the number for Capital City Accounting in the phone app and pushed it. She placed the call on the speaker. After several rings, a light buzz filled the speaker.

"Larry Stewart?"

"Yeah, who's this?"

"Detective Carla McBride, remember me? We spoke last week about a check going to George Ballard."

"Yeah, what about that?"

"I'm sure you've heard about your cousin's death, right?"

"Of course, I'll be attending the funeral. What's does that have to do with the checks?"

"When we talked last week, you wouldn't tell me who ordered you to stop the checks. So, we met with Barry, and he eventually told us he ordered you to stop the checks."

"Then why are you calling me?"

"Listen, Chase, Bambi's son, likely murdered your cousin, and now, Rich Masterson is dead. It was probably murder disguised as an accident. A couple of weeks ago, Bryan Walters was also murdered, the same way as your cousin. Now, Philip Devaney is not answering his phone. In my opinion, he's the next man up to die, then his dad. You may even be in danger."

"Me…umm…"

"Mr. Stewart, I have a gut feeling you're not telling me everything, are you?"

"Uh, umm, I received a strange phone call several weeks ago. The voice was muffled. All they said was revenge was coming if the checks didn't resume. I called Barry about it. He dismissed the threat and told me not to worry about it."

"Is there more?" Silence. "Dammit, Larry, what aren't you telling us? You're in danger, sir."

"Okay, Bambi and I had a thing together. I believe I'm the one that ended up getting her pregnant." As silence flowed over the speaker, gasps traveled around the table. No one expected that. "We began having sex regularly. One day we got into a big fight. I don't remember what it was. Anyway, I broke it off. Then Barry spilled the beans that she showed up at that party with the Diamond Brotherhood. I could've killed him back then, but let it go…uh…"

"There's more, right?"

"George found out about that party. He was once a

member of the Diamond Brotherhood. He knew what went on at those parties. The next thing I know, George met with all the fathers and threatened to expose what happened that night. It would have destroyed everyone's life and maybe sent their sons to jail. They weren't going to let that happen. I'm not sure whether George knew that Bambi and I were sexually active at that time."

"So, he blackmailed the fathers thinking one of their sons was Chase's father."

"You could call it that. George was a smart man. I'm not sure how it happened, but the fathers set up a trust fund with George as the administrator. Each father put in a large sum of money, and it grew over the years. Everything was fine until Barry told me to stop the checks."

"How do you know all of this?"

"My dad, Joseph, started this company and took me in after I got my CPA. When he unexpectedly died several months ago, I inherited the business. That's when I found out what happened back then. The file I found details everything about that night."

"Mr. Stewart, you need to seek a safe haven. Are you married?"

"No, my wife died a couple of years ago."

"Sorry to hear that, but you need to disappear. Just go somewhere, and don't tell anyone until this is over. If Chase knows you are his father, he'll come after you."

"Seriously, I've got a business to run. I'll take my chances, Detective McBride."

# CHAPTER 56

Turning left onto Banfield Lane, the street looked normal and peaceful to everyone. Pulling in front of Philip's house, Carla cut the engine. Carla, Bernie, and Chief Evans sat cautiously, staring at the house. It appeared lifeless; the driveway was empty. Exiting the car, they walked up the driveway to the garage. Bernie peeked through the windows of the garage door, nothing inside.

Walking up onto an expansive porch, Carla immediately noticed the front door was ajar. Informing Bernie and Chief Evans, she called for backup in silent mode and waited for them to arrive. The police station was only five minutes away. Once Officers Pete Wiesmann and Dave Justice arrived, Carla assigned them to secure the back entrance. Notifying Carla, they were ready, Bernie knocked on the door and announced himself. Silence. He repeated himself. Silence once more. With his service weapon drawn and flashlight beaming, he pushed the door open. They entered the great room, all clear. It took them only a few minutes to clear the remainder of the downstairs. They moved up the stairs to the second level, all clear. While Carla examined the bedrooms, Bernie and Chief Evans returned downstairs looking for anything to help them find Philip and his father.

Striking out, they returned to the police station where Carla and Chief Evans rejoined Beth, Mayor James, Angela, and Geronimo in the interrogation room while Bernie called Philip's pharmacy. Mayor James immediately stood up, wanting an answer. Carla just shook her head several times.

Mayor James exclaimed emphatically, "What now, Detective McBride."

"Bernie is checking with his pharmacy. Is there any other place Philip and his dad could be?" A few minutes later, Bernie entered the room, shaking his head. "Mayor, think hard, okay?"

Thick silence smothered the room as he walked around the room, scratching his head. After a minute or two, he faced Carla looking calm and composed.

"His father's cabin on Lake Jackson."

"Okay, maybe it's our last hope to save them. Where on Lake Jackson?"

"Take the main road in, at the stop sign, turn right, go a mile. It's a rustic place, and Devaney's name is on the mailbox. The cabin is down on the lake with a gravel driveway leading down to it."

"Let's go, guys. Everybody else stays put."

Angela interjected, "Detective McBride, I'm going. You may need me."

"I said, sit tight. I'm not putting your life in danger. Plus, I don't trust you. I still believe in my gut; you have something to do with this."

"You're wrong, dead wrong."

"Am I? Just sit tight, and don't do anything stupid, okay?"

Angela nodded, and Carla, Bernie, and Chief Evans left. About twenty minutes later, Carla made a left turn onto the lake's main road, with Officers Wiesmann and Justice following. Reaching the stop sign, she turned right per the mayor's instructions. One mile later, they reached the gravel driveway leading to the cabin. On the mailbox was the name Devaney. After Carla turned onto the gravel driveway, she could not see the cabin. Several sharp turns through the forest blocked her view. As the driveway straightened out, the cabin came into view.

As she drove slowly, the gravel crunched under the tires. Eerie silence captured their thoughts, while outside, the wind whistled among the naked trees. Halfway down the driveway, it straightened out. The lake house was just about one hundred yards away. A white sedan parked in front of the house heightened the silence inside the car. Pulses raced, and heavy breathing bounced off the windows as anxiety and tension grabbed their souls.

For some odd reason, Carla glanced in the rearview mirror. Four-letter expletives blasted the windows. Bernie and Chief Evans turned around to see a Porsche fifty yards behind them. Quickly stopping, the Porsche caught up with them and stopped. Not wanting to alert Lenny and Chase, Carla called Angela. After a brief conversation, Carla continued toward the house, finally stopping about ten yards from the cabin. Seconds later, Geronimo pulled in behind them.

Before exiting the car, Carla radioed for backup. Outside the car, everyone grabbed Kevlar vests out of the trunk. After taking the bullhorn out of the trunk, she turned it on. With everyone ready, she announced herself;

an errant shot rang out. Ducking down beside Carla's car, they discussed their options.

Suddenly, Angela got out of the Porsche, approaching Carla. "Let me try. What do you have to lose?" Realizing Angela was probably right, she handed the bullhorn to her. "Lenny, this is your sister, Angela. Put your weapons down and come out. I can help you." Silence flowed from the cabin. "Lenny, it doesn't have to end this way." Silence met her plea once more.

Carla's phone rang, startling everyone. Caller ID indicated it was from Philip. After placing it on speaker, erratic breathing flowed from it. "Philip, are you okay?" More silence, more erratic breathing, then muted mumbling. "Who is this?"

"Where's Angela?"

"I'm here, Lenny. Are Philip and his father, okay?" Silence. "Lenny, are they okay?"

"Umm, yeah, for now."

"Good, you need to give up and end this if you want to stay alive. Is Chase there with you?"

"Yeah…umm…"

As Angela continued her conversation, Carla instructed Officers Pete Wiesmann and Dave Justice to position themselves behind the cabin. All the while, Angela continued talking to her brother, hoping to occupy him. Bernie and Chief Evans had moved in position, flanking the front door. Everyone was ready to storm the cabin if needed. That was risky, but at this point, the odds of a positive outcome were slim.

"Lenny, the cabin is surrounded now, and unless you give up, this situation will not end well." Silence. "Lenny, it's over. Do you understand that?"

Carla had had enough. She grabbed the phone from

Angela. "Lenny, this is Detective McBride. You've got five minutes to decide if you want to live or die. I'm setting a timer. When it reaches double-zero, we're coming in."

The line went dead. Carla's timer began the final countdown. With three minutes left, Angela grabbed the bullhorn. "Lenny, this is Angela. I'm coming in." Carla glared at her at such a stupid idea. "Detective McBride, I'm your only hope to end this without more people dying. I don't think he will harm me. I'm going in. I got this."

"What about Chase?"

"I don't know about him. Wish me luck."

"I can't let you do this."

"You don't have a choice."

"Geronimo, talk her out of this."

"Detective McBride, Angela is her own woman. When she's made up her mind, no one is going to change it. Trust me, she can handle herself."

"Angela, once inside, you've got five minutes. I hope you know what you are doing."

"Umm, I got this, or this is the end for me. It's my choice, okay?"

# CHAPTER 57

Grabbing a Kevlar vest out of the trunk, Carla tossed it to Angela. Fully protected, Angela took the bullhorn and announced she was coming in. She began her descent to the cabin. Moving cautiously, Angela stepped onto the porch. Bernie and Chief Evans flanked the door, ready to act. After they nodded, Angela's moment of truth flashed in her mind. She had always wondered what made her come back to her childhood home. Maybe this was it, to save her brother's life or end hers.

Standing at the front door, she took a deep breath. With her heart pounding furiously, she announced she was coming in. After starting the timer on her phone, she opened the door. She had five minutes of life remaining because if she couldn't get them to surrender, an impending firefight would likely take her life. After she entered, Lenny and Chase stood behind Philip and his dad. They were bound and gagged but appeared unharmed.

Surveying the insides of the cabin, it was rustic.

Down a hallway, Angela saw several doors, probably to the bedrooms and a bathroom. In the main living area, curtains covered one window on the left side of the room. The window on the front was similar. She glanced at her phone, four minutes until all hell broke loose. As she approached Philip, Chase pointed the gun at her, and she froze. Ignoring him, she directed her gaze at her brother.

"Lenny, you've got four minutes to save yourself and everyone in here. Do you want me to die because that's what is going to happen?"

A defiant silence met her gaze. While glancing at Chase, anxiety covered a stoic and absent expression. She wondered whether he cared about living. Focusing back on Lenny, his eyes told her there was a glimmer of hope.

"Lenny, look at me. We are down to three and a half minutes, and you need to decide. Do you want to live or die?"

As Lenny focused on Angela's concerning demeanor, his glistening eyes turned cold and hollow. She knew things were quickly deteriorating. Three minutes remained until the doors and windows would implode, giving way to a hellish furry of bullets. Philip and his dad felt Chase and Lenny's presence behind them. Their eyes wandered around the room, searching for a glimmer of hope. Two minutes remained until death claimed another soul.

Outside Carla felt the anxiousness, the intenseness of the moment. As time ticked away, it took her back to the Black Rose Case. The outcome of that day replayed vividly in her mind. She took a life that day, and now, unless something changed, she might add another kill to her belt feeling that guilt once again. After holding the bullhorn up to her mouth, ninety seconds echoed among the hills. She saw Bernie in place and wondered what he was thinking. It brought her back memories of when she killed Adam Prescott. Bernie had taken fire for the first time, and now, he was facing a similar situation with life and death consequences.

Inside, Angela stared at Lenny, and his hollow eyes screamed death. She wondered if this was where it all was going to end. Over the bullhorn, two minutes roared in her ears. Lenny was beginning to show signs of uncertain anxiety. On the other hand, Chase seemed calm but distant, not caring about what might occur.

"Lenny, Chase, you heard that, didn't you? You've now got less than sixty seconds until they crash in, and your lives will be over, possibly, even mine."

As Chase's hands began to shake erratically, his eyes turned glassy with uncertainty. Holding the gun closer to Philip's father's head, it appeared he was ready to end it all as his trigger finger twitched. Angela glanced at the phone—forty seconds glared back at her.

"Lenny, talk to Chase. Please don't do this. Mom wouldn't want this, would she?"

"Shut up, Angela. Don't believe her bullshit. She's playing you, Lenny. Can't you see that?"

"Lenny, I'm pleading with you, don't listen to him. I can help you both."

Locking eyes with Angela, he nodded. She had struck a chord in him. Her phone screen flashed twenty seconds until all hell would crash through the doors and windows, ending life as she knew it. As anxiety grabbed her soul, her pulse raged out of control. Suddenly, she collapsed, crashing to the floor. Her hands immediately grabbed her chest as she struggled to breathe.

"Lenny, uh, please help, uh, help me. I think, uh, I'm having, uh, a heart attack. Help me…please, I beg you."

Flashing in his mind, Lenny remembered when his mother needed his help one day. He acted and revived her, saving her life. Looking at Angela grimacing with pain and gasping for air, a voice in his head controlled his emotions. Out of instinct, he rushed over to aid her, to save her life. As he neared her, a swift, powerful leg-whip caught him off guard. With nothing to break his fall, his head crashed hard on the oak floor. Lenny lay motionless as the seconds ticked away.

Completely surprised by this action, Chase charged Angela. Outside, double-zero glared at Carla. She signaled to Bernie their moment of truth had arrived. With the door unlocked, there was no need to crash through it. Bernie quickly opened the door with Chief Evans following. Chase aimed his gun at them. One shot rang out, then another. As Chase's gun hit the floor, he grabbed his chest. Crimson blood flowed through his shirt covering his hands.

Carla entered the cabin seeing Bernie on his knees over Chase. With blood-soaked hands, he pressed harder and harder, trying to save him. On the floor, Angela stared at Lenny lying motionless. Off in the distance, sirens blared. Geronimo entered the cabin, quickly consoling Angela, sitting up beside her limp brother. Chief Evans tended to Philip, and his dad, untying them and leading them outside.

The sirens in the distance grew closer and stopped. Paramedics rushed in attending to Chase, however, Bernie's life-saving efforts were all in vain. Bernie watched death claim another bothered soul, and now he would have to deal with the guilt of his first kill. Lenny began to move his head around, rubbing it constantly. He finally noticed a white sheet covering Chase. Paramedics began to evaluate Lenny's condition. After placing him in a neck brace, paramedics put him on a gurney. Minutes later, he was on his way to the regional medical center.

# CHAPTER 58

After being admitted for observation, Lenny, with Angela and Geronimo by his side, rested peacefully in a private room guarded by Officer Pete Wiesmann. Carla and Bernie arrived about thirty minutes later to question him. However, the doctor treating him declined their request. It wasn't until later that afternoon the doctor allowed them to question him. As they entered the room, Lenny was sitting up in the bed. Angela sat beside him, holding his hand, comforting him. A quiet conversation between them was interrupted by Carla and Bernie's presence. After Angela introduced them to Lenny, Carla informed him they were recording the interview.

"Lenny, tell them what you told me, you know, tell them the whole truth, okay?"

As Angela squeezed his hand, a quirky smile painted Lenny's face. He nodded and began. "Yeah, of course, Angela. A year ago, Chase and I met at a drug rehab center in Missouri. We became friends, and that's when we discovered our parents were from the same town,

Oakmont. Our friendship grew to more than just friends. Anyway, he received a call from his grandmother about his sick grandfather, and we visited him before he died."

Pausing, he sipped on cold water as he rubbed the back of his head. Focusing on Angela's mesmerizing eyes, he continued.

"On his death bed, his grandfather, George, set all of this into motion. George had never gotten over his daughter's death. Even though Joni was not his biological daughter, she was still his pride and joy."

That revelation stopped everybody in their tracks. As gasps filled the room, they gave way to smothering silence. After taking several sips of water, Lenny sighed.

"Yeah, he's not her father. According to George, Greg Devaney is Joni's biological father, and he was certain Greg didn't know. Angela, this is also where I found out that I'm not your full-blooded brother, but I suspect you knew that? You've probably known that for a while, haven't you?"

Heartstrings exploded in Angela's soul as she swallowed hard, then rubbed her glistening eyes as Lenny squeezed her hand.

"It was hard to believe. I was angry. Chase was angry. Before George died, he told Chase about the checks and who his father was. After George died, we stayed with Karen for a while and learned the checks no longer were coming and that Karen would have to sell the house. She had nowhere to go. That's when Chase told her he would take care of things."

Angela's heartstrings continued to flow as she held her brother's hand. "Lenny, who was Chase's father?"

"Larry Stewart, Chase contacted him after the checks stopped."

Carla interjected, "Yeah, we know that. What happened after that?"

"Chase went ballistic, said he would stop at nothing to get the money for his grandmother. That's why I sent Angela the warning note. Chase had planned to eliminate everyone tied to this. He told me if I didn't go along, he would kill me. I believed him."

As Carla's eyes bored holes in Lenny's soul, she could only wonder whether any of this was true. She met Angela's gaze, trying to read her thoughts and body language. She then locked eyes with Lenny.

"Yeah, Detective McBride, I know you don't believe me. This might change your mind. Chase said if I didn't go along with him, Angela would be the first person he would kill. I couldn't let him do that even though we aren't blood related. I had no choice but to play along with him, hoping he wouldn't follow through with his threats."

While squeezing Lenny's hand again, Angela broke down. Geronimo walked around the bed and stood behind Angela massaging her neck and shoulders as tears rolled down her cheeks. All the while, Lenny held his emotions in check. Carla remained silent as Lenny continued his story.

"Chase had planned to eliminate every member of the Diamond Brotherhood who raped his mother that night. George told him who they were. Chase thought as he eliminated each person, that would scare Larry Stewart, his birth father, enough to resume the checks. Guess that didn't work out either, did it, Detective McBride?"

"According to Mayor James, Bryan Walters didn't rape Bambi, how do you explain that?

"Umm, maybe George didn't know that I don't know.

Angela, I'm so sorry I should have tried to stop him, but he would have just killed me and then come after you. I was hoping I could convince him to end this, but I was wrong."

"Lenny, it's okay. We'll get through this. I will help you like I did when we were growing up, remember." Lenny nodded and smiled at Angela as she directed her gaze toward Carla. "Detective McBride, what's next for Lenny?"

"Angela, it's up to the district attorney. I'll give him this recording. We'll just have to see where this goes. It doesn't look good for Lenny at this point. He could've done something."

"Yeah, I understand, but he was trying to protect me."

Angela and Geronimo remained while Carla and Bernie returned to the police station. Mayor James had impatiently remained in the interrogation room with Beth during this ordeal. After entering, Mayor James' pale expression said it all. Although still wired from the ordeal, Carla explained to the mayor what went down. She told him about Lenny's confession. He maintained quiet at every revelation, even when he heard Bambi was not George's biological daughter.

"Mayor James, you knew that Greg Devaney was Bambi's biological father, didn't you?"

"Yeah, George and I were good friends. He told me that after Bambi was a few years old, Karen wanted to have another child. Umm, they tried, without success. Finally, he had his sperm count checked. That's when he found out he was sterile. He put two and two together and figured out Bambi couldn't be his daughter, but he still loved her as if she was his. Anyway, later he figured it all out."

"How so?"

"Karen had been dating Greg Devaney. When they broke up, George immediately began dating her. He had a mad crush on her. One thing led to another, and they became sexually involved. When she turned up pregnant, he thought it was his, and they got married. Karen let it go, hoping her dirty little secret would remain hidden forever."

"How do you know all of this?"

"Karen called me, said she told George before he died. I guess she was feeling guilty and needed to cleanse her soul. Greg had no way of knowing Bambi was his daughter, or he wouldn't have, you know."

"Yeah, you know you could've prevented some of this. Your buddy's blood will be on your hands forever. Shame on you, mayor. I expected something better of you."

"What about Angela, you know, she shows up after thirty-five years, and look what happened. How do you know she's not behind this? She had plenty of motive."

"Mayor, I haven't ruled her out. We'll see what the district attorney decides to do about Lenny. Then we'll proceed accordingly regarding Angela."

"Well, good."

"You know, even if she is involved, it won't wash away the bloodstains in your soul. It might be time you take a look in the mirror. You might not like what you see, Mayor James. You…"

"Carla, that's enough. You've made your point."

"But chief, he—"

"I said that's enough. Now get the hell out of here before I really lose my cool and end your career."

A few days later, Lenny was released to in-home

incarceration under Angela's responsibility until the district attorney reviewed the entire case. With an ankle monitor, Angela's home was his jail cell until the district attorney rendered his decision. Meanwhile, Carla and Bernie continued to mull over the possibility that Angela was somehow involved and might have even orchestrated everything to get revenge for all past sins committed by the Diamond Brotherhood.

Over the past several weeks, Carla and Bernie continued to interview Angela and keep tabs on her and Lenny's whereabouts. They had only circumstantial evidence and convincing the district attorney to move forward on arresting her again was on very shaky ground. Even Lenny's involvement was on shaky ground. Given that forensics never found his fingerprints or DNA at any of the crime scenes, District Attorney Barnett decided against taking any action and ordered Lenny's ankle monitor removed.

What bothered Carla more than anything else was the possibility that Angela, a behavioral psychologist, could have convinced or controlled Lenny and Chase, both vulnerable and troubled men, to carry out her or their plan of revenge. When Carla and Bernie interviewed her for the first time, her book titled, *Manipulation Through Hypnotherapy*, laid on a table in plain sight. Based on all the skeletons out of the closet, Angela, Lenny, and Chase all had a motive for murder. Unfortunately, everything was a big if, and big enough, that the district attorney decided against further any action involving Angela and Lenny in any of the deaths.

# CHAPTER 59

Carla and Bernie were disappointed with the district attorney's decision. However, life had to go on for them, and they turned their attention to Beth's cold case. She was instrumental in this bizarre case, and now it was their turn to assist her. Before doing so, Carla wanted to speak with Angela one last time. There was always something about her that bothered Carla, call it female detective intuition. Angela was clever but also conniving and seductive in a strange way. Carla always felt she knew more about everything but getting it out of her was difficult. She may have orchestrated the perfect plan to get revenge and get away with murder. Perhaps the answers were in her book, Carla thought.

Bernie wanted to sit this one out, taking some time off. He decided to take Carla's advice and take Lydia to The Greenbrier Resort in White Sulphur Springs, West Virginia. Beth and Scott took off to Florida for some fun and celebration as they recently got engaged.

With Carla's tank on empty and the weekend ahead

of her, the last item on her agenda was visiting Angela. Arriving late Friday afternoon, she pulled in front of her business. Exiting her car, she scanned both sides of the street for Angela's car or Geronimo's Porsche; neither was in sight. After approaching the door, she pushed the doorbell. She remembered the chimes ringing from her first visit. A minute passed, nothing but silence rang out from within. Her impatient demeanor grabbed her soul, and she pushed the doorbell several times. After the chimes stopped ringing, the empty silence punched her in the gut.

Strolling around the house, she tried her best to peek inside. Although blinds covered the windows, she found one that allowed a line of sight inside the house. Everything looked the same, and she returned to the front of the house as Angela's receptionist drove up and exited her car.

"Selena, right?"

"Detective McBride, what do you want? I'm busy."

"Angela and Lenny, where are they?"

"I'd say that was none of your business. They are free to go anywhere they want, for as long as they want, right, detective?"

"Well, yeah, but…"

"As I said, I'm busy."

"When are they coming back?"

"That's none of your business, but I don't know. Now, if you don't mind, I'm going to take the mail inside, lock up and leave."

Carla realized she would not get anywhere with her and left. She and Chris were having dinner with Laura and Walt tonight at the country club. Arriving at her apartment, Carla poured herself a shot of her liquid lover,

Jameson. Although she believed in her gut, this case involved Angela somehow, she knew she had to let go. Sometimes you win, sometimes you don't, comes with the territory Chief Evans always told her.

Dinner was at Seven PM. Chris was picking her up at 6:30, time enough for a quick glass of wine. Chris arrived promptly and rang the doorbell. Carla, dressed in her favorite red dress, flung her arms around him. After finding his lips, her exploring kiss ignited his hormones and left him gasping. Meeting her gaze, he wanted more, but she shook her head.

"What, we have time."

"Later, prince charming, I promise you."

"You know, you drive me crazy sometimes."

"Yeah, I know, but you love me, right?"

"Of course, how was your day?"

"Kind of shitty in a strange way. But hey, it's over now."

"Yeah, and it's time to celebrate. I have two glasses of Caymus Zinfandel on the counter."

After walking to the counter, Chris picked up both glasses and handed one to her. Raising their drinks, they clinked together, getting the night off in glorious fashion. With only time for a few sips, each put their wine on the counter.

Fifteen minutes later, Chris pulled into the parking lot at Avondale Country Club. After exiting, Carla saw the ambient lights emanating from the Sunroom. Laura and Walt were already seated and waiting for them. Entering through the side door, they entered the Sunroom. Laura and Walt rose to greet them. After hugs and kisses, they relaxed in silence. However, like many of their dinners, that didn't last long. A bottle of Caymus Zinfandel took center stage, waiting to bless them with notes of purple plum, spice, and jammy fruits.

As each glass received the zin's many nuances, Chris put the empty bottle back on the table. After their usual toast, the evening was off and running. Within minutes, Carrie arrived and replaced it with a bottle of champagne in an ice bucket. She put it just off Chris' left. While there, she took their dinner orders and left. Walt always began the evening conversation and began.

"Honey, tell Carla and Chris about your day."

"Guys, nothing special about today, no fireworks in court. It was a great boring day."

"Okay, honey. Chris, what about your day?"

"Well, we're just getting ready for Thanksgiving Buffet extravaganza and then our annual lunch with Santa. It's always a fun time of the year. Okay, Walt, what's going on in the newspaper business?"

"Yeah, just putting together our entries for the Kentucky Press Association Awards. We've had a great year, and I expect us to be the top dog again."

"Okay, Carla, I've saved the best for last. How was your day?"

"Well, Walt, you're so kind. As you know, we've wrapped up the case involving the Diamond Brotherhood. I still believe in my gut Angela Clark orchestrated everything. However, the powers to be didn't feel the same. I went to visit her, and she and her brother are gone."

"Gone, where?"

"Yeah, Walt. Gone, gone, gone. Her receptionist didn't offer much about that. She didn't know when she would be back, and honestly, I don't think she even cared. I wonder if she will ever be back. The killing is over, end of story, case closed. Can we just drink our wine and move on to something more pleasant?"

"Wow, Carla, don't be such a damn sourpuss."

Although Walt didn't see the bird, she flipped it at him under the table. His ankle felt her wrath. While silence moved in, the Caymus Zin tried its best to liven up the evening. Salads arrived, breaking the tension smothering the table. Grasping each other hands, Chris offered up a short blessing. Then another toast helped destroy the stillness among them. As meaningless chatter moved around the table, smiles replaced the stoic expressions in the Sunroom.

Carrie kept a close eye on her boss. As soon as they finished their salads, she rounded up the salad plates and left. Within several minutes, their main entrée arrived. Penne pasta in an exquisite marinara-mushroom sauce accompanied by a basket of fresh Italian bread graced the table. By this time, the stale silence finally lost its battle with laughter and light-heartedness. The zin paired well with the pasta, as did the Italian bread and dipping oil.

With their entrée finished, and their wine glasses empty, Carrie cleared the table and left. She returned with four champagne flutes. As she poured the Moët-Chandon Imperial, eyes around the table lit up. They always had champagne to finish the night, but never this one. With glasses in hand, Chris raised his toward the center of the table. Eyes still in awe-and-shock mode, all four glasses waited in anticipation.

"Here's to us. Here's to health, love, and happiness."

In unison, the glasses clinked, and a hearty cheer rang off the windows of the Sunroom. Chris leaned in and kissed Carla as Walt did the same to Laura. Chris stood up unexpectedly. With all eyes on him, he knelt, gazing into Carla's sparkling eyes.

"Detective Carla Anne McBride."

"Chris, please, it's Carla. What the hell are you doing?"

"Umm, right. You have always been the love of my life, even though I don't think you ever realized it. I want to spend the rest of my life waking up next to you."

"Chris, please don't…"

"Too late, will you marry me and accept my love till death do us part?"

"Geez, Chris, I…I don't know. You know how I am…umm…you know, right?"

"What the…are you serious?"

As a flirtatious smile crossed her face, she replied, "Gotcha! Of course, honey, I will marry you."

"That wasn't funny at all."

"Yeah, I know, but you should have seen your face. It was priceless, honey. Come here, let's seal this commitment."

"First, give me your hand."

As he pulled out the ring, its brilliance, its awe, and what it represented left her gasping. After sliding it on her finger, quivering emotions took over her soul. A long but delicate kiss sealed the deal. Raucous applause erupted from the sitting area just outside the Sunroom.

"More champagne, boss?"

"Umm, Carrie?"

"Yeah, Carla."

"Just so you know it, I'm the boss from now on. Let's get this party started."

# CHAPTER 60

After such a momentous event on Friday evening, Carla also took a few days off. Over this past weekend, she got engaged and Chris moved in with her, which helped her forget how the last case ended. Things were quiet and back to normal when she returned to work on Wednesday. After checking her mailbox, the sight of an empty slot brought a smile to her face.

Arriving at the desk, Beth and Bernie were hard at work. After positioning herself, Carla glared at them. With her elbows on the desk, she made sure her left hand was in full view. She was ready to flaunt her massive diamond. They sat unaware as the diamond shined brightly. Clearing her throat, Bernie glanced in her direction, as did Beth. Silence flowed toward her. She cleared her throat once more, catching Bernie's insincere scowl. After glancing up at Carla, Beth laughed.

"Geez, McBride, what's your problem? Got a frog in your throat this morning?"

"No, dickhead. Can't you see it?"

"See what?"

Finally, Beth caught its brilliance, "Holy shit, Carla, is that for real? Is that what I'm thinking? Bernie, look at the rock on her finger?"

By now, the gleam and sparkle in Carla's eyes mirrored the ring on her finger. Sticking it toward Bernie, he smiled.

"Well, it's about time, congrats."

"Yeah, congrats. Did you set a date yet?"

"We did, Beth. May 11th, next year."

"Umm, that's pretty quick, partner."

"Yeah, Bernie, Chris set it, didn't want to prolong the inevitable, or better yet, give me a chance, you know, to get wet feet."

"Well, congrats."

"Yeah, thank you both. And by the way, you're both invited. We're thinking about a destination wedding, who knows, maybe a cruise, just somewhere exotic away from crime."

"Umm, can't wait. Guess I'll have to get in shape so that I can wear my speedos."

"Seriously, dickhead, no speedos allowed."

As a smile crossed Bernie's face, Chief Evans stopped by their desk. He could not ignore the happiness exuding from Carla. She extended her left hand toward him, and he smiled and congratulated her.

"In my office now."

"Seriously, what did I do now?"

"In my office, McBride."

"It's not those federal boys again, is it? Did John Dickerson escape again?"

With impatience painting his face, a pissed-off scowl met Carla's bewildered eyes. He pointed toward his office and walked away. Beth and Bernie wondered what the hell was going on and watched her follow him to his office. The closing of the door echoed down the hallway.

"Chief, what is it? What have I done, now?"

"Nothing."

"Then what is it?"

"I received a call yesterday afternoon from a Detective Jerimiah Washburn."

"Yeah, who's that?"

"He's with the Jellico Police Department, you know, Jellico, Tennessee."

"Chief, I know where Jellico is. What did he want?"

"He said he just wanted to talk with you?"

"Okay, about what?"

"Not sure. Here's his contact information. Let me know if it's anything important, okay?"

"Yeah, of course."

Carla returned to her desk, where Beth and Bernie were anxiously waiting. Carla was still absorbing this situation when Bernie stared into her soul.

"Well, McBride, what have you done now?"

"Bite me, dickhead. What makes you think I did something wrong?"

"I've seen that look before."

"Nothing, I did nothing wrong."

"Well, then what is it?"

"He got a call from a Detective Washburn in Jellico, you know, Tennessee. Where we interviewed Karen Ballard."

"Yeah, I know where Jellico is."

"Don't be such a dick, Kowalski. He told the chief to have me call him later this afternoon. That's all I know.

What do you say, we discuss Beth's cold case in the conference room in about ten minutes?"

After two hours of intense discussion, they broke for lunch. McGruder's was unusually quiet, and that fit Carla's demeanor. After sliding into their favorite booth, Sam arrived to take their orders. Immediately, she noticed the rock.

"Detective McBride, that's one hell of a rock. When's the big date?"

"Next May, maybe a destination wedding on a cruise ship."

"Congrats. Chris is a lucky man."

Bernie interjected, "I wouldn't go that far, Sam."

"Bite me, Bernie."

Smiles and laughter moved around the booth while Sam took their orders. After a quiet lunch, they returned to the station. Beth and Bernie continued to compare notes on the Angel Hardesty cold case while Carla stared at Detective Jerimiah Washburn's contact information. As her pulse quickened, she informed them she would be in the conference room for privacy.

After entering the room, the closing of the door provided her with the privacy she craved. She pulled out Detective Washburn's contact information and thought for a moment what he wanted. Baffled, she dialed his number, placing the call on speaker. After several rings, a twangy dialect filled the speaker.

"Detective Washburn, here. How may I help you?"

"Detective Carla McBride here. Chief Evans said you wanted to speak with me?"

"Oh, right, right. Thank you for returning my call."

"Of course, how may I help you?"

"I'm investigating a suspicious death at the former home of Karen Ballard."

"What, you did say former home, right? Suspicious death, who?"

"Yeah, get to that in a minute. Umm, Mrs. Ballard died suddenly about a week ago, a massive stroke. The house is in foreclosure, now." Silence smothered the room as Carla sighed heavily. "Detective McBride, you still there, everything, okay?"

"Yeah, I'm here. Sorry to hear about Mrs. Ballard's passing. We had a good visit with her a month ago or so. Umm, how did you get my number?"

"Oh, about that suspicious death. A realtor found a body inside her house."

"Who was it?"

"Lenny Clark." A gasp, a loud thud, and then silence shattered the conference room as her pulse skyrocketed. "Detective, are you okay?"

"Yeah, I didn't expect that. You mentioned a note?"

"Right, right. First of all, on the outside of it was your contact information. That's how I knew where I could reach you."

"The note, what did it say?"

"Right, umm, nothing."

"Seriously, nothing at all?"

"Well, it didn't make any sense to me. Maybe it will to you."

"Okay, go on?"

"I thought it was kind of weird. A circle with the initials LJ inside. Why leave a note if you didn't want to say something?"

"Yeah. What was the manner of death?"

"He was hanging from the railing at the top of the

stairs. Although it appears like suicide, the coroner found a needle prick on his neck. Sounds like murder to me."

"Damn, I knew it. I just couldn't prove it, shit."

"Knew what, prove what?"

"Angela was behind all of the deaths involving the Oakmont Diamond Brotherhood."

"Angela, who?"

"Umm, Angela Clark. She finally got revenge for her cousin, Bambi, for her mom and herself. And now, she killed the only person that could implicate her. Lenny is her brother, well, not really. She grew up thinking he was, but eventually found out he was only her half-brother instead. He was the result of a rape, you get the picture, right?"

"Uh-huh. Diamond Brotherhood, what's that all about?"

"It's a long story."

"Detective, I got all the time in the world. This murder is a big deal down here. Do you know where this Angela might be?"

"Umm, no idea. Just put out a BOLO for a pearl white Porsche 911 with the vanity plate STUD. You just might find her with Preston Geronimo, the owner."

"Umm, well now. You know, that won't do any good."

"Why is that?"

"Well, state police found that beautiful piece of machinery at the bottom of a steep ravine. It appears the car exploded on impact. The remains inside have not been identified yet, and honestly, might never be."

"Huh, one body or two?"

"Well, it's hard to tell if anyone was in the car."

"Hmm, interesting. Where's the note?"

"I've got it here."

"Take it out and smell it, okay?"

"Seriously?"

"Yeah, just smell it?"

"Okay, this is a first for me."

As several deep sniffing sounds softly filled the speaker, a smirky smile beamed across her face.

"Uh-huh, you know, I recognize this scent. My wife wears it. I believe it's, umm, called umm…"

"Umari Seduction."

"Yeah, yeah, right. How'd you know that?

"It's where this whole story began."

"Huh, what do you mean?"

"Ah, nothing. Good luck with your investigation and finding Angela Clark."

# CHAPTER 61

While ending the call, footsteps moving down the hallway grabbed Carla's attention. The sound of the distinctive stride echoed off the walls. Getting up and leaving the conference room, she and Mayor James collided. Her folder and its contents flew all over the floor.

"Sorry, Mayor James, I didn't see you."

"That's okay. I'm on my way to meet with the chief. I'll pick up those documents for you. I shouldn't have been looking at my phone. Distractive walking, I guess, sorry."

"No problem, mayor. Did you say you had a meeting with the chief?" He grumbled under his breath. "Great, I was headed there as well. So, I'll join you."

"Uh, what's going on?"

"Mayor, in the chief's office now."

Expecting the mayor, Chief Evans was standing in his office. He entered, followed by Carla. A questionable scowl met her angry eyes and disposition.

"McBride, what the hell is this about?"

"Chief, before you blow your top, hear me out, okay? Take a seat, mayor."

"This better be important because Lester and I have some important business to discuss, you got it?"

"Yeah, chief, I got it, but so do I. Detective Washburn, you remember him, in Jellico, right?"

"Yeah."

"Well, I called him."

"And?"

"I'll make this short, and then the mayor is going to answer my damn question, right mayor?"

While shrugging his shoulders, the mayor's nonchalant disposition ignited Carla's Irish temper, and a loud boom rocked the walls.

"Listen close, mayor, Angela's brother is dead. Did you hear me, dead, just like Bryan, Barry, and Rich?" A palish tone grabbed the mayor's complexion as he deflected her angry and dagger-like eyes. "Yeah, murdered, and it appears Geronimo may be dead, perhaps at the hands of Angela." As stoic expressions flew back at her, she continued. "Mayor, I didn't get a chance to ask you before all hell broke loose when everything went down at the cabin."

"What are you talking about?"

"You said Bryan went into the other bedroom the night the Diamond Brotherhood partied and raped Bambi, right?"

"I don't recall saying that."

"The hell you don't. I recorded that interview. Would you like to hear it again?"

"No, I still don't know what you're talking about."

She pulled out her iPhone and played the audio clip. The mayor's distinctive voice flowed from the phone. A couple of minutes later, she stopped the playback. Glaring into the mayor's soul, he tried his best to deflect her intense eyes.

"Mayor, now that we confirmed what you said, who was in that bedroom? I'm not leaving until you tell me."

As he sat quietly, his pulse exploded. While swallowing hard, he searched for some sense of calmness. With his respiration increasing, beads of sweat dotted his brow. While her eyes bored into his soul, he wiped the glistening coolness off his forehead. Chief Evans watching the mayor fidgeting in his chair, glared into his soul as well.

"Lester, answer…the…damn…question."

As the room grew quiet, the mayor's forehead glistened under the fluorescent lighting once more. He glanced at Chief Evans, then at Carla, and hung his head low.

"Lester…answer…the…damn…"

"Okay…okay, Chief. Angela…Angela Clark."

"Did anyone else go into that bedroom that night?"

As a deadly silence grabbed the room once more, Lester looked up to the ceiling, rubbing his forehead, searching for calmness and forgiveness.

"So, you raped innocent Angela Clark?"

"Umm, well, not exactly."

"What the hell does that mean?"

"It wasn't intercourse, you know, it was…"

"It was what?"

"Umm…you know, we didn't force her to do anything. She wanted—"

"Damn you, mayor—no wonder she was out to get Bryan. Mayor, you know, Angela may still be out there somewhere. Think about that long and hard. You better watch your back."

"What are you saying?"

"There was a note on Lenny's body. A big circle, you know, like an 'on-deck circle' on a baseball field, you remember, right?" He nodded. "Inside it was the initials LJ."

"LJ, what the…"

"Yeah, mayor. At first, I didn't get it, but I do now. Based on everything I now know, Chase and Lenny went after the guys who raped his mother, hoping they could scare his biological father, Larry, into resuming the checks. He would've been next if they had pulled everything off. Angela wanted revenge because of what you and Bryan made her do in that bedroom. Furthermore, she did it for her mom. She wanted revenge for Bryan's father, Alex, who raped her mother, fathering Lenny. I still believe she orchestrated everything and hoped Chase and Lenny would take the fall if they didn't die in the process. With Chase killed in the shoot-out, she saved Lenny in hopes of letting him take the fall. However, when the district attorney decided not to prosecute him, she killed Lenny, and maybe Geronimo. That way, she's home free."

"That's ridiculous, right, chief?"

"Umm, Lester, maybe, maybe not."

"You're serious, aren't you, detective?"

"Yeah, and unless I can find her first, you're the next man up. You know, she may never come after you. She may want you to live the rest of your life looking over your shoulder, wondering when your time is up. Of course, that's if she's alive."

As Carla left the chief's office, she put the case to

bed. Although there were still some unanswered questions burning inside her, she knew she had done her best. She hoped for some quality time off before her big wedding day. Unfortunately, she knew that wasn't likely to happen since the next case was front and center on Beth's desk. After calling Beth and Bernie, she met them at McGruder's. Jameson, her liquid lover, called her name. The mayor's nonchalant disposition riled her soul to the point that she didn't care what happened to him. All she knew was Jameson's amber love could temporarily erase the mayor's smirky grin out of her mind. That's what mattered to her now.

After a couple of drinks, she headed home. Chris met her as she entered their apartment. As usual, a loving embrace and welcoming kiss greeted her. Although she had two drinks already, he poured them each a glass of red wine. As they caught up on each other's day, she noticed a package on the table by the door.

"Chris, that package on the table—what did you get today?"

"Oh, that. It's for you. Kind of strange, though."

"How so?"

"There's no return address on it. I'll get it for you, okay?"

"Thank you, honey."

After handing her the package, he nestled beside her as she studied it front and back. No return addresses on anything always sent her pulse soaring. Furthermore, the postmark was just several days ago. That sent her mind wondering. By its shape and touch, she assumed it had to be a book. She wasn't an avid reader by any means and hadn't ordered a book in quite some time. After pulling the book out of the cardboard package, her rosy complexion quickly soured, and anxiety rocked her soul. She'd seen the book before and remembered Angela's recommendation when they first met.

"Honey, were you expecting this book?"

"Not at all. This is a complete surprise."

"*Manipulation Through Hypnotherapy,* that's an interesting title. Wait a minute, wasn't Angela Clark one of the main suspects in your last case?"

"Yeah…yeah, she was. This is totally bizarre given she might be dead."

After opening the book, the elegant, cursive inscription on the first page caught her off guard. She'd seen that writing before. While the scent of Umari Seduction took her breath away, her pulse exploded in her soul.

"What does it say, honey?"

*"Carla, I can call you that, right? Until our paths cross once more, and you know they will, all the best, Angela."*

# ACKNOWLEDGMENTS

My wife, Bonnie, is always the first to read my original manuscripts. We discussed the good and the bad. When she finished this novel, she hated my ending. I wasn't surprised because I didn't like it either. So, we discussed it, and I went back to the drawing board. In the end, I created a new ending that we both agreed was better. So, I thank her for her honest suggestions.

I would be remiss if I didn't acknowledge my youngest brother, Rick. Upon visiting him in February 2019, I told him about my first three novels and securing a publishing contract. I informed him about my idea for book four in The Detective Carla McBride Chronicles. He offered some suggestions, which I embraced in writing the novel. Although I didn't use all of them, some are reflected in the finished product. He also suggested a title, given my baseball background. In the beginning, his suggestion, *Next Man Up*, was going to be the title. However, after many revisions and other titles to consider, I chose a different one. Anyway, thank you, brother.

# A LOOK AT BOOK FIVE:
## ENIGMA

Detectives Carla McBride and Bernie Kowalski join forces with Beth Pendergast again in a test against their patience and experience when a twenty-year-old cold case is brought to the forefront.

All hands on-deck, a major curveball is thrown their way that takes the investigation well beyond their beloved Oakmont community. And legendary Detective Ace Hutchinson—who was the original lead investigator on the case—becomes a major player.

Only thing is…nobody is sure whose side he is on. Standing in the way of closing this decades-old cold case are a multitude of suspects, persons of interest, and unexplained reasons complicating an already-perplexing investigation.

*Can Carla, Bernie, and Beth navigate an illusive case's twists and turns in order to unravel an unexpected mystery for the ages? Or will they fail on their final quest to deliver justice…*

*AVAILABLE MARCH 2023*

# ABOUT THE AUTHOR

Author Nick Lewis lives in Richmond, Kentucky, with his wife, Bonnie. He graduated from Marshall University in the fall of 1970. Upon graduating, he taught school and coached football for one year at Eidson Elementary. He then switched directions and began a forty-year newspaper career. He held circulation and marketing positions at four different newspapers in Ohio, West Virginia, and Kentucky. In 2004, he was appointed publisher of *The Richmond Register* in Richmond, Kentucky. He retired from that position in June 2013 and began his quest to become a full-time author.

In January 2014, Nick created The Detective Carla McBride Chronicles. The first book in the series, *The Gold Fedora*, debuted in October 2019. *The Black Rose, Chasing Truth and Redemption,* and *Quandary* completes the series to date. Book five in the series, *Enigma*, is forthcoming. He has another published novel, *When Eagles Soared*.

When Nick is not writing and revising manuscripts, he enjoys golf, gardening, and creating new adventures with his wife of fifty years. Bonnie plays an essential role in his journey of writing novels. He is an avid Marshall University football fan with three grown children, three grandchildren, and two cats named Zorro and Ziva.

CPSIA information can be obtained
at www.ICGtesting.com
Printed in the USA
BVHW081120140223
658470BV00025B/261

9 781685 492434